ROGUE BEAST

KYLIE GILMORE

Rogue Beast: © 2020 by Kylie Gilmore

Cover design by: Michele Catalano Creative

Published by: Extra Fancy Books

ISBN-13: 978-1-947379-30-5

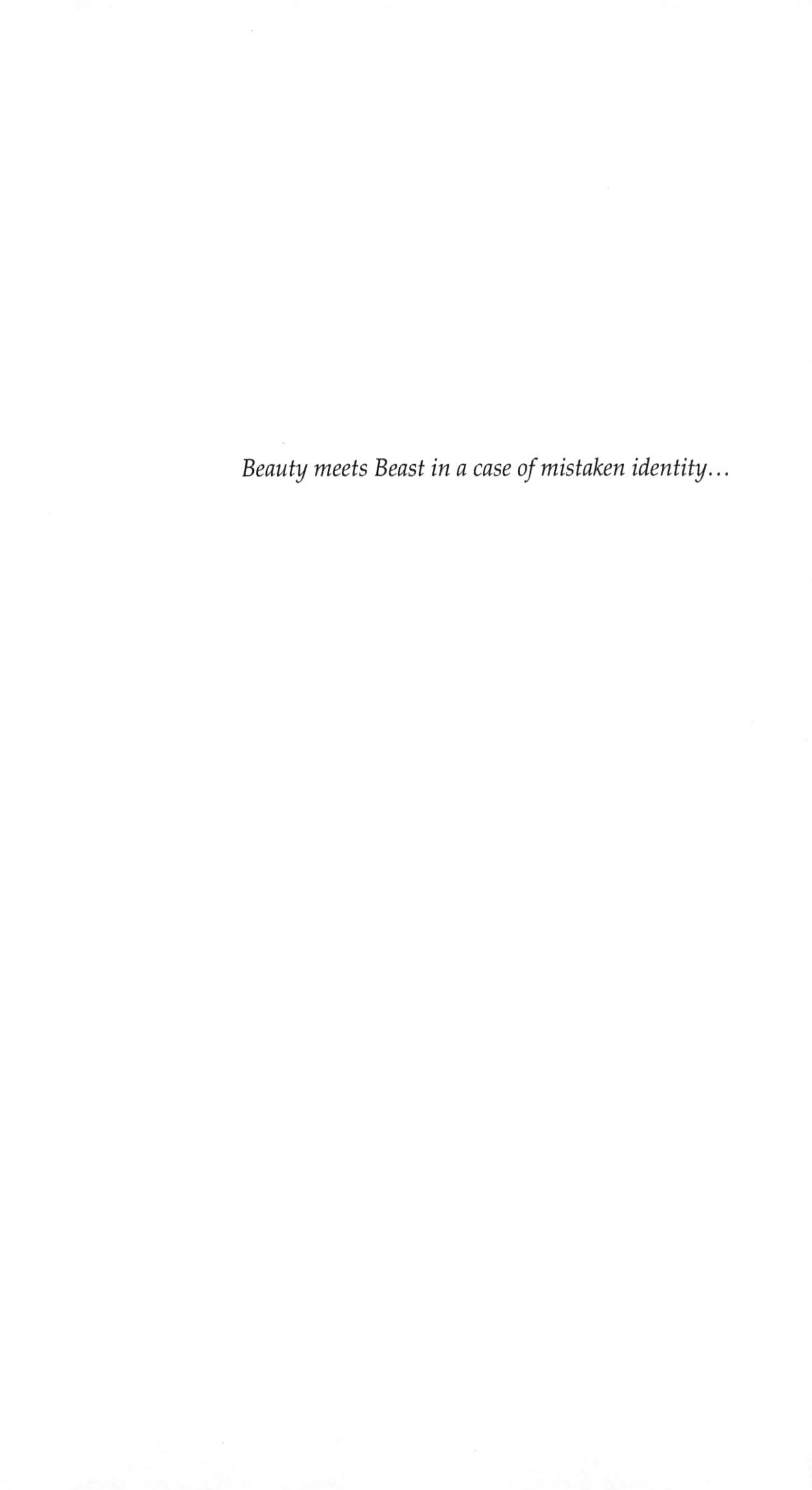

Beauty meets Beast in a case of mistaken identity…

1

———

Harper

My phone vibrates with the text I've been waiting for all day: *Bodyguard is on his way to you.*

I dash out of the soundstage, walking as quickly as I can in high-heeled ankle boots through the fenced-off parking lot of trailers. Goosebumps rise on my skin despite the warm September day in Manhattan. I fought the idea of a guard for a long time—I'm a very private person—but when a man broke into my apartment two weeks ago, startling me from a sound sleep, to ask me to whip him, that was the final straw. Ever since I played a tough-as-nails CEO on my previous show, I've had more than my share of harassment from men. They're either attracted to that toughness, or want to bring me down a peg. *It's called acting, guys!*

Seriously, it's one thing to have a guy shouting at you on the street or grabbing for your hair or clothes in a crowd—all of which I deal with—and a whole different thing to have a home invader. The even more disturbing part is how he managed to get past the lobby's night watchman and knew how to disable my apartment's security system. My new bodyguard is the key to getting a sound sleep again.

Oh, there's Trina talking to him. She directs him toward my trailer and dashes off in the opposite direction. My knees wobble as my bodyguard swaggers toward me. He's a *beast* of a man. My mouth goes dry, my pulse racing. He's mid-twenties, tall, six feet plus, and bulky with muscles. His physique is shown off to perfection in a snug black T-shirt and faded jeans. His dark brown hair is clipped short, drawing attention to his sharp cheekbones and square jaw. Black sunglasses hide his eyes. *Tough. Hot. Sexy AF.* Did *not* expect that.

I take a deep breath and slow my pace. I need to be calm, cool, and professional when I meet him. Joe Sullivan and I will be spending a *lot* of time together. He's moving into the apartment next door tomorrow at my request. It's critical we get off on the right foot. Today's a taping day for our new sitcom, *Living Gold*, with a live studio audience. I'll feel better knowing my new bodyguard is on set with me in case there's any aggressive men in the audience obsessed with my previous character, Amanda.

The funny thing is, I'm not tough at all. It's a failing I've worked on my whole life. I can play tough, thanks to General Joan Ellis, my grandmother who raised me. *Harper! Chin up, shoulders back, never show weakness!*

Ma'am, yes, ma'am!

Except I would've caught hell for responding back. She really missed her calling as an elementary school teacher. The military could've used her in command of the troops, instead of attempting to bring a shy, sensitive girl up to her standards. And failing miserably.

Joe walks right by my trailer, not knowing he missed it, and I dash ahead to greet him, a professional smile pasted on my face to hide the raw lust. "Hi, I'm Harper. So nice to meet you. This one is mine." I gesture to the trailer. "Follow me. I'd like to chat before taping starts." I go on ahead, unlocking the door, and head inside, holding the metal door open for him.

He doesn't join me. Instead he pushes his sunglasses to the top of his head and just stares. His eyes are a striking aquamarine. *My God. He could be in movies.* My stomach does a crazy flip, heat flashing through my entire body. I've never had such a visceral reaction to a man on first sight. This could be a problem. I'm his boss. Also, I have a boyfriend. Colton's been in England for three weeks now filming a movie. I should call him.

"Please come in," I say.

"You're Harper Ellis." His voice is deep and smooth like my favorite dark chocolate, giving me a similar jolt of pleasure. Better, if I'm being honest.

"Yes. Welcome." It occurs to me he sounds a little surprised. I thought he knew who hired him, though I do look different today from the character I used to play. Amanda Boxer wore business suits and sensible pumps. My new character, Lexi Gold, is a wealthy fashionista, so I'm in a sleeveless Vera Wang black shift dress, with a sheer top above the cleavage, that ends mid-thigh with high-heeled designer ankle boots. The biggest difference is my hair. I used to wear a straight-haired dark brown wig as Amanda because it was too much work for the show's hairstylist to straighten my curly hair, and it caused too much damage to it in the process anyway. I was on the show for three years, so I appreciate my stylist having the foresight to save my hair. Apparently, shoulder-length curls don't say tough CEO.

My new guard takes the two steps into my trailer, and the space suddenly shrinks with his large presence. He checks out my trailer while I check out him. He's *exactly* what I need to scare off creeper men. His neck is thick and corded, his shoulders wide, and his biceps are so large his arms don't lie flat at his sides. His thighs look solid and strong, long legs leading to black work boots. Probably steel-toed for maximum fighting power. *Perfection.*

He rubs his hands together. "So…nice to meet ya. I caught *Capital Asset* a few times." That's my former show. Amanda Boxer was a ruthless hedge fund CEO.

My lips curve up in approval. Not because he watched my show. It's his rough-sounding Brooklyn accent. (I know accents well, part of my training.) I couldn't have asked for a better fit for this gig. When those local creepers come at me, they'll have to deal with one of their own.

Suddenly I realize I'm being rude, checking him out for my own needs. Obviously he's already been vetted by my assistant, who went through all the résumés. My only requirements were strong, competent, and not too old.

"Can I get you a drink?" I ask, gesturing toward my mini-fridge. "I have bottled water and diet iced tea."

"Sure, I'll take a water."

I brush by him on the way to the mini-fridge, catching the scent of a sexy, musky cologne. *Must be professional.* I get the bottled water and hand it to him, careful to keep from touching him in the exchange.

"Thanks," he says, unscrewing the cap with a quick movement. Strong, so strong with those large hands. He lifts his brows, eying me as he guzzles water. I might be staring.

I look away. We're going to be working closely together, so I shouldn't hold back on the hospitality. This is an important occasion. My first bodyguard ever is going to risk life and limb to keep me safe. The least I can do is share my secret stash. Not my drinks, the good stuff. We're building a professional relationship here.

That's right. Ignore his sexy scent, his stunning body, and beautiful eyes. I open the cabinet above the microwave, carefully push aside the camouflaging red plastic cups on the top shelf, and retrieve a small Ziploc bag. The shelf wobbles. I should call maintenance about that.

I open the bag, telling him, "I'm not supposed to have this. My wardrobe is set with a lot of designer stuff for my exact size. It's a big deal if something doesn't fit." I lift my gaze to his, getting a jolt when our eyes meet. "Would you like one?" I have three individually wrapped squares of dark chocolate with cherry. I'm normally careful to make them last the entire show season, but he's more important than my love of chocolate.

Joe shakes his head. "Real nice of ya to offer, but it's not in my diet either. I try to eat clean."

"Of course, completely understand." I quickly put the chocolate back in the bag, even though it smells so luscious all I want to do is stuff it in my mouth. It's near dinner, but I can't eat until the taping is over. Otherwise, I'll get sluggish, and my performance will show it. I shove it back on the shelf so quickly I accidentally tip the shelf, and red plastic cups tumble out. "Oops! Wobbly shelf."

"I could fix it."

My eyes widen. "Oh. Do you have the right tools?" Maybe he has one of those Swiss Army knives that morphs into a dozen useful gadgets.

One corner of his mouth lifts as he leans close to inspect the shelf. My breath catches at his proximity. *Ridiculous.* I need to chill. As soon as he shifts to the empty cabinet next to my stash cabinet, I retrieve the Ziploc bag and all of the cups so he can work his magic.

He reaches in and does something to the other cabinet shelf and then with another quick movement fixes my wobbly shelf. He turns to me. "I borrowed a couple of bracket pegs from the other cabinet, since you weren't using it. I'll get you some more. Then you just push them in here. See the predrilled holes?" He points to them in the cabinet.

I peer around him. "Yes."

"You just pop those babies in there. Here, I'll put your stuff back." He gestures for the cups and Ziploc bag I'm still holding. I stare at him, surprised by Mr. Fix-It. Not only is he gorgeous, he's so helpful and genuinely nice. I really expected more of a killer instinct from a bodyguard.

I hand him the stuff, and he tucks it back exactly as I had it. "Thank you."

"No problem. Anything else need fixing around here?"

I blink. My new bodyguard could be my handyman too. I'd never have to let a strange man into my apartment or trailer again. *So awesome.* Then I remember myself. We're supposed to be getting the awkwardness out of the way—my awkwardness—by having a professional conversation, client to bodyguard. "That's all, thanks." I gesture toward my sofa. "Have a seat."

He ambles over to the sofa with a relaxed stride. *Wish I could be that relaxed.* I'm usually a little high-strung before a taping, but this is also an unusual situation for me, working with my first bodyguard. Though I have to admit he's not at all like I expected. I thought he'd be this tough scary man who would take some time for me to get comfortable having around. He's not giving off any scary vibes at all.

I like him already.

I take the seat next to him, crossing one leg over the other. He's drinking water again, his Adam's apple going up and down hypnotically. *Stop staring!*

I focus on his eyebrow, avoiding getting lost in his aquamarine eyes again. "So, I'm not sure if Trina clued you in, but this is my first time having a bodyguard. Please bear with me as I get used to having a shadow. I know for sure I want you on set when we bring in the live studio audience on Fridays. We've got nine more weeks of taping, and then I'm not sure where I'll be after that. A lot depends on if the show gets picked up for another season as far as what future roles I can take. But if we both feel it's working, I wonder if you'd be open to travel?"

He rubs the back of his neck. "Hafta think about that one."

I hold up a palm. "Sorry. I'm rushing ahead. We'll play it by ear. You stick close on taping day and accompany me to and from work. I know I'll sleep better at night knowing you're next door." I recently bought the next-door apartment with the intention of knocking down the separating wall to expand my own, so it worked out well to have the nearby space.

His lips curve into a small smile, and my pulse thrums through me. "Sounds like we'll be spending a lot of time together. It's good to get to know each other. Gotta say, you don't sound as tough as you do on TV." *Living Gold* hasn't aired yet, so he's referring to my CEO character.

I try to keep the irritation from my voice. "That's because Amanda Boxer was a character I played, not me." I don't know why people don't get that.

He leans close. "It makes me realize what a great actor you are."

"Oh." I run my finger along the seam of the sofa cushion, staring at it. I'm not great with compliments, having received so few growing up. General Joan did *not* coddle.

He leans back on the sofa and continues, "You seem sweet in real life."

"Well, sweet doesn't help in a fight."

He grins, his aquamarine eyes twinkling. My stomach does another crazy flip. "Probably not, but I like it."

My cheeks heat, my heart kicks hard, and my brain completely checks out on me. I'm all discombobulated with the compliments and the sexiness. *Professional. Keep it professional.*

"You're exactly as I hoped," I say. *Except gorgeous.* I should've been more careful with my list of bodyguard requirements and requested a nongorgeous type.

He cocks his head. "How am I what you hoped?"

I gesture with both hands around his massive shoulders and biceps. "Jacked."

"Funny. Jack is my brother."

I laugh a little. "I meant—"

"I know what you meant. I like to keep fit in my line of work. Prevents injuries."

I nod. "Makes perfect sense. I hope I didn't make you uncomfortable, talking about your muscles." My cheeks flame. *God, Harper, could you be a worse boss, ogling your new employee?*

He gives me a panty-melting smile, his teeth flashing white against a sexy five-o'clock shadow. "I'm perfectly comfortable."

I'm dying here.

This is not at all embarrassing.

"Good," I say softly.

Our gazes lock. I'm enthralled, aching to get closer. The attraction is like nothing I've ever felt before. If we had an on-screen chemistry test, the director would go nuts for us as a couple. *You need him. Don't screw this up.* I can't look away, caught in something more powerful than myself. *Oh, God, it's mutual. The attraction is mutual. Ah, hell.*

I tear my gaze away, scrambling to figure out how to navigate a professional relationship when I'm as lusty as a teenager coming face-to-face with my crush. And my crush is into it.

"What do you like to do when you're not working?" he asks.

I attempt to sound casual and normal. "I love books and music, especially live performances."

He shifts toward me. "Yeah? Me too. I hit up as many music festivals as I can."

I smile. "Cool." I've heard music festivals are fun, but with the large crowds it's impossible for me to attend like a normal person. I only went once when a headliner, who was a friend of mine, invited me. I watched from backstage with her security detail.

A sharp knock on my trailer door startles me, and I leap up. "They probably want me on set. We should go."

I head for the door and open it, expecting one of the production assistants. Instead it's a scary-looking man with a shaved head and a neck tattoo, wearing a white button-down shirt open to mid-chest, revealing another tattoo over one of his pecs. Good thing I've got Joe here. How did this scary guy get past security?

His brown eyes are intent on mine as he offers his hand to shake. "Harper Ellis, I'm Joe Sullivan."

My bodyguard.

My stomach drops. "What?" I whisper over the roaring in my ears.

"Your new bodyguard," he says. "I got a little lost on the way to your trailer. Hey, you okay? You look kinda pale."

The complete stranger I let into my trailer brushes by me and steps outside. "Real nice to meet ya, Harper. Save some of that chocolate for Joe." He winks, turns, and walks away.

I slip back into my trailer and make my way to the sofa, flopping down in a cold sweat. My real bodyguard waits outside.

Who the hell did I let into my trailer?

2

———

Garrett

As exits go, it was a pretty good one, but the look of horror on Harper's face has me making an about-face. I know I was in the wrong. It's just that I didn't want to spoil the moment by admitting I wasn't her bodyguard. Plus, the chemistry between us is electric. She wants me. Not bragging, either. I could feel it, see it in her eyes, hear it in her voice. I'm good at reading people. I want her too, so if we could just get past this misunderstanding…

I check in with her guard, letting him know I'm on set because my sister-in-law Josie is the star of *Living Gold.* I'm sure he doesn't want to get on the bad side of the star at his new place of employment. After he confirms it with the head of security, he lets me through.

I knock on her trailer door and wait, the blood pumping through my veins. My first time on set has been an adventure so far. With potential for—

The door flies open. Harper's hazel eyes flash pure fury. God, she's beautiful. From her mass of curly dark brown hair to her smoking hot body in that slip of a dress all the way down to her sexy toned legs.

"Who are you?" she demands. "How did you get on set?"

"Is there a problem?" her guard asks, stepping closer.

"I'm on the list," I tell her. "Can I come in? I'll explain everything."

She gestures me impatiently in, telling her guard, "It's fine."

I step inside, letting the door quietly shut behind me.

She slams her hands on her hips. "So? Explain."

I hold my palms up. "I'm Garrett Rourke. My sister-in-law is Josie Abbott, and I was on my way to my reserved seat in the studio audience when I ran into you." *And you invited me in.*

She purses her lips. "Why don't I ask her that right now, hmm?" She grabs her phone from the sofa and texts rapidly, her brows drawn down in concentration. She lifts her head. "No reply yet."

"Sean's probably distracting her." *More like hooking up with her, but hey, they're madly in love and married, so why not?* "Have you met my brother Sean? Strong family resemblance." People from the neighborhood say you can tell a Rourke son because we resemble our dad, with his same dark brown hair, angular cheekbones, and build. I'm the only one who inherited his aquamarine eyes, which supposedly is the sign of a true ruler of Villroy. Yup, I've got royal blood. My dad abdicated the throne to Villroy to marry my mom, a commoner. Even if he hadn't been banished from the kingdom all those years ago, I still wouldn't have ruled as the youngest of six sons. That's me—baby of the family, even at twenty-six.

She lowers her phone and studies me for a moment. "You do resemble Sean. A lot." She puts a hand to her forehead. "Ugh, I feel like *such* an idiot. I assumed you were my guard when I saw my assistant talking to you. I thought she was directing you to my trailer when she was probably directing you to Josie's trailer."

"Yeah."

"And I practically dragged you in here. This is my fault."

"Nah, honest mistake." I smile, which makes her blush. She's sweet and a little shy, an appealing combination and not something I expected from an actor. Josie is loud and extremely outgoing.

She shakes her head.

I lift a palm. "If it helps, I'd like to be your bodyguard. If I didn't already have a job, that is. I work for my family's construction and real estate development business." That sounds more impressive than it is. I work on crew, no fancy title like my older brothers have. When the business was passed on to us from my uncle, my oldest brother was named CEO. As we grew with the real estate development business, he handed out corporate titles to my older brothers. Everyone but me. I know he sees me as the young inexperienced one, even after eight years of hard physical labor. Though part of me suspects it's also because I'm the best at my job. I can do every aspect of construction with an attention to detail that guarantees happy clients.

Harper sinks to the sofa. She checks her phone, reading the screen before meeting my eyes. "Josie's excited you're here and so happy we met. There's a bunch of celebration emojis." She holds up her phone to show me a dancing cheerleader, fireworks, and a champagne bottle.

I grin. "Sounds like Josie."

She sets her phone down next to her on the sofa and covers her face with her hands, peeking at me between her fingers. "I'm so embarrassed."

I step closer. "Don't be. I should've said something, but it felt like we were connecting, ya know? I didn't want to spoil the moment by admitting I wasn't who you thought I was."

She drops her hands, revealing bright red cheeks. You never see her blush on TV. Could she blush on cue? Acting is such a strange and fascinating world. I can't get over how different she is in real life from her character Amanda.

She blows out a breath. "Okay, well, I guess I have only myself to blame for accosting you and foisting water and chocolate on you."

I chuckle. "That's what clued me in to your sweetness. You only had three little pieces of chocolate, yet you offered me one."

She stares at my chest. "Just trying to be welcoming to the newest member of my little entourage."

"Who else is in it?"

She waves airily. "No one all the time like a bodyguard, which is why I was trying to make nice. I've got a publicist, agent, manager, and assistant hustling for me."

"Cool."

She stands. "Guess I should let the real Joe in and welcome him to the team." She shakes her head, muttering, "I'm making a mess of this guard thing."

"Lemme give you my number. I don't live far from Josie and Sean. In fact, I house-sit for them when she's away on a job." I want her to know how much Josie trusts me so she knows she can trust me.

"Oh. Uh…" She blushes even more, if that's possible, the blush spreading to her neck. "Actually, I have a boyfriend. Colton Young. He's away right—" Her phone rings to the tune of the Rolling Stones' "I Can't Get No Satisfaction." She gives me a small apologetic smile. "It's him. He's filming a Rolling Stones biopic. Sorry. I have to take this. Err, help yourself to a bottled water to go."

Even giving me the brush-off, she wants to give me something. "Sure, thanks." I can always use water after working on a hot day. We got an early start today on site to avoid the worst of the heat. I walk over and open the mini-fridge, which has a neat line of bottled waters on one shelf and diet iced teas on the other. I grab a water and glance at her listening intently to whatever Colton's saying, her brows knit together.

I head for the door and stop, one hand on the knob. I can't resist taking one last look over my shoulder at her. Something about her pulls at me. She's looking off in the distance, frowning before saying in an ice-cold voice, "Let's just cut to the chase and end it now. Goodbye, Colton."

She looks to the ceiling, blinking back tears.

I can't leave her in distress. "You okay?"

She squares her shoulders and lifts her chin, a steely look

taking over her face. It reminds me of the tough CEO she played before, which means it's an act.

"You seem—"

"I'm fine," she says through her teeth. "Colton was just being kind—his words—giving me a heads-up that he's now with his costar." Her lips press tightly together. "He didn't want me to be blindsided."

Cheating ass. He doesn't deserve her sweetness. "That sucks."

She crosses her arms, hugging herself. "Yeah, well, the good news is he's hoping after we both see other people, we'll really know if we're ready for a commitment. Silly me. After six months together, I thought we did have a commitment."

Total dick move. "Breakups are rough."

She nods jerkily. "He says they went out in public, which means it'll be in the press and all over the internet." She sighs. "I have to call my publicist to do damage control. Not for the first time because a guy…God, I am *so sick* of—sorry." She holds up a palm. "You don't deserve to hear me vent."

"Vent away."

She presses her lips tightly together, slowly shaking her head.

I never considered the public nature of relationships for well-known actors. That must suck even more.

The door to the trailer opens, and her guard pokes his head in. "Just got word that you're needed on set. They're bringing the audience in twenty."

She takes a deep breath. "Okay, thanks, Joe." She turns to me. "That's my cue."

"My cue too. Josie got me on a special list, so I'm allowed on set early."

She stares at me for a moment, then shakes her head. "What a day I'm having."

I follow her out, and she locks the door behind her. The three of us head over to the soundstage on Chelsea Piers. Joe's quiet, on alert, scanning the area as we cross the blacktop, stepping over taped-down wires running to the trailers.

A woman wearing a headset waves urgently for Harper to go inside the soundstage. She hurries ahead, Joe keeping up with her. She waves over her shoulder at me. "Nice meeting you. Bye!"

"Sure, bye." She's hustled inside, and I'm stopped and questioned by the headset lady. A few moments later, she waves me in.

I head for my reserved seat in the front row of the audience bleachers and spot Josie on set talking to Harper and another guy. Josie always stands out with her red hair and bubbly personality, gesturing enthusiastically. After they finish their conversation, I lift a hand to her. "Josie."

She throws her arms up in a V like a cheerleader. "Garrett! You made it!" She hurries over, and I meet her halfway. She hugs me and pulls back, her blue eyes shining. "I'm so glad you could come. This is going to be a great episode. Sean's just getting something from my trailer. He'll sit with you." She gestures around the set, which is the interior of a mansion —living room, stairs that lead nowhere, and an adjoining kitchen. "Well, what do you think?"

My gaze catches on Harper, who's heading off the set. "It's been amazing so far."

"Oh? I hear a note of *I got to meet Harper Ellis* in there," she says in a teasing voice. "Are you a fan? I just *love* her! One of the best scene partners ever."

"Yeah, she's very talented, but I think she's upset. She just broke up with someone after six months."

Josie's eyes widen. "She and Colton broke up? I had no idea. It just happened right in front of you?"

"I overheard her on the phone. Maybe check in with her?"

"Right. Totally will. After the taping, though. I don't want to throw her off her game." She frowns. "Poor thing." She goes up on tiptoe and kisses my cheek. "I gotta go before they call in the audience. Enjoy!"

She heads off, intercepted by my brother Sean halfway. She greets him enthusiastically like he's just arrived, though he's probably been here the whole time. That's just how she is with him. Sean is damn lucky to have a woman who adores him heart and soul the way Josie does.

I'm ready for that big love like they have. If only I could

find the right woman. Harper comes to mind as someone with potential. But I know better than to step in as her rebound. Those kinds of relationships never work out. It's about luck and timing, mostly. Though I secretly wish it were about fate because then it would just happen, and nothing I did, no choice I make, would ever be wrong. Fate would take the wheel and bring me the One. Call me a romantic.

But I have good reason to be. The One is a real thing. I've seen it with my parents. My dad could've been king, living the high life in a palace on a beautiful island. Instead, he gave up everything to marry "the best woman in the world." His words, which he often says to her and to anyone who'll listen. That's what I'm holding out for. When I know with absolute certainty that I would give anything to be with the best woman in the world for me, that right there is the One.

Sean bounds up the steps to the bleachers and slaps me on the back as he takes the seat next to me. He resembles me with short dark brown hair, a bit of scruff, except he's got our mom's blue eyes. "Hey, Beast, heard you met Harper. Lucky you, meeting a star your first time on set." My older brothers nicknamed me Beast because of my muscles. Sue me for wanting to keep fit. Guess it's better than my old nickname. Mom called me her teddy bear.

"Yup, lucky me," I say.

"What's the matter? Did she blow you off?"

I nearly choke on his choice of words. The attraction was intense. If she hadn't told me she had a boyfriend, I would've sworn she was into me as much as I was into her. "No, we had a nice talk."

He elbows me. "Nice, huh? That's Beast code for you're into her. You like the nice girls."

"Doesn't everyone?"

He leans back in his seat. "They're not bad. You should ask Harper out. She and Josie get along, so we could double date."

"She has a boyfriend. Well, she did. They just broke up."

"Perfect. Step in there."

I give him a sideways look. "Ever hear of rebound?"

"Ever hear of ask her out before the next hot actor comes along to turn her head?" He leans in, speaking in a conspiratorial tone. "This is a different world filled with nonstop beautiful rich people. You gotta move quick." He would know. He runs the Royal Rourke Foundation US and mostly networks through Josie's Hollywood connections to raise funds to better the Brooklyn neighborhoods we work in. It's part of our family business mission to give back by creating parks, playgrounds, and other things to enhance the neighborhood in every development project we take on.

Still, the *beautiful rich people* angle doesn't mean much to me. "If that's what she's into, then I'm not right for her anyway." I'm a construction worker, nothing more, nothing less. Though sometimes looking at Sean's awesome life makes me think about something different for myself. I've been working for my family's construction business since I graduated high school and, lately, I've been feeling restless. I like working with my brothers, but I can't help but think—is this it for me?

But what the hell else would I do with only a high school diploma and no marketable skills beyond tools? I can't see myself doing what Sean does, networking his ass off to raise money for the charitable arm of our family business. Not that he needs my help. Besides, my family is important to me. Only one of my brothers has ever left the business, and he'll likely be back. Family sticks together no matter what. My dad drilled that into us. He lost his family through banishment and wanted his new family, us, to stay close. I won't let him down.

Sean socks me on the shoulder. "When did you get so mature? Aren't you supposed to be sowing your wild oats?"

"That gets old."

"Yeah, I know what you mean. I hit that stage and started getting pickier about who I spent time with."

I feel someone staring and turn to see Harper just behind the living room set. She whirls and runs into Joe, who's standing behind her. She's not used to having a bodyguard. I can see her blush from here as she says something to him and dashes out of sight behind a long wall of hallway. Joe follows.

Maybe I should go to more of these tapings. If nothing else, she's immensely entertaining.

Yeah, that's the reason.

                                    3
                                  ─────────

Garrett

The next morning, Saturday, I take a shower after my usual run, get dressed, and flop down on the sofa to check my phone for messages. My heart kicks up speed. Harper texted me late last night after I shut my phone off. A bunch of texts, actually. She must've gotten my number from Josie. I always work out in the morning before checking in with the world, so this is all news to me. Holy shit.

Harper: *A reporter surprised me outside my apartment building, asking me about Colton and his new lover. I panicked and said we mutually decided to see other people and I was glad I met you.*

I said your whole name. It just came out. I'm so sorry. Not cool.

I feel terrible.

There's going to be press about it. Just ignore it, okay? My publicist will make it all go away.

Sorry.

I stare at the screen, unsure how to respond. While I'm sitting there trying to figure out what this all means, Sean texts me. *Sly dog. You said you weren't following up with Harper.*

There's a link to an article. It's one of those gossip entertainment sites, and there's a large picture of Harper and

Colton with a jagged split down the middle. Right next to it is Colton with his arm around another woman, a beautiful petite blonde. The article goes on and on about how the perfect Hollywood couple are now through because of a stronger love between Colton and his new costar, Taylor. I skim the article, searching for my part in this. Finally, I find it, in a quote from Harper: "I'm doing okay. We mutually decided to see other people a few weeks back, and I'm very happy I met Garrett Rourke."

I set the phone down on the coffee table and stare blankly for a moment. She dragged my name into it without asking me ahead of time. That's bad.

I stand and pace the living room. On the other hand, she apologized, and she only said she was happy she met me. She didn't say we were a thing.

But it was implied, wasn't it?

I stop in front of the ugly piece of modern art on the wall that I somehow got stuck with and glare at it. This piece of "art"—purple and red scribbles with a yellow dot in the center—belongs to my brother Connor, who left it behind. He won't let me throw it out because our brother Jack gave it to him as a birthday present, and he won't take it with him because Con's wife says it doesn't go with their decor. Now I'm saddled with it. I take it off the wall and turn it around.

Back to pacing. Maybe it's flattering that Harper mentioned me. Maybe she truly is happy she met me. This could be an opportunity. Did fate intervene, tying us together?

I'm grasping at straws. I grab my phone and text her back. *Just got your texts. Thanks for the heads-up.*

Harper: *Really sorry. Are you mad?*

I think for a moment. I want her too much to be mad, and what does that say about me? This is such a bizarre situation. I've only been mentioned in an article once before when my oldest brother, Dylan, got married in Villroy. It was the first time our family had a wedding in the kingdom after my dad's banishment, so it was big news. The reconciliation between the Villroy Rourkes and the Brooklyn Rourkes is relatively new.

I text back. *I'm fine.*

I need to talk to Josie before I pursue anything further with Harper. Josie's an excellent judge of people, she knows how the industry and the press machine works, and she'll be straight with me. I text her, and she promptly invites me for dinner, which I accept.

I take a seat on the sofa and decide to do a little investigating. I tap over to Google on my phone and type my name to see how far this thing with Harper traveled. I let out a low whistle. She must be an even bigger name than I realized because there's *tons* of articles about the split, and a few wondering who I am with links to a picture of me in a group photo from Dylan's wedding. There's a red arrow pointing to my head to pick me out among my brothers. This is really weird.

When I arrive for dinner at Sean and Josie's brownstone in the Park Slope neighborhood of Brooklyn, a bottle of red wine in hand, Josie answers the door. "Come in! I'm so happy you could make it for dinner." She takes the offered wine. "You are so sweet! My favorite." She tilts her head, offering me her cheek.

I bend down to kiss it. "Thanks for the invite."

She gestures for me to follow downstairs to the kitchen. "Sean's on cooking duty tonight."

Great! Josie is a disaster in the kitchen. She keeps trying, though. Relentlessly optimistic, this one.

"What are we having?" I ask.

"It's this neat fish dish, where you wrap it in parchment paper and cook it with vegetables."

"Mediterranean fish en papillote," Sean says, sounding extremely sophisticated. The thing about Sean is that he was just like me, a regular old construction worker, but he didn't let that define him. He got heavily involved in fundraising efforts for Habitat for Humanity and started meeting a different circle of people—educated, wealthy professionals. He's a bit of a chameleon, changing to fit in depending on the circumstances. When he's in town, he'll still step in on crew on occasion if we need him at work, but otherwise he's knee-deep in Rourke foundation work, or accompanying Josie on set. She makes more than enough money for both of them.

"Take a seat," Josie says, indicating one of the scrolled iron swivel stools at the kitchen island. "You want a glass of this delicious wine or one of Sean's beers?"

I grin. "You hafta ask?"

Sean jerks his chin at me from the island, where he's chopping vegetables. "How ya doing?"

"Good." I give his shoulder a squeeze on my way past him and take a seat.

Josie shakes her head, smiling. "You don't have to bring wine just for me." She fetches me a beer, opens it, and searches for a glass.

I wiggle my fingers at her. "Gimme. I'll take it straight from the bottle."

She hands it over and gets to work uncorking the wine. Jazz plays in the background over speakers in the ceiling. Sean went all out on renovating this place. The appliances are top of the line too.

A few moments later, Josie joins me at the island and clinks her glass against my bottle. "Cheers!"

"Cheers."

I try to think of the best way to get her view on the Harper situation without sounding like I'm *too* interested. Josie is the kind of person who'd get overly excited and try to play matchmaker. I'm not sure what I want to happen with Harper. I'm part mad she brought my name into it without asking me, and part flattered that she'd want me tied to her in the public eye. Is she the kind of person who throws people under the bus to make herself look good, or was it just a onetime panic response? I want to believe she's a good person.

Josie nudges her shoulder with mine. "I texted Harper your number after our taping yesterday, and now I hear you're dating. I'm so happy for you. I just knew you two would be a good match."

"Josie," Sean says with a note of exasperation in his voice, "you didn't tell me you did that."

"What?" she asks, looking between us. "They're both single and awesome. Why wouldn't I want them to connect?"

I clench my jaw. I offered to give Harper my number before the taping, she declined, and then Josie sent it anyway. Did Harper think I asked Josie to do that? So fucking embarrassing, like I'm desperately pursuing her. I've never desperately pursued any woman. That's what my charm is for.

"You shouldn't have given her my number," I say. "I don't need dating help. We're not together either. She told the press we're a thing without asking me ahead of time." I narrow my eyes at her. "I'm not liking being blindsided by the two of you."

"Ohhh, I didn't realize that's how it went down with her," Josie says, conveniently ignoring her own wrongdoing. She cocks her head. "Huh. That's not like her. Maybe a reporter ambushed her, and she panicked."

I take a swig of beer. "Yeah, basically. That's what she said."

She squeezes my arm. "Are you mad?"

"I'm not sure," I admit.

"Because he's into her," Sean says. "I told him we'd go on a double date."

Josie claps, her eyes lighting up. "That would be awesome. And if you got married, she could be my sister! Oh, you guys, you know I've always wanted a sister."

I stare at her. *Is she nuts?* "Josie, we literally just met."

"And you have sisters-in-law now," Sean points out, taking a roll of parchment paper from a drawer.

Josie beams at him. "I know, but I'm greedy."

He sets the roll of parchment paper on the island, cups her jaw, and kisses her. "Love you," he says gruffly.

She practically dances in her seat. "Love you too!"

I take a long draw on my beer, ignoring the stab of jealousy. I'm happy for them, for all of my brothers with their forever loves. It's stupid to feel like I'm the one left behind. Youngest is always last. So what? It's not a race.

Josie takes in my no doubt somber expression and gets serious. "I don't think she meant to hurt you by bringing you into it. You have to understand the kind of spotlight she's under. People know her from *Capital Asset*, and she was in two teen shows before that. She started working when she was fifteen, so the public feels like they know her. They want to know who she's with and what she's doing with her life. It can be a lot of pressure. And this thing with Colton…" She shakes her head. "I think people feel sorry for her being cheated on, so she spun it away from that. She's probably trying to make it look like it was a mutual decision to make things more equal. Your name popped up because she'd just been talking to you." She lifts a finger. "But subconsciously she wants to be with you."

Hope spears through me, and I ruthlessly tamp it down. Harper only talked about me to save face. I hadn't realized she was known to the public for so long. I only knew her from that one show. I don't keep up with celebrity gossip, and I missed those teen TV shows. They were probably for girls.

I feel Josie staring at me. "Okay, I get why she'd want to even the playing field after Colton sprang his new girlfriend on her. Ya know, this acting thing is really a double-edged sword. You get to do the work you love, but there's a price, giving up your privacy."

"Exactly. And she's had some weird stalker incidents since playing Amanda Boxer. The last thing she wants is to appear weak in any way."

My gut tightens. "What kind of weird stalker incidents?"

"The most recent one was a guy breaking into her apartment, asking her to whip him."

"Jesus."

Sean shakes his head. "Sicko."

"What happened?" I ask. "What did she do?"

Josie straightens in her seat. "I give her a lot of credit for quick thinking after being woken from a sound sleep. She told him he had to be tied up in the closet before she'd do it, and he had to wait for her command. So she tied him up with her jump rope in her bedroom closet, and then she left the apartment and called the police. They found him still eagerly waiting for her."

My gut twists. "She must've been terrified." Sweet Harper facing an intruder alone. No wonder she hired a bodyguard. Shit. That's why she looked horrified when she realized I wasn't her guard. She didn't seem scared, though, and she still invited me into her trailer to explain myself. Maybe she could tell I wasn't a danger. I would never hurt a woman.

Josie continues. "Yeah, and there's been others. Guys are attracted to tough Amanda like she's some kind of dominatrix, or they feel threatened and want to put her in her place. Usually it's just verbal harassment, but there've been a few incidents where a guy grabbed her by the hair or ass."

A cold fury settles over me. I hate that she felt threatened by these men just because she's on TV doing her job. I almost wish I were her guard because I'd kick every guy's ass that tried to get near her.

"I can't believe this is all over a character she played on TV," I say. "Don't they know the difference between fiction and reality?"

She lifts a shoulder. "I know. Not that it excuses that kind of behavior anyway. No woman should be harassed for being who she is whether that's tough or gentle."

"True," I say.

"Absolutely," Sean chimes in.

Josie gives him a sweet smile before turning back to me. "Anyway, I just want you to understand where she's coming from. She's really the sweetest person, but even someone sweet, when they feel threatened, will do whatever they need to do to protect themselves. She needed to not look weak and alone. I'm sure that's why she blurted she was with you."

"I'm fine with it." And I really am. I'm more worried about her safety. "Now I get why she hired a bodyguard. Why don't you hire a bodyguard?"

She smiles at my brother. "I've got Sean. No one's going to mess with him."

Sean's chest puffs out for a moment before he tucks fish

and vegetables into a parchment pouch. "The moment I think it's called for, we'll hire a guard. So far, Josie hasn't attracted that kind of attention. I do look out for her in public, and this place is wired for security." He gives Josie a stern look. "I already told her once we have kids, a guard is nonnegotiable."

Josie blows him a kiss.

I can't help but feel bad for Harper. To feel threatened like that, to have her home violated. The stuff of nightmares. It could've been so much worse too.

Josie turns to me. "You two should go out for real now."

I hold up a palm. "She was just saving face."

Josie presses on. "You guys are both so sweet. I think you should go for it."

I lean close to get in her face, making sure she gets how serious I am. "Josie, she's got enough going on. I'd just be adding to her stress after our run-in yesterday, her breakup, and the fallout from the press." Not to mention feeling threatened by random men. That's just wrong.

Sean and Josie turn curious eyes on me. "Your run-in?" they say in near unison.

"I thought you just had a nice talk," Sean says.

I rub my scruffy jaw and fill them in on Harper's mistaking me for her guard, along with her extreme embarrassment when she realized it. "I don't want to stress her any more."

"Oh my God, this is all so adorable!" Josie exclaims. "A case of mistaken identity."

Sean shakes his head, smiling, and continues assembling parchment packets.

"I doubt Harper thought it was adorable," I say.

Josie picks up her phone and starts texting.

I stiffen. "You're texting her, aren't you?"

She smiles, still texting merrily. "I just told her you're here for dinner, and you asked me to pass along that you hope she's okay."

It sounds like the right note to hit without putting any pressure on her. "I guess that's alright."

Josie texts for so long the hair on the back of my neck stands up. She did something, didn't she? A step too far.

"Are you talking about me?" I ask.

Josie puts her phone down and gives me her wide-eyed innocent look. The woman is never innocent of anything. "No big. Just let her know how awesome you are from my insider point of view, and that if she wants a friendly ear, to get in touch with you anytime to chat."

I clench my jaw. "I didn't agree to that last part. She'll think I asked you to do that and feel pressured." *And it makes me look desperate again.* "Come on, Josie. Do ya think I can't get a woman on my own? You're making me look bad."

She turns to my brother. "It was a harmless add-on, right, Sean?"

Sean puts dinner in the oven, saying, "Don't get me in the middle of your sneaky matchmaking ways."

Josie turns back to me and lifts her chin. "I'm not sorry. You should be thanking me."

I bite back a sharp retort.

She flutters her lashes at me. *Ridiculous.* I'm still mad.

I narrow my eyes at her and take a pull on my beer. My phone vibrates with a text.

Harper: *I'm okay, but thanks for the offer to chat.*

"It's her, right? What'd she say?" Josie asks eagerly.

I take a sip of beer, playing it cool, ignoring the sting of rejection. I guess a little hope snuck in there. "She said so long."

"Oh." She rubs my arm. "Sorry, Garrett. I guess it wasn't meant to be."

Whatever. I'm tired of hoping for things that don't work out. I've decided fate will put the right woman in my path. Harper Ellis simply isn't her.

"How do you feel about an older woman?" Josie chirps. "The woman who plays the matriarch of the family on my show is single. She's not that old either, fortyish. They use makeup to age her."

"No!" Sean and I say in unison.

Josie presses her lips together. "She's nice, and so are you. I don't see anything wrong with it."

Sean gestures toward me. "Beast needs a woman who—"

"I don't need anyone's help," I grumble.

Josie brightens. "Ooh, remember that nice Catholic girl your mom tried to set Brendan up with?"

We all crack up. Poor Brendan. Just when my brother brought home the love of his life, there's Mom introducing him to Faith. Josie sure knows how to lighten the mood.

"Maybe?" Josie asks me.

"No!"

4

Harper

My phone vibrates with a text on the dining room table, where I'm eating dinner, and I stare at it, my pulse accelerating. Is Garrett following up with me for more? Do I want him to? I can't deny the chemistry between us was like nothing I've ever experienced before. And I really do like him. At the same time, I'm still hurting from Colton's betrayal. I should've seen this coming. My ex, John, used me for a step up in the industry too. It's just that Colton was so different from John, so casual and relaxed about everything, I didn't think he had that kind of ambition in him. Guess he hid it well, and look how great it worked out for him. He went from a part in a music video to starring in a movie thanks to our "It" couple status. I haven't even starred in a movie! Just small forgettable supporting girlfriend roles.

I ignore my phone, not ready to deal with whoever it is in my current state of mind.

I'm so sick of user men. John had been a guest star on *Capital Asset* during our first season. He poured on the charm, the gifts, the affection. I let my guard down, let him into my heart. We went everywhere together, even lived together. The press loved us, and as my profile grew playing Amanda, the buzz around us grew. I thought everyone saw what I did—a madly-in-love couple. A wedding was surely in our future. John's career started building with supporting roles in two movies, and I was happy for him. But the moment he was offered the lead in a new superhero movie, he cut ties. He told me it was just the way the business works, nothing personal. *Nothing personal to the woman you dated for a year!* I never guessed how ruthlessly ambitious he was, until he showed his true colors.

Twice burned, and I won't let there be a third time. I'm going to focus on work and that is it. My agent says I'm a TV workhorse, reliable to help any show shine, but I want more than that. I want a juicy part in a movie. The roles just aren't coming my way. Maybe I should date myself to leapfrog into a better role. Sure worked for John and Colton!

I drop my head in my hand. I have to stop picking the wrong kind of guy. I need to listen to my gut more for warning signals that something's not right. I read a book today about women who make bad choices in men. *Yes, I'm that desperate for answers. I'm smart, yet I keep doing this.* One of the reasons women choose the wrong men is because of abandonment issues, which I definitely have, since my mother left me as a newborn and wasn't part of my life. I always suspected my strict grandmother drove her away, not approving of a nineteen-year-old accidentally pregnant by a married man. My father never wanted me. He had another family, and my very existence threatened what he had. My throat closes tight, my eyes hot. *Unwanted, unlovable.* I wipe at a tear and take in a shaky breath.

No wonder I'm screwed up about men and relationships. My father was a cheater who never once tried to contact his daughter. I learned young—men cannot be counted on. They won't stick. And, somehow, I have to keep learning this lesson by choosing the wrong men.

So, okay, now that I know why I have this destructive pattern, I can be smart and end it. I'll choose the right kind of man next time. A good trustworthy man. Once I'm ready to go back to dating, that is, way, way in the future.

One thing's for sure, I'm never going to have a kid by accident like my mom. My child will be planned for and very much wanted with a loving family surrounding her. She'll never feel worthless or unlovable. *Fantasies.* Who knows if I'll even be married before my fertility window passes? But if it's meant to be, I'll do it the *right* way.

I exhale sharply and pick up my phone to read my text. Not Garrett. I deflate and tell myself I'm relieved it's my manager.

Saw the press. Did you know Garrett Rourke is from the royal Rourke family in Villroy? Congrats on snagging a royal! Good PR.

I hadn't put that together. I try not to read gossip sites, not wanting to read anything bad about myself. That's why I hired a publicist as a buffer. So a guy from Brooklyn is a prince or a duke or something. Is that common knowledge? I'm about to do a search on his name when I stop myself. That would only bring up the latest trashy talk about me and Colton, where I mentioned Garrett. I shouldn't have done that. It's just he made a good impression on me, so his name just popped out. And my adrenaline was through the roof when that reporter showed up just as I was entering my apartment building. I don't like men staking me out where I live.

I swear the next guy I date will have zero ties to the industry. A writer would be nice. He'd probably be quiet and have lots of books. We'd spend our Sundays reading in a quaint cottage on the water. In the meantime…

I send a quick response to my manager and get back to dinner. Joe moved in next door, so I feel safe here alone. After dinner, I'm going to have a relaxing Saturday night in and read my go-to comfort book *The Scoundrel and the Governess* by Alice Segal. See how I'm already preparing for my role as wife to a writer by reading so much? It's not being antisocial, it's called rehearsing for my future dream life.

Just as I settle into the cushy corner of my sofa with my e-reader, I get a call. I check the screen and immediately tense—Dana, my bulldog publicist. I hired her mostly so she could spin press *away* from me unless I'm obligated to promote something. I'm not a good public speaker. Which is to say I completely freak out for days ahead of time and get through it in a sweaty, heart-pounding race to the end, after which I collapse. It's *not* pretty. I much prefer saying lines written for me as a character than facing the public as myself.

I answer the phone, immediately taking control of the conversation. "Hi, Dana, were you able to make any headway tamping down the Garrett part of the story?"

"I've been following it closely, and, truth is, I'm *loving* this royal guy you threw into the mix," she says. "Completely topped Colton's newest sweet young thing. Sorry. I know you cared for him, and you guys looked great together, but everyone said he was not the kind to stick. If it helps, I'm sure he'll cheat on Taylor too."

"It doesn't." I grip the phone tighter. "You said you'd help get Garrett out of the story."

"It exploded with the royal angle. No way I can contain it. I say we roll with it. Now that Colton's out for the gala next Saturday, might I suggest you invite this royal? You need a gorgeous hunk of a man in a tux at your side. Colton's absence will be too conspicuous. You'll spend the whole night fielding questions about him, and neither of us wants that."

I stiffen. I forgot Colton was set to fly in for the event. No way I'm roping Garrett into it. The poor man! First I accost him and drag him into my trailer, assuming he's my guard, and then I blurt his name to a nosy, well-connected reporter. He's been through enough because of me. The gala is a black-tie fundraiser dinner for an organization close to my heart—Best Friends Care. They train service dogs and match them to people who are disabled physically and/or psychologically. A lot of veterans with PTSD benefit from a therapy dog. My uncle suffered from PTSD and never got the help he needed. He suffered greatly before he committed suicide. A therapy dog might've saved him.

"Dana," I say firmly, "I'm not going to ask Garrett to what will likely be a boring event for him." I don't want him to feel used either. It's a terrible feeling when you realize someone you thought was your friend (or your love) just wants something from you.

"He's a royal. It's right up his alley."

Garrett looked like a regular guy in a T-shirt, jeans, and work boots. He works construction in his family's business. I just can't picture him as a royal doing photo ops and cutting ribbons. He's too rough and tough looking for that, which is partly why I thought he was my guard. I close my eyes, embarrassed at the memory. *My tough, hot, sexy AF guard. Not.*

He fixed my shelf.

No, I'm not going down this path.

"I'll go solo," I say. "Or maybe I'll bring a friend." I'm only an hour and a half away from where I grew up in Summerdale, New York. I could ask one of my hometown girl friends. "A woman in a tux at my side could deflect the Colton gossip." I stifle a laugh.

"Harper," Dana says in an exasperated tone.

I often exasperate her. We're at cross purposes—I work hard to keep my life private, and she works hard to keep me in the public eye. She knew what she signed up for with me.

She continues. "I looked up these Rourkes. They're hot as hell."

At least one of them is. Still not going there.

"I'm not using him for a photo op," I say.

Dana continues as if I haven't spoken. "And even though Garrett's in the background of this wedding picture floating around—wearing a black tux, I might add—it's clear he's *superior* eye candy with all that muscle."

Like a bodyguard. Then I get an idea. "I have Joe now. It's perfect. He's going with me anyway as my guard, so I'll just put him in a tux, and it'll look like he's my date. Problem solved." I smile, pleased at my clever thinking.

"You're not using your guard as a date. He's recently separated from his wife, not yet divorced. That's *not* the PR we want for you. Don't you read the daily memos Trina sends out to keep us all in the loop?"

I grimace. My assistant is very industrious, but who can keep up with daily memos? I trust her to do her job. She's been with me for three years now.

"Okay, forget about the memos," Dana says. "I'm happy

to read them for you. Your job is to get that royal man candy on your arm for next Saturday."

I break out in a cold sweat at the thought. Could I skip the event entirely? No. I want the press to take note of Best Friends Care, and my presence will help draw attention to the cause.

"Harp, we good? Date for Saturday's gala?"

No. "I'll come up with something."

"I'll get in touch with Prince Garrett Rourke for you, okay? I know you can get uncomfortable with this kind of thing." That's her polite reference to my shyness. I don't pursue men. *Except when I mistake them for my guard apparently.*

"I don't think anyone calls him Prince Garrett." *Do they?* Josie didn't. Boy, is she a major Garrett fangirl. I'm betting she loves everyone in the Rourke family with great enthusiasm. That's just her. "Don't get in touch with him. I'll figure something out."

Her voice takes on an urgent tone. "You have to go. You're getting an award for your contribution. It's because of you they were able to go international with their organization. That is a big deal. You can't turn them down at this late date. I've arranged a ton of press for this."

"I'm going! Don't worry."

She lets out an audible breath. "Okay, okay. We want the focus on the cause, not on your cheating ex. If you show up with a date, the message is, you're fine and you both love this cause. Don't make it harder on yourself than it needs to be. And he's easy on the eyes. No one will feel sorry for you after that."

My breath catches. "They feel sorry for me?"

"More like pity. You know I tell it like it is. It's career suicide to be pitied. No one will enjoy rooting you on as Amanda Boxer, Lexi Gold, or any other character. You can be tough, you can be a wealthy socialite, but you cannot look pathetic and weak. You can't be pitied. Understand?"

Pathetic and weak! My upbringing kicks in, and I square my shoulders and straighten my spine. I was raised to be strong and I am. I was betrayed by Colton and did nothing wrong.

I keep my tone even. "I'm going solo. Goodbye, Dana."

"Think about it, please," she says in a strained voice. "Ciao."

I hang up. I'll look even stronger and tougher going alone. I don't need a date to even the score between me and Colton. I will rise above.

~

I walk to my trailer for lunch after our Monday morning table read for *Living Gold*, looking forward to some quiet time to myself. I halt, surprised to find Dana sitting on the trailer steps. She's in her forties with sleek black hair in a bob and more energy than anyone I know. Except maybe Josie. That woman is nonstop.

"Surprise!" she exclaims, rising from her perch on the top step.

I give her a one-armed hug so I don't spill my take-out container of sushi on her. "I can't believe you flew all the way from LA to see me. Is this about the gala?"

"Hey, I like to check in with my New York contacts on the regular. Not everything is about you, though you are my favorite client."

I unlock my trailer door and head inside. She follows, unusually quiet.

Once we're both seated on the sofa with drinks, I offer her half my lunch.

"Already ate, thanks," she says. "You go ahead."

I pull the built-in table in the adjacent wall closer, set my lunch on it, and open the lid of the take-out container.

"So how's things here?" she asks. "Are you enjoying playing Lexi Gold?"

I get out my chopsticks. "I love it." On *Living Gold* I get to play against type as a single mom with a vulnerable side, which is the main reason I took the role. The premise of the show is that the wealthy family (the Golds) have a maid problem. Namely, the former maid's illegitimate daughter— played by the comedic genius Josie—just inherited the mansion from the recently deceased patriarch, who had an affair with her mother. Sitcom gold. Ha. Gold.

Dana's quiet again. She's working up to something.

I eat my lunch and wait.

Finally, she says, "Wouldn't it be great to bring that sensitive fashionista persona into the public eye at the gala? Instead of being pegged as that tough bitch, you become the socialite with a heart of gold."

"What's wrong with being myself in public?" I take a bite of sushi. I do my job, get in, get out, as polite and professional as can be. Not that it's easy for me, but at least it's honest.

She nods and takes a long drink of water.

I lift my brows in question.

"Nothing, of course," she finally blurts. "You're wonderful, very sweet, just that sometimes you're so reserved it makes reporters fill in the blanks. Empty expression on your face can mean tough or aloof or angry."

"My so-called resting bitch face. Screw 'em. Let them think what they want."

She laughs nervously. "See, that's why I'm the publicist and you're the talent. So who's your date for the gala?"

I narrow my eyes at her. "Tell me you did not fly out here just to harass me about a date."

"Of course not. I have other business in New York. I just stopped by to make sure you take the next right step."

I shake my head. She totally came out here to harass me.

"This is bigger than you," she says. "This is about putting the spotlight on Best Friends Care. Everyone wants to know about this new guy you said you were seeing; therefore, everyone will listen when you talk about this great cause. We'll come up with a noncommittal sound bite to shift the attention from him to the service dogs."

I sigh. She knows how much this organization means to me. I helped foster puppies for them in LA years ago when they were just getting started in that one location. As my name recognition grew, I was able to help them grow. Soon they had training centers across the country and now across the world.

I put my chopsticks down, my gut knotting. It's not that I don't want to see him. I just don't want him to feel used. And it's embarrassing what I've put the man through. I can't let that hold me back. I can get over my embarrassment for the cause. "Fine. I'll ask Garrett—"

She pumps a fist. "Yesss!"

I hold up a palm. "But I'm going to tell him he's under no obligation, especially after I dragged his name into the press." *And dragged him into my trailer.* Then I remember what he said when I asked him why he let me think he was my guard: *I should've said something, but it felt like we were connecting, ya know?* I don't know many guys who would speak so openly. Maybe there is something there—a connection. If I'm willing to take a risk. My gut churns. I need to pay attention to my gut, and it's telling me not to get in deep. I'm not ready for it.

She stands and kisses my forehead. "He won't say no, trust me. You're a catch."

I give her a wry look. "Don't be alarmed if I show up by myself on Saturday."

"Not a chance. I gotta go. I've got a meeting with Josie today too."

"You do? Is she your client now?"

She crosses her fingers and holds them up. "Not yet. She wants to see if I can amp up the spotlight for the Rourke foundation fundraiser at the Met. I'm all over it. Ciao!"

She leaves in a rush, the scent of her citrusy perfume lingering behind. Zippy like her. I told Josie I'd go to her fundraiser mostly because she asked, and I felt I couldn't say no. I just hope Dana doesn't insist on a royal date for that event too. It's the Saturday after the gala, and two glitzy events back-to-back is too much to ask anyone, let alone a guy you just met under embarrassing circumstances.

I'm suddenly too nervous to eat. I decide to text Garrett and just get it over with. I type out a long text explaining Best Friends Care, and why it would be nice to have him there. I add that he's under absolutely NO OBLIGATION. All caps to emphasize the point.

Then I wait.

He's probably busy. I take my phone off vibrate, so I won't miss the notification, and go back to lunch, keeping my phone within reach just in case. I'd really like to have an answer before I go back to work. We'll be blocking on set, scripts in hand, so no phones allowed. I don't want to be angsting over this all day. I put myself out there. Okay, I went kicking and screaming to this point, but part of me hopes he'll want to go just for me. I exhale sharply. This is another reason I keep getting tangled up with the wrong men. I always hope the next guy will be different. And I so want me to be enough, not just be a step up in someone's career.

My phone rings, and I jump. He *called* me. I really prefer texting. It lets me think carefully about what I want to say and compose the perfect message. Who knows what I'll blurt in the heat of the moment?

"Hello?" I say cautiously.

"Hey, good to hear from ya, Harper." His deep smooth voice melts me, making me feel soft and gooey inside. I'm chocolate. *Wait, what?*

"Hi." I don't trust myself to say anything more.

"Hello," he says warmly. "You texted a long note, so I thought the phone would be better."

Adrenaline fires through me as I realize this is the part where I have to ask him on a date. "Yes. Like I said in my text, I was supposed to go with Colton to the gala, and there's all this press—for a really good cause, service dogs for people who really need them—and there's going to be a ton of press. Did I mention that part in the text? About the press? I can go alone, no problem, but if I have a date, it would be nice, especially if you also say service dogs are a good thing. To the press, I mean. No pressure, just as friends united for a good cause."

"Will the press be there?"

"Uh…yeah." *Didn't I mention that?*

He chuckles. "I'm teasing. You said press, like, four times. Sounds like you're concerned about them."

"I want the spotlight on Best Friends Care, not on me and

my cheating ex. The spotlight would be on us, of course, but then we'd redirect it to the service dogs."

"I do think service dogs are a good thing."

My heart races because that almost sounded like a yes, and I'm not sure how I feel about that. *Why did I let Dana rope me into this?* "You're under no obligation to go. None whatsoever. In fact, it will probably be a horribly tedious night. I have to make a speech that will not be *at all* entertaining. It'll be painful and awkward. For me too. I'll be stressed the whole night about it. Public speaking is not my thing. I need to be a character to be comfortable out front like that—"

"Harper."

"Yeah?"

"I'll go."

"Why?" I blurt.

"I like you."

"Which part did you like best? When I accosted you, or the part where I pretended we were dating without consulting you?" *Seriously, what guy wants that?*

He laughs.

I grip the phone tighter. "Didn't you hear what a horrible date I'll be? I'm going to be stressed the whole night about my speech, which will be boring. When I can speak, that is, after coughing and choking on my own spit."

"You're funny."

I sit straighter. "I'm dead serious."

"Alright. But you know what I got out of this conversation? I heard a woman who's brave enough to face her fear of public speaking for a greater good. That's the kind of person I'd like to spend time with. And it's a good cause, like you said."

My heart thumps harder. "It's black tie." *Last chance to bail! I can take it. Really.*

I can hear the smile in his voice. "I'll rent a tux."

A surge of warmth goes through me. "Thank you. I really appreciate this. I'll have my driver pick you up. And let me know if I can return the favor in some way."

"Next time I have a black-tie event, where *I* need to make a boring speech, you're the first number I'll call."

I laugh. "Okay."

A loud buzz saw goes off in the background on his end.

"I should get back to work," he says. "But I wanted to ask you a question. Hold on."

I tense again, not sure I want to answer any personal questions. It gets quiet in the background, and I wonder if he walked outside to continue our conversation.

"Does Sean still work with you there?" I ask. I'm curious because I see him on set a lot.

"Sometimes. He spends more time on the philanthropic side now, working remotely so he can be with Josie."

Wow. That is so sweet. "I'm going to his fundraiser at the Met."

"Cool," he says. "Need a date for that too?"

I smile. Maybe he doesn't see me as that woman who keeps putting him through stuff. "You're willing to commit to two dates in a row with me? What if you have a terrible time on Saturday, and then you're stuck with me the next Saturday?"

"What if I have a great time?"

My stomach does a topsy-turvy flip. "What if."

"So my question is, do I need to pretend we have a relationship for the press?"

Easy question. "If you wouldn't mind, it would make everything a little easier. It's up to you, though. Only if you're okay with it. We can say we're just friends. It's true anyway."

"I'm fine with the fake relationship thing. Anything I should know?"

I let out a breath of relief. His agreement means less explaining to reporters, which is always a good thing. "I'll come up with a story and fill you in on the way there. Thanks again, Garrett."

"You should call me Beast. Everyone does."

"Because you're a beast of a man with your bulky muscles?" I cringe. *I can't believe I just said that.*

"Nailed it," he says with a laugh.

"And what will you call me?"

"Beauty."

My breath stutters out. Beauty and the Beast. So romantic. And the thing is, I always saw myself as Belle with her love of books. I might harbor secret princess fantasies. Not something the general who raised me would've tolerated. I love my grandmother, but she's a difficult woman. Joan Ellis spits nails for breakfast. I indulged my princess fantasies by watching movies at friends' houses.

"Thank you, Beast."

"See ya Saturday, Beauty."

5

Harper

I ride the elevator of my apartment building down with Joe, my new shadow, to the car that'll take us to the gala tonight. I'm tense about my speech and desperately trying to take it down a notch. I did warn Garrett I'd be a mess. The driver already picked him up, and he's waiting in the back seat. I'm still a little surprised he agreed to go. Most guys are in an event like this for the PR, and—dirty little secret here—when I don't have a boyfriend, the date is often a setup between our publicists. Garrett has nothing to gain by being seen with me. In fact, he's doing me a favor, helping me save face with a fake relationship. Maybe Josie sang my praises, who knows; I'm just glad to have a drama-free date. I'm stressed enough about my speech. I've rewritten it five times. I'm worried I'll say the wrong version or Frankenstein them together in a way that doesn't make sense.

When I reach the sidewalk, the driver, Michael, steps out to open the door to the back seat for me. I only hire a car service in the city since it's such a hassle to park. I drive myself around in LA. Joe sticks close behind me.

A woman passing by on the sidewalk turns to the guy she's with and says loudly, "Is that Amanda Boxer?"

"I think it is!" he says. "What's her real name?" He calls out to me, "Hi! Harper Ellis, right?"

I give a little wave before carefully slipping into the back seat of the car, managing the layers of toile on my pink Caroline Herrera dress and being extra careful not to knock my head. I don't mind being recognized. I just don't want to be accosted.

Joe gets in the front seat, greeting Garrett in the back before facing front. The car pulls into traffic, heading for the hotel where they're holding the gala.

I turn to Garrett, and my breath stutters out. Wow. He was made for formal wear. His wide shoulders and broad chest fill out his tux jacket perfectly. The black material and white shirt contrast with his stunning aquamarine eyes. He's clean-shaven, the sharp angles of his jaw prominent.

"Hi," I say breathlessly.

He flashes a smile. "Hi. You look beautiful." He touches one of my teardrop diamond earrings. "Are these real?"

"Yes. They're on loan from an up-and-coming jeweler who wanted the exposure." My hair is swept into an updo to draw attention to them. Everything is carefully orchestrated for an event like this. The earrings are beautiful, an intricate design of white gold and diamonds.

"Funny how people who can afford nice jewelry get to wear it for free."

"All part of the PR machine. Anyway, you look great. The tux suits you."

He shoots out a jacket sleeve, snapping it tight. "I'm told I clean up nice." He winks. "I should probably buy a tux. I've had to wear them for four of my brothers' weddings. One of them had a courthouse ceremony, so I got a pass for his. Plus, I'll need one for next Saturday's Rourke fundraiser." He searches my expression.

It hits me that he's asking. He wants a second date already. I can't get sucked in. It's too soon. I swore I'd take some time before I got involved with anyone again. Besides, I'm sure he won't have much fun at these kinds of events. I never do. I only go to help causes I believe in.

"Tonight's going to feel long for you," I say. "It's more like work than a party."

"Will I be swinging a hammer?"

I laugh. "No, not that kind of work." I relax a little. He's a construction worker. There's nothing he could possibly gain from a connection with me. I have to remember that so I don't shut down and make tonight more difficult than it needs to be.

"How're ya doing? Nervous?"

How strange. I was so caught up in him I forgot to be nervous about my speech for a few minutes. "I'm worried I'm going to blurt out different versions of my speech. I rewrote it and memorized it five times."

"Just bring it with you to the podium. If you start to feel off, no one would mind if you check it."

I take a deep breath, nerves racing through me as I imagine myself trembling at the podium. "I have this fantasy of me moving freely onstage like I'm in a TED talk, you know? All confident, owning the space."

"You could play the part of a TED talk speaker. Turn it into a performance."

"I can't. The words are from the heart."

He shifts, leaning closer for what suddenly feels like an intimate conversation. "So this cause means something important to you. Not just something you do for PR."

"Yes." I tell him about my uncle's PTSD, and how I wish he could've benefited from a therapy dog. He's surprisingly easy to talk to.

He gives my arm a squeeze. "It's amazing the effect the unconditional love of a dog can have on a person. Do you have a dog?"

"I don't. I move around a lot and work long hours. I just feel like it wouldn't be fair for the dog to be left alone so much. One day I will. I've always wanted a golden retriever."

"Sweet dog."

"Yeah, my friend had one growing up." My breath hitches as our gazes lock, warmth spreading through me. I blink and look away. "So I should fill you in. When we arrive, there's a red carpet we'll walk down on our way in. Lots of cameras and flashes going off. Just stick close to me. I'll do all the talking. Though it would be great if you could chime in that you also support this organization. People want to see who I'm with, and our job is to use that spotlight and turn it to Best Friends Care."

"Got it."

I risk a glance at him. Still stunningly gorgeous in his tux, and he smells wonderful, like fresh soap and man. *Be strong, Harp. Friendly not flirty.* "Don't answer any questions about our relationship. I'll handle that, but just so you know, the story is that Colton and I agreed to take a break a month ago. You and I met three weeks ago through Josie."

"Easy enough. Are we exclusive?"

I consider that. "We're exclusively dating because that's what I do." *And what my boyfriends agree to as well, though few have remained faithful. Men suck.*

"I always think it's kinder to end it before moving on to the next person."

My lips part. A man who believes in monogamy as basic human decency. Outstanding.

His lips curve up, his eyes sparkling with good humor. "Why do you look so surprised? Did you think I was a player?"

I open my mouth and close it again, not wanting to admit my current low opinion of men. "I don't know you well enough to make any judgments. I was just surprised at how openly you express yourself."

"Score one for the Beast."

"Oh, you're way too nice to be a beast," I blurt.

He smiles, his eyes warm on mine. "Thank you."

Heat rushes through me; butterflies dance in my stomach, every nerve ending alive. It's just like when we first met, except it's beyond lust now. *Be smart. Protect yourself.*

His gaze drops to my neck and then to my bare shoulder and back to my eyes. My skin heats everywhere he looks. Imagine if he actually touched me. "People would probably say this is just a rebound relationship. They'd know it wasn't serious."

I face front, needing to put some distance between us. "I'm not responsible for what people say. We stay on message, and that's all we can do."

"Do you usually only date actors?"

I turn back to him. "Usually that's all I meet. I briefly dated a cameraman when I was twenty. He tried to sue me for emotional distress when we broke up. Now my dates are vetted first by my publicist."

"I was vetted?"

"In a way. After I mentioned you to that reporter, my publicist looked into you. She shared about your royal connection, but that's not why I asked you. I needed a date to the gala, that's all." I grimace because that sounds like I'm using him as a quick substitute for my cheating ex, which I kinda am, but I really do like him. He's so much nicer than most guys I meet. "In my mind you're here because of the Josie connection. And I enjoy talking to you."

"I'm glad she connected us. Feel free to call or text whenever."

My heart kicks harder. It sounds like he wants to get to know *me*. Not just the trappings around me, or even how fast he can get under my dress like most men. Am I being foolish hoping he's different, or is he the real deal?

"Thank you," I say softly. "That's sweet."

"Okay if I hold your hand?"

I blink, stunned that he asked. I'm not shy about getting physical once that ball's rolling. In fact, I find it hard to stop myself, and then my emotions get all tangled up in the sex, and next thing you know, I'm nursing a broken heart. Suddenly holding hands feels like a slippery slope.

He offers me his palm. His hand is large and calloused from his work. *What would those hands feel like on my bare skin?* My boyfriends usually have soft hands. Some of them even get manicures. "I figure we've been dating for three weeks, so we should get comfortable with each other."

Slippery slope! Defensive walls up!

I place my hand in his, and he closes his hand around it in a warm clasp. A hot shiver races down my spine. It's not nerves. I'm excited. From something as innocent as holding hands.

He leans close, his deep voice rumbling in my ear, drawing another shiver. "I'll hold your hand like this as we walk the red carpet. Unless you prefer my arm around you."

Pure lust floods my body. I can't think straight between his heat, his nearness, and his intoxicating scent that makes me want to bury my face in his neck and breathe deep.

He draws away, studying me for a moment. "Or we could do the gentleman arm." He releases my hand and offers his arm.

"Let's play it by ear," I say, boggled by the insane effect he has on me. We're just holding hands!

"Sure, no problem."

"Tell me more about you," I say, dying of curiosity. "Just in case it comes up. I should know."

He shares freely. It's clear he loves his family as he describes them, telling me about his parents' great love and his five older brothers. He's just started telling me about how proud he is of his family business when the car pulls up to the hotel for the gala. I'm unbelievably disappointed. I love hearing about his world. It must've been wonderful to grow up the youngest with all those people looking out for you and loving you. I spent my childhood trying to grow a thicker skin to earn General Joan's approval. It's impossible to change your nature like that, but I sure can play the part. Acting started at an early age for me.

Actually, I became an emancipated minor to pursue my profession at fifteen. My grandmother gave me the "freedom to fall on my face," and here I am. Hmm…maybe I should thank her for that. She gave me what I needed to survive in this tough business.

The car door opens, and the gathered paparazzi and reporters buzz with excitement. The driver helps me out while Joe stands guard. Garrett appears at my side. I paste on my happy-to-be-here expression, take Garrett's offered arm, and start down the red carpet leading to the hotel entrance. Joe follows behind.

I stop several feet from the drop-off area, where the bulk of camera-toting people wait, strike a pose, and smile.

"Is that Garrett Rourke?" a reporter asks.

"Sure is," Garrett replies with his panty-melting smile.

The cameras click furiously, zooming in on him. His shoulders draw back, seeming to enjoy the attention. He turns to me, still smiling, his eyes warm on mine. The crowd falls away. All I can focus on is that beautiful smile and the warmth in his eyes as though he really enjoys being with me. Just regular me, on the inside.

"Over here! Over here!" someone yells, gesturing us farther down the carpet.

I continue our walk, feeling Garrett's eyes on me. *Is he checking if I'm okay?* I've done this tons of times. It's the speech I have to give later that's the hard part.

We stop again to talk with reporters holding out microphones from local channels, as well as a few entertainment channels. Dana told me to talk to everyone.

They yell questions at me, mostly about what happened with Colton, and is it serious with Garrett?

I smile and take control of the conversation. "We're so happy to be here tonight in honor of Best Friends Care. Service dogs for anyone with a disability, whether that shows on the outside or the inside, can be life changing. I'm a long-time supporter."

"Great cause," Garrett chimes in. "The unconditional love of a dog is like nothing else in the world. Beyond emotional support, these dogs can fill in gaps in abilities, helping people lead a fuller life. Who wouldn't want that?"

I mask my surprise. That was a great speech, and I didn't tell him to say that either. He's a natural in front of the cameras.

The reporters go crazy for Garrett, coaxing him closer for pictures, peppering him with questions ranging from his favorite kind of dog to what he's appeared in and what he thinks of Amanda Boxer. It's insane. They assume he's an actor since that's mostly who I date. Garrett's relaxed as he good-naturedly fields questions. He even says he has great respect for the character of Amanda Boxer and greater respect for the woman who played her.

I'm melting.

"Amanda!" a man yells as he wedges himself in between reporters. "Why're you such a bitch? I'll teach you better."

I go ice cold. Joe moves quickly to deal with him.

Garrett glares at the man, his voice deadly calm. "Step away, man."

The guy throws up his middle finger, notices Joe at his side, and takes off.

I give Garrett's arm a tug, letting him know we're done here. I'm queasy with the reminder that, even with a guard and a big guy like Garrett on my arm, there's always going to be some men who try to get to me.

Garrett gives me a nod before saying to the reporters, "It's a great cause, guys. Donate any way you can, no amount is too small. Or too large."

"You're large!" a woman reporter says. "Looking good filling out that tux."

I narrow my eyes at her.

Garrett takes it in stride, saying with a wink, "They call me Beast."

No-o-o. That's the headline right there—Beast. They're going to be all over that.

I give his arm another tug, and he follows me inside the hotel. We're quickly escorted through the lobby to a private side door and down a long hallway leading to the ballroom. Joe's right behind us.

I speak under my breath, "You shouldn't have told them your nickname."

"Why?"

"Because it gives them too much fodder. That's going to blow up instead of the cause."

He grimaces. "Shit. I'm new at this. I'll be sure to talk up the cause the rest of the night. They'll be out there when we leave too, right?"

"Most likely."

"Okay, I'll fix it. I'll say the message and shut up. Are you okay about that asshole who yelled at you?"

"It happens a lot. That's why I have Joe." I glance over my shoulder and give him an appreciative smile.

He remains stone-faced, but jerks his chin at me. Tough guy.

Garrett glances back at Joe and nods at him before turning back to me. "Must be a lot of guys with little dicks walking around with something to prove."

I smile. "That makes me feel better thinking of it that way. You did great out there. I'm just wound a little tight right now. They loved you."

"I didn't mind all the questions and cameras as much as I thought. It was fun playing the part of Harper Ellis's love interest."

I laugh a little. Though I'm surprised a guy like him, with no experience handling the press, actually enjoyed it. "I'm sure it's easier to play the part than to be that role."

"Why? Because you're so tough?"

I'm not lovable. I glance up at him, hearing the smile in his voice. "Right."

"Too late. Your sweet tooth gave you away when you offered me your chocolate squares hidden in the cabinet. Three bitty squares. You have a mushy center."

I shake my head. "I told you I offered you that chocolate to get to know my new guard."

He pulls his shoulders back and puffs out his chest. "Yup, all that weight lifting finally pays off." He grins. "Kidding. It's been paying off with women for years."

"I bet."

"You prefer your men scrawny like Colton?"

I burst out laughing. Colton is lean and works so damn hard to show any muscle definition at all.

We stop as our guide uses his hotel security card to open the door for us. We step into a glittering ballroom. There's a large dance floor, multiple white-tableclothed tables for the fundraising dinner, and a raised dais at the front for the honored guests. Nerves race through me, already anticipating standing up there for my speech.

"Our seats are up front, but we should mingle first," I say. "There's more press here covering the event too, but they won't be nosing into my personal business. These aren't the gossip hounds."

"Great." He lifts his chin, looking like a classic leading man with that square jaw. "A chance to redeem myself."

I need to stop thinking of him in the acting world. He's a construction worker. A regular guy.

I go up on tiptoe to whisper, "You've already done something wonderful just by showing up here."

He dips his head and kisses my cheek, surprising me. "Sweet. I'm gonna call you sweetheart for the rest of the night. You can call me—"

"Garrett."

"Lamb chop."

I giggle.

"What? Lamb is a type of beast, isn't it?"

"Somehow I don't see you as a cuddly little lamb."

He drops an arm around my shoulders and tucks me against his side. "I can be cuddly."

I can't help my smile as I meet his eyes. "You're one of those snugglers in bed, aren't you?"

He keeps a straight face. "I prefer the term spooning."

Suddenly I want to know what that would feel like to have his large body spooning mine, his strong arm wrapped around my middle, his erection pressing urgently against—

"So thrilled to see you, Harper," a feminine voice says.

I whip my head toward Carol, the executive director of Best Friends Care, my cheeks heating from my wayward thoughts. Garrett eases his arm off my shoulders. I miss it already. "Hi, Carol, good to see you too! I'm happy to be here. This is Garrett Rourke. Garrett, this is Carol Lemke. She's the mastermind behind this organization."

"Oh, you," she says affectionately, fluffing her red curly hair off her shoulder. "I wouldn't say *mastermind*. But you can go ahead and say it if you want."

Garrett chuckles. "It's great what you're doing. I'm sure you've changed a lot of lives for the better."

She smiles, taking us both in. "Now that we're international, we've placed nearly half a million shelter dogs."

"I didn't realize these were shelter dogs," Garrett says. "That's even more impressive. So you have some kind of training program for the dogs?"

I listen proudly as Carol shares how they choose the dogs for temperament and how eager they are to do the work. It gives them purpose. It's a win-win for the dogs and the lucky people who get to have them.

"Do you ever place puppies?" he asks.

"We do. Those require a foster family to socialize them until they're ready to begin training."

"I'd love to do that," he says, and my heart squeezes. That's exactly what I did back in LA before I started working steadily. "If I were home more, I'd sign up for that. I'm gonna mention it to my parents. They've got an empty nest and a lot of love to give."

I'm beginning to suspect he has a heart of gold. I really hope that's the case because I'm all mushy inside.

Carol beams a smile at him. "Go to our website and tell them to fill out the volunteer form. Oh, here, I have a card." She pulls one from her purse. "Give this to your parents. Tell everyone you know. The city shelters are too full as it is." She smiles at him some more. He seems to have that effect on people. "So nice to meet you, Garrett." She turns to me and whispers in a conspiratorial tone, "I like this one."

"Me too," I whisper back.

She smiles, her eyes dancing merrily as she waves farewell, off to mingle with someone else.

Garrett's arm drops over my shoulders, and he kisses my temple. "Sweetheart."

A laugh bubbles up. "Lamb chop."

"You said you were gonna be so tense tonight because of your speech, but you seem happy."

It's you. "I'm in denial."

"Ah. Acting skills pay off."

"Come on, I'll introduce you to the board of directors and everyone else I know."

"Sounds like I passed the Harper Ellis test. You didn't even prep me."

"You're a natural."

And he is. I can't even believe how well he's working the room—smooth, sincere, enthusiastic about the cause. And with me? He's warm and affectionate. I may have brought the perfect date. A trickle of unease goes through me. No one is as perfect as he seems. There's got to be a catch somewhere. I need to be careful he doesn't take more from me than I want to give.

I won't be betrayed again.

6

———

Harper

We're sitting at the head table now, and they served us our dinner first. I can barely eat, knowing I'll be called up to the podium for my speech soon. I force down some rice, my movements jerky, every muscle tense. Garrett hasn't noticed my quiet meltdown as he eats his meal with gusto. I wish there were a magic button I could push to fast-forward to after my speech. Nothing could quiet my nerves now, not even the gorgeous man at my side. I can only pray I don't hyperventilate halfway through my speech.

Please, God, let me be coherent for the cause.

A large hand lands on my shoulder, and I jump. Garrett speaks under his breath. "Hey, just your three-week boyfriend here touching you like normal."

"Sorry. It's almost time for me—" my voice chokes on my own spit and I cough "—speaking." I grab my glass of water and guzzle it.

He gestures toward the death grip I have on the index cards in my lap. "Lemme see the speech."

I open my hand, revealing several crumpled index cards. "I should review them." I smooth them out as best I can with trembling hands and flip through them, barely comprehending the words.

"Maybe you should've had a glass of wine. Or two."

I exhale sharply. "It's ridiculous that I still get stage fright. But it's me, not tough Amanda up there, you know?" I push my plate back and set the index cards on the table, staring at them. There's several crossed-out words and arrows pointing to new sentences. I should've started a new set of cards so there wouldn't be any confusion.

Who am I kidding? I could have the most perfect speech in the world, and no one would hear it over my reflexive coughing, stops and starts, and occasional squeaky voice. Why is this so hard? I make a living speaking in front of the camera. But that's all pretend. This is the real me—an awkward bundle of nerves.

"Should I get you some wine?" he asks.

I shake my head. "I'll be a drunken shit show up there if I have even one glass. I'm really careful to eat healthy and only have a glass of red wine once a week with steak. You know, for health reasons."

"What would help?"

"Someone else doing this?" My voice hits a high note.

He takes my hand in his larger one and gives it a gentle squeeze. "Sweetheart, this is a cause you believe in. All you have to do is tell them why. Then every single one of the potential donors sitting here tonight will open their hearts and their wallets."

I glance at the sea of faces out there waiting to hear my speech. The sophisticated, wealthy elite in their finest formal wear. I'm supposed to motivate them to the cause. *Carol should be doing this speech!* She's the one who did all the hard behind-the-scenes work. I suck in air, my breath coming in short pants.

A giant screen unfolds behind us. They're going to project my image up there so everyone can see me up close, a quivering leaf.

I grab my cards and force myself to read slowly enough to comprehend.

"Is that big screen there so they can see you, or is there a film or something?" Garrett asks.

I don't look up from the cards. "Just me."

"Be right back."

My eyes widen. He's leaving me alone here? I didn't realize how much his quiet presence was holding the panic at bay. I break out in a cold sweat. "Where're you going?"

"I'm just gonna ask Carol a question. I'll be right back, promise."

I nod like a bobblehead doll. *Right back. He'll be right back.* "Okay."

Back to my cards. A bead of sweat runs down my forehead, and I brush it away before it can land on my cards and blur the ink.

I hear the mike at the podium being adjusted. Carol's up there. I swallow hard. *It's time.*

Oh, Garrett's back, sitting next to me. He looks so calm. I stare at him, trying to soak in that calm. He smiles, but I can't manage to smile back. My lips feel numb.

Carol speaks with great confidence and enthusiasm. "Harper Ellis is our celebrity ambassador and so much more. She's been with us since we were a single office in LA when she was a teen. She gave generously from the start. As her career gained momentum, so has her generosity. Tonight we honor her with our lifetime supporter award for her part in helping our organization grow. We're now global and reaching so many people in need of loving companionship and assistive living skills."

She gestures for me to come up. Polite applause breaks out. I stand abruptly and stride on stiff legs to the podium.

Carol aims a small remote at her laptop, glances over my shoulder, and returns to her seat. The audience *awws* in unison, staring at the large screen behind me.

I glance over, my lips parting in surprise. There's a picture of a pack of golden retriever puppies. My heart rate slows to a normal beat, taking in those adorable dogs. That's what's at the heart of this important cause. Puppies just like them will be loved in their foster homes, trained for important work, and provide years of unconditional love to people who need them. One day I hope to have a golden retriever of my own.

My hand goes to my heart as understanding dawns. I beam a smile at Garrett. It was him! I told him earlier that I wanted a golden retriever. That's why he left to see Carol. He asked her to put that picture up there, knowing it would put me at ease and draw the audience's attention to the puppies instead of me.

He smiles back, and it's like a warm hug wrapping around me.

Thank you, I mouth silently.

He nods once and gestures for me to continue. I take a deep breath before turning back to the audience. I hold up my index cards. "I don't need these. I'm just going to speak from the heart and tell you why I love Best Friends Care, and hopefully you'll see why you should too."

And I do. My heart's in my throat as I share about my uncle, and then I return my gaze to the puppies for a calming moment before describing all the admiration I feel for what Best Friends Care has accomplished in the twelve years I've been involved with them. My voice chokes and cracks a few times, but it doesn't matter. I said everything I wanted to say, concluding with, "Please give from the heart for this important cause that can turn a person's and a shelter dog's life around."

The crowd erupts in thunderous applause. It's not for me, it's all for Carol's hard work and dedication. I smile and gesture toward her as she approaches the podium. "All credit for this great organization goes to Carol Lemke."

She joins me, saying into the microphone, "Thank you, Harper. As you've just heard, Best Friends Care does good in the world, and we're hoping you'll support us. There's a device on your table to donate, and we'll see the numbers tally up here." She points to the screen that now says zero and then flips suddenly to ten thousand dollars. "Oh, thank you!" She looks out to the crowd. "Thanks for getting us started."

Awesome! I gesture for everyone to keep going. People start pulling out credit cards at every table. I check the screen as a cheer goes up. *Whoa.* It's already at a quarter million.

I did it!

With a little help from the pups and one very intuitive man.

Garrett

Harper drops into her seat next to me, flushed pink, her eyes bright. She's been working for this cause since she was sixteen. That's impressive commitment. She's impressive, the kind of woman I've been looking for—sweet, generous, hard-working. I'm so damn proud of her.

She grabs her water and finishes it in one long swallow.

I lean close. "You did great."

She beams and surprises me with a quick hug. "It wasn't quite the TED talk I hoped to perform, but the puppy pic really helped me relax. Thanks for thinking of that."

"Happy to help the cause."

We smile at each other for a dizzying moment before another cheer goes up. I glance back at the screen, where donations are piling up. These people are loaded.

After the fundraising part of the night finishes—hitting a jaw-dropping two million—a band starts playing, and everyone flocks to the dance floor for a slow dance.

"Come on," I say, taking her hand and drawing her out of her seat.

Her gaze holds mine for a charged moment. "Are you asking me to dance, lamb chop?"

I grin. "That's right, sweetheart."

I guide her onto the dance floor, settling my hand on the small of her back, enjoying the feel of her bare skin heating under my palm. Once we're there, I take her hand in mine and lead in a waltz.

"Did they teach you to dance like this at the royal palace?" she asks.

"An ex. All those music festivals are usually full of women who love to dance. One of them asked me to go to ballroom dance lessons with her."

"How long did you do that?"

"Eight weeks. The instructor said I'm a natural." I dip her over my arm and slowly bring her back up. "I've got rhythm."

Her eyes are huge, her lips parted. "I feel like I'm in a musical."

I laugh. "Good. They're usually happy shows, right? All that singing and dancing."

"Usually. Have you seen a lot of Broadway shows?"

"No, just one. My friend's parents brought me along to see *The Lion King* when I was a kid. It was amazing."

She beams. "I love that show too. I saw it as an adult."

"Excuse me," a guy says. "Can I get your picture for the society pages?" He's holding a camera.

I check in with Harper. She looks surprised too.

"I thought there was only press here to cover the event as a news story, not the society pages," Harper says.

"Yes, but I told my editor we have a royal here, and she wants a picture of him for the society page. I'm with th*e New York Times*." He turns to me. "Do you mind?"

The New York Times*! Me? I'm not a big-deal royal.*

"You know I'm not in any danger of taking the throne, right?" I ask the guy. "I'm way down the line."

He smooths my lapel. "You look princely in that tux, and it's the first time anyone's seen you at a major event. The bachelor prince and the beautiful actress. Our readers will die for it."

I check in with Harper. She thinks it over for a moment and finally agrees.

The photographer waves us on. "Just go back to dancing like you were, smiling at each other, flirting. It's perfect."

We resume dancing. Harper smiles the fakest smile I've ever seen.

I lean down to her ear. "Harp, can I call you Harp? You look like you just watched someone else get your Oscar."

"I do not," she says hotly. "Besides, I've never been nominated for one."

I straighten. "I give you the most constipated award."

She giggles. "You're terrible at flirting."

"Sweetheart, I'm not even trying."

She softens at the *sweetheart*, her hazel eyes locked on mine. Every nerve ending goes on alert, the chemistry arcing powerfully between us. Raw lust rushes through me.

"Perfect!" the photographer says, snapping picture after picture. After he's satisfied with the results, he thanks us and takes off.

Another slow dance begins, so I pull her closer and continue dancing.

She sighs and then seems to remember herself and puts some space between us. "You're such a good dancer I'm afraid I got a little too close."

"No such thing."

"Garrett," she says softly, "you're a nice guy, but this is a friends date."

Nice guy. That's female code for *I'm not attracted to you.* Which is a lie. The chemistry here is so obvious we attracted a photographer. I don't buy that my connection to the throne is all that interesting to New York's elite. We're the wealthy royal family's poor relations. Our business is doing well, but most of the profits are funneled into buying the next property. We're still in the building-the-business stage. That guy wanted our picture because Harper and I have this palpable connection. Why is she trying to deny it?

"And why are we on a friends date instead of an actual date?" I ask.

She blinks a few times. "Why?"

"Yeah, why?"

She stares at my shoulder. "Because that photographer reminded me why I need to be careful. I just broke up with only the latest in a long line of terrible choices in men, and I know you didn't have anything to do with that, but I have baggage, okay? I'm not ready to get involved with anyone right now."

That's honest, and I appreciate that. More importantly, it's nothing personal against me.

"Fair enough," I say.

Her lips part in surprise. "Really?"

I whisper in her ear, "Did you expect me to walk away because sex is off the table? I can go slow. I think you're worth it."

I lean back to read her expression.

Her eyes are shiny with unshed tears. "You're not like the guys I usually meet."

I grin. "That's the best thing I've heard all night. Besides your incredibly motivating speech. It's because of you they raised two mil."

"No," she says, smiling.

"Yes. Carol even skipped her boring old speech knowing she had to seize the Harper Ellis moment."

"Stop," she says, ducking her head.

I tip her chin up. "You really can't take a compliment."

"I'm not used to them."

"Then I'll give you more until you build up a tolerance."

"Sort of a desensitizing program?"

"Exactly, sweetheart."

She beams up at me, leaning a little closer in our slow sway of a dance. "You really are a beast of a man."

Flashes go off. I turn, surprised to see several photographers snapping pictures of us. She pulls me off the dance floor, stopping in a quiet corner, angled away from the photographers.

"What's the deal with all the pictures?" I ask her. It's a little strange that the reporters in here, who were supposed to be less about gossip and more about substance, keep taking our picture. How many society pages could there be?

"I don't know. My publicist said she arranged a lot of press for the cause. It's just starting to feel more personal. Probably because of the Colton thing. We're a story. She usually keeps out the gossip types though. I'm getting a little creeped out."

"You want to leave?"

"No, I'll stick it out. We'll just be careful not to do anything that draws attention."

"Like ballroom dance?"

She laughs. "Yes."

I grin. "So gazing adoringly into your eyes is out?"

She gives my shoulder a little shove. "You're ridiculous."

I waggle my brows at her. "Am I, or are you so turned on right now you're ready to tackle me to the floor and rip my clothes off?"

She laughs, and then she can't stop laughing, tears coming out of her eyes. Joe shoots me a curious look, standing nearby as usual. I shrug. I had no idea I was such a comedian. People are starting to stare.

I stare too, a little offended. "Are you done cracking up at the idea of me naked?"

She gets serious. "Sorry. It's just that I have a vivid imagination, and I saw it all like an animated cartoon. Like me with big hearts in my eyes, leaping in the air and then tackling you. But you're so big it's ridiculous." She laughs some more. "Sorry. It tickled me."

I feign irritation, letting out a huff and staring at the ceiling. Then I tickle her, and she shrieks in surprise. I wrap her in my arms, hugging her and shielding her at the same time from curious eyes and cameras.

"Are we making a scene?" she asks my chest.

"It's my bad influence. You can't take me anywhere."

She smiles up at me, and my heart thunders. I want to kiss her so bad. But I said I'd give her time, get to know each other as friends, so she can see she can trust me. And it can only help if we build something deeper. Then I'll know for sure I'm not just her rebound guy.

"Let's go back to our seats," I say, dropping an arm over her shoulders. "We're less interesting there than on the dance floor or giggling in the corner, and we'll have a chance to talk more."

"I do not giggle," she protests. "I'm very serious."

"Uh-huh."

"You tickled me. I'm not used to that."

"Don't forget your hilarious giggles over the idea of me naked."

She giggles again. "Just the animated version in my mind."

"Stop picturing it," I order.

She fights back a laugh, her hazel eyes dancing with amusement. *Sweet woman.* I want her so damn bad.

We're intercepted several times by guests on our way to our table. Most people just want the chance to meet her. She's animated and enthusiastic, encouraging them to get involved with Best Friends Care in any way they can. Every compliment they give her, she deflects and draws their attention to the cause, even while she's signing programs and taking selfies. She gives them what they want, but it's never about her. No big ego here when there easily could've been with the way people fawn over her. I like that. She's not caught up in fame, which means she could be with a regular guy like me. It worked for Sean and Josie. Of course, they met when Josie was a struggling out-of-work actress. Still, I have hope.

By the time the evening ends, I know without a shadow of a doubt. She was put in my path for a reason. It's fate at work here.

7

———

Harper

The next morning, I wake and stretch, my mind flashing back to last night—Garrett. He called me sweetheart. He said I'm worth taking it slow. What a revelation this man is!

I grab my phone from the nightstand and sit up, propping the pillows behind my back, and power it on. A few moments later, a series of texts from my publicist appear.

Dana: *OMG, you did it. You made the* New York Times *society page! You two look amazing together. Everyone loves the royal angle. You have to take him to more events. They're speculating you'll be the next American princess!!!*

There's a series of links. Pictures and stories from inside the fundraiser, as well as from the red carpet. Almost all of them focus on Garrett with the occasional story reminding people of me and Colton. Everyone wants to know more about the "secret prince of Brooklyn." Some are asking what he's been in; some speculate he's a model.

I press my lips together, my stomach turning sour. Where are the articles on Best Friends Care? That was the whole point of the gala. I do a search, hoping to find something. There's only a few short articles that sound as vanilla as a press release about how much the evening raised. At least it's something, but I'd hoped there would be a bigger reach to get the public involved. I shouldn't have brought him. I wanted to go solo. Of course, then the focus probably would've been on Colton and what happened with us.

Why can't people focus on what's important? My love life shouldn't be anyone's concern but my own. I know it's part of the deal being a public figure, but come on.

I need to know what Garrett thinks about all this, so I text him. *You're famous.*

No response.

I blink away tears, irritated by them. It's just baggage. Garrett was wonderful last night.

After a shower, I curl up on my sofa to watch an old movie in my favorite soft T-shirt and fleece pajama bottoms. I always need to recharge after a big event like the gala. My phone chimes with a text, and I grab it off the coffee table.

Garrett: *You're the famous one, sweetheart. I just stood in your shadow.*

I can almost hear his deep smooth voice through his words and find myself smiling.

Garrett: *There's a group of guys with cameras waiting by the front door of my apartment building. Are they there because of me? If so, what should I do? I have to go out today.*

He honestly doesn't know why the paparazzi staked him out?

Duh. He doesn't have a publicist texting him links to articles. And I doubt he has a Google alert on his name. Why would he? No one ever reports on a guy working on a construction site.

Me: *Those guys are paparazzi. You're all over the internet right now. Everyone wants to know more about the secret prince of Brooklyn.*

Garrett: *Seriously?*

Me: *Yes!*

I send him some of the links Dana sent me. A few minutes later, he texts again.

Garrett: *They're saying I'm a model.*

He's proud of his part in the family business—they do

important work—so I imagine he's not happy with people pegging him as a model. I reassure him.

Me: *They make up crap all the time. Don't take it to heart. It means nothing.*

My phone rings, surprising me. It's him. My heart races with excitement.

"Are you mad at me?" he asks the moment I answer.

I still, surprised. "Why would I be mad at you?"

"Because there's a ridiculous amount of stuff written about me, and you're barely mentioned." He sounds snappish.

My hackles rise at his tone. "I'm mentioned too. I don't think—it's fine."

"You *are* mad at me. I'm fluent in woman speak. Fine is never just fine."

I can feel myself shutting down in self-defense. He's fluent in woman speak because of all his *many* girlfriends, obviously. "Good for you on learning the female language so well."

"Uh-huh. Look, you asked me to this thing after your asshole ex left you hanging. I'm not sure how any of this is my fault. I'm only interesting to the public because of you."

"You're a royal. That makes you inherently interesting."

"So are my five older brothers. So are my seven cousins. And every other Rourke relative I have."

"Yes, but they weren't with me last night. You were." Does he regret being in the spotlight with me because everyone is making assumptions about him? Is it the paps staking him out that's the problem?

Or maybe he's just another user and he's angry thinking I called him out on it somehow. Classic user behavior, turning the whole thing around on the other person. I *so* wanted him to be different.

I'm confused.

"Garrett—"

He lets out a long whistle. "I sure was wrong about you. Here I was thinking you're not about fame, no big ego here. Lady, there's not enough room in the city to hold your ego."

I gasp. "Excuse me?"

"You *hate* that they're focused on me. And you're mad because you think I wanted this. All I wanted was a date with someone I thought was a kind, compassionate, caring person. Now I see how it really was for you last night, just a big PR campaign to make you look good."

"That's not true!"

"I'm so disappointed in you."

My gut twists. "I do care about the cause. A lot. I told you why."

He lets out a long breath. "Now I've got these weirdos downstairs. Do I talk to them? Do I ignore them?"

"You can ignore them, but they'll follow you."

"Well, they'd better not follow me to my parents' house for dinner tonight. That's going too far."

"Then you need to give them a statement and tell them that's all you'll be saying."

"What kind of statement?"

"Whatever you feel like giving them. It's up to you. Just don't mention me."

"Ridiculous," he mutters. "All because I went to that gala."

Guilt stabs at me. He does regret it, and it's my fault the paps staked him out. The least I can do is shield him from what I have to deal with. "You don't have to go to the Rourke fundraiser with me next Saturday."

"Wow. Thanks for the uninvite to my own family's fundraiser. This just gets better and better. So glad I agreed to this whole *friends on a date* bullshit. Bye, Harper."

I jolt at the harsh goodbye. He hung up on me!

I let out a shaky breath. Somehow the conversation got away from me.

This is exactly why I didn't want to get involved with anyone so soon. I'm still hurting, and that makes me extra defensive and vulnerable to hurt. I rub my temple at the headache forming there. He was really defensive and harsh too.

You know what? I don't need the guilt trip, the *I'm so disappointed in you* garbage.

Garrett Rourke can suck it.

Garrett

Harper Ellis can suck it.

Where the hell does she get off? I did her a *favor* after she dragged my name into it, pretending we were a couple. This is the thanks I get? I jog downstairs, on my way out for my morning run. She's pissed off because she thinks I stole her spotlight. I was amazed the press thought I was a model since it's not something I ever considered before. And then she puts me down, saying it's crap and means nothing. I bet she thinks I'm using her to get a leg up in the entertainment world when *I'm* the one who was used. She's lumping me in with her ex. And I treated her well too. To think I really hoped this was the start of something good between us.

Now that I think about it, modeling could be something to consider. My mom did modeling when she was younger. She made enough to pay for college. It could be a lucrative side gig for me. I'd never leave my family's business. I eagerly followed in my brothers' footsteps with a tool in my hand from the time I could walk (the kiddie version). This is what we do as a family. But wouldn't it be great to have the money to buy the house I've always wanted instead of renting? Harper's too wrapped up in her own stuff to see what it's like for other people.

I open the front door to the apartment building, step outside, and camera flashes go off in my eyes as reporters yell questions at me.

"What does Colton think of the two of you?"

"Will Harper Ellis be the next American princess?"

"Any projects in the works starring you and Harper?"

I cross my arms over my chest. "I have one thing to say, so listen up. That's all you're gonna get from me today. Harper and I parted as friends. End of story."

I jog down the sidewalk, heading toward the park. The fuckers trail behind me, still shouting questions.

I pick up speed, and after a while, they stop. Pays to be in shape. *You're welcome, Harper. Now you're free of the guy you thought was using you.* From here on out, it's my own efforts that will determine my future. I'll talk to my mom about modeling tonight.

I clench my jaw, pissed all over again about Harper putting me in the same category as her asshole ex. I should've known a celebrity would have a big ego, thinking everything's about her, hating to share the spotlight. I don't have time for that bullshit.

My mind flashes to her trembling hands just before her speech.

The way she offered me one of her last tiny squares of chocolate.

Okay, so she's not *all* ego. She's a real person with insecurities just like everyone else. I'm still not going there. I'm insulted, and I deserve better after how well I treated her.

I stick to that righteous feeling all day. Until I arrive at my parents' house for dinner that night. My dad takes one look at me and says in his naturally authoritative voice, "We need to talk about this press, son."

And I know right there I won't be feeling so righteous anymore.

He gestures for me to take a seat on the dark blue living room sofa. My mom waves to me from the kitchen, where she's preparing her famous pot roast and potatoes. It's an open floor plan—living room, kitchen, dining room all in a row, as is typical of Brooklyn rowhouses. They keep the pocket doors separating the spaces open.

I smile at her and take my seat. "I'll be in to help in a bit." I'm eager to talk to her about getting started in modeling. I have to strike while the iron is hot. On my current pay, it'll take years before I can afford a house.

"Sounds good," she says, smiling at me.

I turn to my dad, who's sitting across from me on the matching loveseat, spine straight, shoulders back. I swear he could sit anywhere—from a barstool to a ratty old recliner—

and look like he's sitting on a throne. You can take away his crown, but he will *always* be king.

"Seems you've become a local celebrity," he says.

"How did you hear about it?" I didn't think my parents read the society pages or gossip rags.

"Mrs. Bianchi told us," he says. "Apparently, she has a Google alert on all of us Rourkes." He barely holds back an eye roll—too undignified—and exchanges a look with my mom. Mrs. Bianchi is our next-door neighbor.

"She's looking out for us," my mom says diplomatically.

"Right," my dad says.

There was a feud. For as long as I can remember growing up, Mom and Mrs. Bianchi were stone-cold furious at each other. Family legend says it all started with a missing serving spoon at a neighborhood potluck dinner at the Bianchis'. This was before I was born, but I heard whispers. Mom returned home and realized she didn't have her spoon, so she went next door to get it. Mrs. Bianchi claimed she'd never seen it. My mom swore that Mrs. Bianchi had seen it since she'd complimented the pattern. Anyway, Mom returned home, furious, and said Mrs. Bianchi was a thief. Things went downhill fast when the Bianchis got a dog, who constantly escaped through their broken fence to take a crap in our tiny yard. From there, it was all-out war between Mom and Mrs. Bianchi, with the two husbands running interference over one grievance or another. But that's all over now, ever since Mrs. Bianchi's daughter, Ariana, married my oldest brother, Dylan. Everyone is friends again. *Friendly.*

My dad turns to me. "It's a strange thing to be a public figure. Your private life is not your own. You must always keep up appearances and never say a bad word against anyone. It will stick with you."

"I didn't say anything bad."

He inclines his head. "I'm just sharing what I know after growing up in the spotlight. Never mistake a reporter's friendliness for actual friendship. You must keep your thoughts and feelings close to the chest. That's not for public consumption. What a reporter wants most is to catch you in a vulnerable moment, to hear an admission of something that they can spin a story out of."

I nod.

His brows knit together, seeming deep in thought. "It's hard for a public figure to know who to trust. Too many people hope to gain from the connection. Everyone wants a piece of you for what you can do for them."

And there goes my righteous indignation. He's speaking about himself, but I instantly see the truth of it for Harper. She's being defensive because she has to be, especially with a guy. Men are a problem for her—stalkers, cheaters, users. It's a wonder she's willing to date at all. Of course, she is young and beautiful. It would be a shame for that to go to waste. Too bad she can't enjoy it like a regular nonfamous person.

My dad continues. "As long as you plan on spending time with Harper, you need to be careful. Smile for the cameras, that's fine. But give them nothing else. We don't want any dirt associated with the Rourke name."

Shit. I hadn't even thought of that. It's only recently that our family was welcomed back to the kingdom. It means a lot to my dad after his banishment. This press stuff is not just about me, it's about my family.

"I'll be careful," I say.

He smiles. "I'm sure she has PR people that keep her on message. Let them do their thing."

"Honey, he's not spending time with her anymore," my mom calls from the kitchen. "There's a new story with Garrett saying they parted as friends. Are you okay, teddy bear?"

"I'm fine," I say through my teeth. Not like it was a real relationship. I was a stand-in to make her look good. There's that righteous feeling. Harper was in the wrong, not me.

My dad wags his finger. "That's the kind of thing you shouldn't share with the press. Now you've given them more grist for the mill."

I tense. "I thought that would shut down speculation."

He shakes his head. "Fuel on the fire. Any new piece of information keeps it alive. Just say 'no comment' from here on out."

This is bad. First the story was about Harper being cheated on, then on our new relationship, and now on our breakup. Is she going to invent another fake relationship to counter our breakup? Show off some new guy her publicist vetted for her at the Rourke fundraiser next Saturday? I bet there's plenty of guys she could choose from among the Hollywood elite. My gut churns at the thought.

"Garrett, are you listening to me?"

I focus on my dad. "Yeah, I get it. Keep my mouth shut."

"You can say things that highlight what you really want them to report on. Like how much you support a cause, or you can talk about the good work you and your brothers are doing with the community garden in your latest project. Just not your personal business."

I clench my jaw. Not much point in all these instructions since I won't be seeing her again. "Okay, I doubt I'll have to deal with much press anymore."

He leans forward. "How did you get thrown into Harper's orbit?"

I snort. "Long story. Short version is, I visited Josie on set for a taping."

"Ah." He leans back in his seat. "Good show. Your mother and I really enjoyed watching a taping a few weeks ago. You're coming to the watch party on Thursday, right?" *Living Gold* premieres on Thursday night, and my parents are hosting a party for our family to watch it together.

"Of course. I want to be there for Josie."

"Josie thinks highly of Harper."

My brows lift in surprise. Family grapevine works fast.

He glances at my mom before leaning forward, speaking in a low tone. "Your mother checked in with her."

"Daniel!" my mom exclaims. "You're not supposed to tell him that part."

His lips twitch. "This is a private conversation between men."

She rolls her eyes.

He turns to me. "What happened that it ended so soon? You're more long term usually."

"Ego clash. Hers." I spread my arms. "Huge ego."

"Ah. I don't have any experience with that, I'm afraid." He winks.

"Ha!" my mom says from the kitchen. "That's because you're the one with the huge ego."

He joins her in the kitchen, wrapping her in his arms and whispering something that has her pushing him away, laughing. They whisper to each other, smiling, and I look away. No need to see the parent nookie.

That's the kind of love I'm holding out for. Maybe I should give Harper another chance. But, you know, she was so quick to push me away. Then again, I wasn't exactly being conversational in our last phone call. I was insulted and hurt and pushed back.

Being home again reminds me of the Rourke family philosophy. Growing up, my dad always said be bold, take risks, you only get one go-round in this life. He risked everything to be with my mom, and now look at them.

I take a deep breath. I'm a Rourke. Time to be bold.

8

Garrett

I'm in a custom-made charcoal gray suit, courtesy of Josie, for the Rourke foundation fundraiser at the Metropolitan Museum of Art. It was black tie optional, so I opted out of renting a tux again. I love the fact that the blazer doesn't pull tight across my shoulders like most do. I'm actually comfortable in this suit. Josie arranged for it through a stylist friend as a thank you for house-sitting when she and Sean were away last summer, but I know the real reason. She's been trying to get me more involved in the Rourke foundation events. Not because I'm so great at networking with the wealthy elite. It's because, well, okay, I'll just come right out and say it—I'm her favorite in the Rourke family. Besides Sean, of course. She's constantly inviting me to stuff. I usually decline, but not tonight. I'm on a mission.

I'm trying to give Harper a little leeway here. She has to be cautious about whom she gets involved with, and I've seen for myself what happens when she's not. It's all out there in big bold colors for everyone to see. I won't seek her out right away. I want to see if she's with another fake date for the PR. If she is, I'm out for good. I don't want to be with a shallow, ego-driven woman, even if she does have some sweet moments.

I take a sip of champagne, scanning the room for her. Everyone's gathered for a cocktail reception in the historic Great Hall, the museum's entryway. It's an impressive space made with limestone in that old Greek style with archways and columns running the length of the hall. Above us is a wraparound balcony, where more people are gathered. I scan the balcony space for a familiar face, taking in all the beautiful people in their fancy clothes, and then check out the three massive domes overhead. How did they get those into place back in the 1800s? Couldn't have been easy. This reminds me a little of Amalie Palace in Villroy. Built to impress.

Harper's been on my mind a lot this week, but I've held off on texting or calling her. I saw her on the premiere of *Living Gold* at our family watch party. She sounded every bit the sophisticated socialite, but when the camera got in close, her eyes showed such grief over the loss of her father. How did she convey so much without a word? It struck me that she must be sensitive, like me. That could be why we connected in the first place.

It's different for people in the spotlight. I get that now. Who knows, maybe I'll be in the spotlight soon too. My mom gave me a contact at her former modeling agency, and I'm supposed to get professional headshots taken on Monday morning. A buoyant excitement goes through me at the thought. A gig of my own. Nothing I've ever done in my life has been just about me. It's always been about the family.

I've already checked in with Josie and Sean. Guess it's time for me to strike up a few conversations and do my part for the Rourke foundation. I spot a guy in a black tux who looks relatively normal. Probably because he reminds me of my brother Brendan. He looks around my age with dark brown hair and a neatly trimmed beard, leaning casually against a column, taking in the scene with a tired look on his face. I bet he got roped into this thing.

I walk over to him. "Hey, enjoying the gala?"

He remains leaning against the column and jerks his chin at me. "Who wants to know?"

I offer my hand. "Garrett Rourke. It's my family's foundation."

He straightens and shakes my hand in a firm grip. "Wyatt Winters. So, are you one of the rainmakers like Sean?"

"Nah, I work construction. It's a great cause. All the funds raised tonight will go toward the community garden in our newest development project. We have a mission to give back to neighborhoods. Mostly in Brooklyn, where I'm from." *There. See how I'm helping the cause?*

"An admirable mission, which is the only reason I'm here. Tell me exactly *how* your company has given back to neighborhoods in the past."

Straightforward and direct. I like that.

So I tell him all about Rourke Management's projects so far, including building a wheelchair-accessible playground, low-rent space for artists and nonprofits, and parks. I'm damn proud of what we've accomplished so far. Our company has won awards for urban excellence and social responsibility.

"We build neighborhoods that people want to live in for generations," I conclude. *That sounded awesome. I should tell Becca to put that in our marketing stuff.* She's our chief strategy officer (and my brother Connor's wife).

He cracks a smile. "Cool. Maybe I should've gotten into building something instead of tech. I'm done being chained to a computer."

"What do you do?"

He stares at his untouched champagne. "I was one of those Silicon Valley whiz kids. Now I'm retired."

I do a double take. "Little young to be retired."

He lifts a shoulder in a careless shrug. "You want to hit up the bar for something stronger?"

"Sure." I hadn't realized they'd set up a bar. I thought cocktails meant just the champagne the waiters were circulating.

"Champagne is a candy-ass drink," he says, setting his glass on a nearby table.

I leave my glass behind too. "Candy-ass, huh? Was not aware of that."

"Oh, yeah. I'm partial to whisky. How about you?"

We make our way through the crowd in the Great Hall.

"Beer will do for me."

"I don't think they serve beer here," he says. "Is this your first gala?" He turns into an alcove, where there's a line for the bar.

I glance around for signs of Harper, but don't see her. "Actually, this is my second event like this in two weeks."

"Boring as hell, right? No offense to your family's foundation."

"How'd you get roped into this?"

He barks out a laugh. "I met Sean and Josie in LA at a fundraiser I was roped into by an ex. This is my last one for a while. I plan to lie low after this."

"Prince Garrett," someone calls.

Strange. There's a prince around here with my name. Sean's reach through royal circles must've expanded, probably through one of our cousins.

I turn to Wyatt as we shift closer to the front of the line. "So how is it you can retire at…"

"Thirty," Wyatt supplies. "The big three-oh. I'm having my mid-life crisis early."

I chuckle.

A bald guy in his forties appears at my side. "Prince Garrett, so glad I found you here."

Why is he calling me Prince Garrett? I've never gotten any royal treatment in New York. That's strictly a Villroy thing.

"Do I know you from Villroy?" I ask. It's possible we met at some point. There's a lot of people coming and going at the palace.

He flashes a dazzling white-toothed smile and offers his hand. "Mark Perlman, your new agent. And you're the secret prince of Brooklyn."

I give him a quick handshake to be polite. I'm not sure what he means by "my new agent." The modeling agent I talked to was a woman.

Wyatt orders a whiskey. "You want one?" he asks me.

"I'll take a tequila."

Wyatt turns to Mark in question, but he declines, waiting patiently by my side.

Once the drinks arrive, Wyatt raises his glass of whiskey toward me and wanders off, leaving me alone with Mark.

Mark puts a hand on my elbow, guiding me to a quiet corner. "So, Prince Garrett—"

"Just Garrett."

"You've got something here. A look. And I don't know if you realize this, but the buzz is really building over you."

I sip my tequila—a high-end label meant to savor—and stare at him. I'm sure he'll get to a point soon. He's a fast-talking, high-enthusiasm kind of guy.

"Ever think about acting?" he asks.

"No."

"No problem. Many men start a little later, once they've filled out in the jaw and body." He gives me a once-over that feels like I'm being inspected as a purebred at a dog show. I'm surprised he doesn't peel back my lips to check my teeth. "Minimum, I can get you into commercials, but, Garrett, I have a good feeling about you. I think you can build on this and be a *major* star. Not just a working actor. I mean a household name, the kind that can headline movies!"

Adrenaline fires through me. Whoa. Imagine that! It's a helluva lot more exciting than my current life, which isn't bad by any means, but…a movie star? Me? *Reality check.* I know nothing about acting. This guy must have me confused with one of the real actors here that Josie invited.

"I don't think I'm who you think I am." I gesture around me. "Throw a stick and you'll find an actor. I'm just a construction worker."

He nods vigorously. "Yeah, yeah, I know who you are. The guy who was at the Best Friends Care gala last week with Harper Ellis. Good call getting with her. Oh, sorry. I heard you parted ways. I can arrange for another actress on the rise to be seen with you to get the ball rolling. Gotta keep feeding the PR machine."

PR machine. Exactly why Harper asked me out in the first

place, and now I don't know what's real or not. That's messed up.

I lift my glass to him. "No, thanks. Nice meeting you."

"Wait! Listen. Too soon on the dating front. I get it. I see great potential here, that's all." He pulls a business card from the inside pocket of his tux jacket and hands it to me. "Consider signing with me. There's an aftershave commercial I can get you in for." He raises a hand near my cheek. "That jaw is perfection."

"Uh, thanks?" I can't tell if he's coming on to me or trying to sign me as a client. I glance around once again for Harper. She's average height and could be hidden behind a big guy, maybe her bodyguard.

Mark continues in an urgent tone. "Do you know how much a commercial pays? Thirty grand for one day's work, minimum."

That gets my attention. "Seriously?" I could do that on the side and have a down payment on a house in no time. That's even better pay than modeling. And I wouldn't have to feel guilty about abandoning my family's business. I could have both.

He grins. "Seriously. And if you're on board, I'll arrange for a personal acting coach. I see great things for you, Garrett. With me on your team, the sky's the limit. Think about it." He walks away.

I look at his card. "Is this a legit agency?"

He stops and turns, a wide smile spreading across his face. "William Morris Endeavor is the top of the food chain."

"Huh." I slide it into my pocket.

He taps his temple. "I can tell you're thinking about it. You won't regret it."

I lift a hand in farewell and wander through the crowd, my mind whirling. It's one thing for the press to say stuff about me being a model, a whole other thing for a legitimate agent from a top agency to approach about signing me for a commercial. Now that I could see giving a whirl. I had no idea a commercial paid so much. It looks so easy too. Three minutes or less with minimal dialogue. Hell, I could do that in my sleep. This could be a great opportunity.

That movie-star stuff is a wild dream I've never considered. For just a moment, I let myself imagine that life—doing a cool action-hero movie, living in a sweet house of my own, never worrying about money, going to the head of every line. Could it be that I was passed over for every important role in my family's company because I was meant for another role in life? I've never felt ambitious until now.

I should talk to Josie about this, get her take on Mark Perlman. I weave through the crowd to find her and stop short.

Harper. And she's alone. My pulse thrums through my veins. Time to make my move.

9

Garrett

She looks incredible in a pink one-shouldered dress that clings to her sexy body. A surge of raw lust has me frozen in place for a moment. I need to be in control, take it slow and easy. I spot her guard, Joe, standing a little behind her. That's going to be hard to get used to, always having a witness, but I'll do my best.

A tall blond guy in a tux approaches Harper. She smiles prettily and talks to him. A rare stab of jealousy hits.

I toss back my tequila, set the glass on a nearby tray, and stride over. "Hello, sweetheart," I say in my warmest voice, tamping down the edge of jealousy threatening to break through. The "sweetheart" is to put the other guy off. *Staking my claim.* Deep down, my instincts are pure caveman.

Her hazel eyes widen. "Garrett."

"Surprised to see me?"

She blinks. "I, uh, just didn't think it was your scene."

"Well, it is." *Not really.* I glance at the guy trying to poach my potential date and turn back to Harper. "My family is the reason there's an event." I jab a finger at the banner by the front of the Great Hall that says Royal Rourke Foundation Gala.

"Of course, sorry."

It's actually my first time ever showing up at one of these things, but I'm too focused on getting rid of the interloper to explain. I turn to the guy. "I'm Garrett Rourke. And how do you know Harper?"

He smiles uneasily. *Good. Aggressive message received.* "We just met, but I feel like I know her from her outstanding performance on *The Zone.*" He offers his hand. "I'm Jeff Briggs."

"Nice to meet ya, Jeff. Harper and I have some catching up to do." I give him a pointed look.

"Garrett," Harper says, sounding somewhere between surprised and appalled.

"We do," I insist, never taking my eyes off Jeff. I will glare him away.

He offers Harper a smile. "Nice to meet you. I'm available if they're casting for *Living Gold.* Jeff Briggs. I'm SAG."

Harper smiles tightly. "I don't have any control over casting. You should go through your agent for any casting notices."

"Of course, I just thought it wouldn't hurt…" He trails off at my glare, turns, and walks away.

"Does that happen a lot?" I ask.

She sighs. "All the time."

"Did you ever approach actors at parties, hoping to get an in?"

She scoffs. "No. I busted my ass going to audition after audition. I would never…" She stops herself, her teeth clenched together. "Doesn't matter. Big news is that you and I broke up." She lowers her voice. "I told you not to mention me to the paparazzi when you gave them a statement."

I grimace. I should start following this stuff more closely. "I thought I was doing the right thing putting them off the story of us. Anyway, sorry. I get now that I should never say anything personal to them. Swear it won't happen again."

She nods. "Thanks."

"Are you still mad I got excited about being a model?" I tense in anticipation because this could be a real problem. "I wasn't trying to steal your spotlight," I add.

"I was never jealous or mad that you were featured. That's not your fault. I was just hoping Best Friends Care would've gotten more press since that's what the whole night was supposed to be about."

That makes sense. I press on just to be crystal clear. "After I said the press thought I was a model, you said it was crap and meant nothing. Kinda a slap in the face."

She blows out a breath. "I was trying to make you feel better. I thought you'd be upset since modeling isn't nearly as important as what you guys do with your development projects." She gestures around us. "Look at where we are tonight because of it. All these people supporting a good cause to build neighborhoods instead of tearing them down in favor of skyscrapers owned by some faraway corporate entity. Josie and Sean told me all about it."

I rub the back of my neck. "That's the problem with texts. Too easy to take the words the wrong way. So you know I'm not a user like your ex, right?"

She looks over my shoulder. "I admit I was confused by our whole conversation."

"Our fight."

"It did feel that way, yes." She meets my eyes, a soft vulnerability lurking there. "I hoped you were different."

I nod, relief making me relax. She wasn't jealous I stole her spotlight. It was just a misunderstanding. "So just you and Joe on a hot date?" I jerk my chin at him standing guard. He scratches his cheek with his middle finger. I bite back a laugh. I really like Joe.

Harper doesn't notice. She's staring at her untouched champagne, her brows knit together. "Well, after the disastrous way things ended after our date last week, I thought it best not to drag another guy into the spotlight." She meets my eyes. "Not that the date itself was bad, just the fallout."

I lean close to her ear. "It wasn't a disaster, sweetheart."

She shivers and crosses her arms. "You can stop pretending we're in a relationship now."

"No more lamb chop?"

She laughs. "I thought you were mad at me." She leans

close to whisper, "You hung up on me. And then the paparazzi staked out your apartment, which was my fault, and then you told them we were over."

I shift to whisper in her ear, "We both got a little touchy. I'd like to try again." I straighten. "How've you been?" Josie told me Harper was a little down at work this week. Part of me hopes it's because she missed me.

She lets out a breath. "Can't complain."

"But if you could complain—" I cup a hand by my ear and lean down "—go ahead and whisper it."

I draw back at her silence. She's smiling.

I grin. "You missed me, didn't ya?"

She shakes her head. "I felt guilty as hell. I never want to be a user. I thought that's what you thought of me, asking you to go with me last minute to the gala, telling you what to say for the cause. And then, well, you know the rest."

"Hey, what did you really get from me other than a sexy escort?"

"Shh, it sounds like I paid you." She lowers her voice. "Like a male prostitute."

"Worst hundred bucks I ever spent. I didn't even get a kiss."

"What? You never paid me anything. Besides, I would pay you, not the other way around." She stops and laughs. "Oh. Sorry, my guilt is getting in the way of your joking."

"I get it about needing to be careful when you're in the public eye. My dad was raised to be king and went through a lot of public scrutiny from the day he was born all the way until he abdicated the throne and was banished. Luckily, that was before social media and the internet, but it was still pretty big news."

"I read a little about it. It sounds like he made a choice he's happy with."

"Married the best woman in the world. That's what he always says about my mom." I tug a curly lock of her dark brown hair. It's soft and springy. "Were you looking up stuff about me?"

"I read through some of the press last week, and a bunch of stuff popped up about your family."

"So yes."

Her eyes sparkle as she bites back a smile. "Only to see how bad the damage was."

"No damage. Actually, look at this." I pull the agent's card from my pocket and show her. "This guy wants to represent me and get me a commercial. You think I should do it? It seems like a no-brainer with the pay for one day's work."

She reads the card, her lips pressed together. "It's a top agency."

"Think I should go for it?"

"Have you ever acted before?"

"No, but it's a commercial. How hard can it be?"

Her eyes narrow. "Acting is a craft. It takes time and many hours of study to hone your skills."

"To say something like 'get a close shave with Sharp Edge'? He says he'll get me in for an aftershave commercial." I rub my clean-shaven jaw. "Apparently, this jaw is perfection."

She hides a smile by sipping her champagne. My charm is totally working on her. "Is that so?"

"Sure is. Touch it." I lean my cheek toward her.

She claps her hand to my jaw in a near slap. "Wow."

"Right?"

She tilts her head. "You know the odds of getting a commercial your first time out? More like after your one hundredth audition, if you're lucky. You sure you want to put in that kind of time?"

I shrug. "I'll go on one audition. If I don't get it, no problem. I'm not quitting my day job. I just like the idea of having some money in the bank to buy a house. Maybe with a yard so I could finally have a dog."

She softens. "That's nice. Really nice."

I execute a formal bow like my royal cousins do. "With your blessing."

She hesitates.

I wait, my eyes intent on hers. I don't want her to think

I'm a user either. If I succeed or fail at this new gig, it's all on me.

"Sure, it wouldn't hurt to go on one audition," she finally says.

"Great. Now how do I get on your show?"

She scowls. "Not funny."

"Harp, I don't need you for connections. I could just as easily have asked Josie for a part on the show." *Not that it ever occurred to me to try acting before.*

She stiffens. "But you didn't, did you? It wasn't until you were on the red carpet with me that the press took notice. A top agent took notice too. Be honest, you're starting to take it seriously as a career path."

"And what's wrong with that? You're the only one who gets to be an actor in a relationship? That's not what your boyfriend history says. Why would I be any different?"

Her eyes flash. "First of all, we're not in a relationship." She backs up a step. "Forget it. This time I'm listening to my gut."

And then she turns and walks away.

Seriously, she walked away!

I thought we were getting along too. What's her problem?

Harper

I'm being smart, I reassure myself as I walk to the European sculpture garden for dinner. Joe trails behind me. My emotions are all over the place with Garrett, and I'm probably extra sensitive to him getting into the industry because of what happened with Colton and John, but I just can't go through that kind of hurt again. I promised myself I'd listen to my gut when it sends a warning signal, and it's churning them out like crazy. God, it's so easy for him too. He has no idea the grueling years of auditions I've been through. I got lucky at fifteen to get a teen TV show and then another. After that, there was a long drought before I was cast on *Capital Asset*. I almost gave up. But I couldn't face going home in defeat, especially when that meant facing my grandmother.

I enter the courtyard, where round tables with white tablecloths are set with crystal glasses, china place settings, and a large floral centerpiece. Marble statues surround the edges of the room. There's a small podium set up at the far end of the room, probably for a speech. Thank God it's not me up there tonight.

Josie stands and waves me over to her table, where Sean is already sitting. It's assigned seating, and I'm so glad to have a friendly face with me for dinner.

As soon as I reach her, she's enthusiastic as always, hugging me like we're long-lost friends. It's so funny because I just saw her last night for our show's taping.

"You're next to me," she says, taking her seat.

I sit next to her and glance at the name card on my other side in alarm. Garrett. I'm about to casually switch his name card farther away when the man himself takes his seat. My cheeks flush. Josie set this up.

Josie beams at Garrett. "I'm so glad you two made up!"

"She can't resist me," he replies.

As if we're in a relationship! I think I was clear about that earlier when I walked away. Now how do I get through an entire dinner with him?

I stare at him, desperately trying to come up with a solution that puts more space between us. I don't want to leave Josie. And this is his family, so he's not going to want to leave. Could I get him to sit over by Sean?

He gives me a slow sexy smile that makes my heart thump harder. "Sweetheart."

I jerk my gaze back to Josie, my mind blanking on a comeback from *sweetheart*. It's like a warm hug wrapped around my heart. Her brows knit quizzically. I can't explain when he's right there. This is so awkward.

Sean elbows her, and she recovers herself, smiling brightly. "Good, good, good."

Garrett rests his arm along the back of my chair, almost

but not quite touching my bare shoulder. I'm hyperaware of him, every nerve ending on alert.

Josie pops up from her seat, signaling to someone across the room, and grabbing Sean by the arm to join her. They leave. Since the rest of the people at our table haven't arrived yet, I decide it's time to define the boundaries here. "No need to pretend we're in a relationship."

A smile plays over his lips, his eyes glowing in the dim light. "I know, darling." His voice is as silky as a caress.

A shiver races down my spine. "So, uh…" *Think!* Lust diverts all energy south of my belly button. *Why must I be so attracted to him?* "You can stop calling me sweetheart and darling because we're not a couple. And friends don't do that." Not that I want to be his friend. I just want to get through this dinner without letting myself get any further tangled up with him. My gut says no. I can ignore every other tingling part.

"Darling gets the axe too? Damn." He shakes his head, his lips pressed together like it's a real shame. He lifts his head, his expression brightening. "How's babe?"

I bite back a smile. "No."

"Honey?"

I snort-laugh and slap a hand over my mouth. "No sweet names of any kind, please."

He slowly nods. "Just friends. Got it."

"I'm serious."

"As a heart attack."

"Right."

He grins. "Okay, lamb chop."

I bite my lower lip, torn between laughing and making sure he understands about the boundary here.

"So, since we're friends…" he drawls in a husky voice.

My heart kicks up, and every part of me fires up in anticipation. I lean in, dying to know what he thinks we'll do as friends.

"Mind if I sit here?" a deep voice asks. A handsome dark-haired guy with a neat beard swipes the name card from the seat next to Garrett, pockets it, and puts his own name card down. Wyatt Winters.

Garrett smiles. "Wyatt, hey, man, sure, take a seat."

I can't help but think about the name card he pocketed. I point to his pocket. "Aren't you going to put that name card on someone else's table? That person could be wandering around wondering where they're supposed to sit."

"Right," Wyatt says, taking out the card and making a small paper airplane out of it. He sends it sailing, and it lands in a floral centerpiece a few tables away.

I gesture toward it. *That is not going to cut it.*

He sighs and stands to retrieve the card. "Your girlfriend is bossy," he tells Garrett and winks at me before walking over to the other table.

Garrett grins at me. "Don't worry, there was a space between girl and friend. I tell everyone I meet. Don't forget the space."

I purse my lips. He's teasing me. At the same time, I feel like I'm losing ground here as he heartily agrees with everything I say. He taps the end of my nose and laughs.

Wyatt returns to his seat and leans around Garrett, offering his hand to me. "We got off on the wrong foot with my terrible manners. I'm Wyatt."

I shake his hand. "Harper."

His eyes widen. "I know you. You're Amanda Boxer. *Badass.*"

"Yes, Amanda is," I say evenly. "Now I play a different role. That's what actors do."

He leans back in his seat. "Sure, I know. I met a bunch of actors in LA and Josie of course. Probably the reason most of us are here. She's something, isn't she?"

I follow his gaze to where Josie is enthusiastically embracing a woman and then gesturing as she introduces her to the group surrounding her. She's like a firefly, her light attracting everyone to her. I'm more like a caterpillar in a cocoon, who emerges only as a completely different creature in my butterfly-actor skin. *Getting philosophical here, Harp.*

"She's awesome," Garrett says. "She's my sister-in-law, like the sister I never had. I've got five older brothers."

Wyatt rubs the top of Garrett's head with his knuckles. "Bet they kicked your ass on a regular basis."

Garrett grins. "Mostly they carried me around and looked out for me, except for Brendan. He's only two years older, and we got into it a lot. We're close now." He turns to me. "What about you? Any brothers or sisters?"

"Only child."

"Lucky," Wyatt says. "I've got three younger sisters." He widens his dark eyes and leans in. "The *drama*. The high-pitched squeals." He shudders. "It's a wonder I've still got my hearing. Most of it anyway."

A group of older women arrive at our table, and after a brief introduction, they resume talking to each other.

Wyatt turns to Garrett. "So, back to the reason we're all here tonight, tell me how you decide what kind of community project you'll do with each development job."

I listen as Garrett explains the process his family's company goes through from scouting out properties of potential value to coming up with a comprehensive development plan, considering what they can do with the space that best suits it. The projects they've done sound really cool. They've won awards too. I can tell he's proud of their work. Of course, it was obvious even when we met. One of the first things he did was talk about his family business.

"So what's your part?" Wyatt asks.

Garrett laughs a little, but it sounds forced. "The youngest brother doesn't get first pick for any exciting position in the company. My older brothers took charge, saying I was too inexperienced. I probably was at the time we took over the company from my uncle. Anyway, I've spent the past eight years working crew. Maybe I'll always work crew until something else opens up."

Like acting. I suddenly understand why he'd want to try something different. He got the short end of the stick, and he knows it.

"Like an older brother retires?" Wyatt asks.

Garrett exhales sharply. "Yeah, we'll all be old by the time that happens. I don't know, man, I just take it one day at a time." He taps the table. "I love working with my brothers."

Wyatt shoots me a disbelieving look and turns back to Garrett. "Ever think of a different line of work?"

Garrett hesitates before saying, "Born into the family business. We stick together. What about you? Now that you're retired, ever think of a second career?"

"Retired?" I echo. "How old are you?"

Wyatt shakes his head. "Why does everyone ask that when I say I'm retired? Can't a guy just take his billions and be done?"

"Whoa," Garrett says.

"No," I say. "You're young—"

"Thirty," Wyatt says.

"Youngish," I amend. "You have years to be a contributing member of society."

"I contribute. I'm here, aren't I?" He gestures around the room. "I'm a philanthropist."

"How did you make billions?" Garrett asks.

I'm curious too, but I was taught never to speak about money. I let my agent handle that.

Wyatt shakes out the cloth napkin folded like a swan and sets it on his lap. "I created a virtual reality system that a certain social media company was willing to pay handsomely for. And I created and sold a few other startup tech companies before that. Made my first million at nineteen."

Garrett stares at him, speechless.

To my thinking that means Wyatt's capable of more. He's an innovator.

"You have to do something," I say. "No one can be happy going aimlessly through life and showing up at the occasional fundraiser."

A waiter arrives offering a tray of champagne. I take one. Wyatt and Garrett decline.

I sip my champagne and look at Wyatt expectantly.

He pulls at his collar. "Worse than my sisters with your tough judgey looks."

Garrett does a double take. "What are ya talking about, tough? She's got a face like one of these goddess statues." He gestures to the sculptures surrounding us.

My heart squeezes. I've never been compared to a goddess. "Thank you," I say softly.

Garrett jerks his chin like *of course*. He seems a little offended on my behalf.

Wyatt leans back in his seat, resting his palms on the table. "I just want to lie low in some dinky town no one's ever heard of and chill. Maybe I'll anonymously donate to help the community where I hide out with a library annex or something like Garrett here does, but otherwise—" he gestures with one hand "—chill."

I consider that. My hometown is a dinky place no one's ever heard of, and it could use some philanthropic donations for the budget gaps. The older hippie generation that founded the town has mostly left, and they could use fresh blood. Someone like Wyatt, an innovative thinker, could help the town thrive. Of course he'd get sucked in. Impossible not to in a town with everyone in everyone else's business. It was a refuge for me to have a community that cared. I donate every year to support the school's arts program, a special place where I discovered theater for the first time.

"Write this down," I tell Wyatt.

He takes an imaginary pencil from behind his ear, wets the tip with his tongue, and pretends to be ready to write on nonexistent paper.

I laugh. "Seriously. Get out your phone and take note. Summerdale, New York. A little over an hour from here in the suburbs. No one's ever heard of it. The people are a little quirky, but if you can deal with a postman who likes to deliver tamales with the mail or a café owner named Rainbow, it's perfect for you."

Wyatt pulls out his phone and dutifully types it in. "Yes, ma'am. My new hideaway." He brightens. "Is there a Mexican community? I love authentic Mexican food, the spicier the better."

"No. Bill's white. He's just a big fan of tamales."

"Damn."

"They're really good tamales, though."

Garrett nudges my arm. "I know Summerdale. My family goes there every Labor Day weekend. We rent a house by the lake."

The hair on the back of my neck stands up. So weird that Garrett's family goes there. I mean, there's always some houses for rent by the lake, but it's not exactly a hot spot. And how did a guy from Brooklyn find it?

Wyatt puts his phone facedown and sends me an aggrieved look. "Garrett here heard of it. Sounds like the secret's out on Summerdale."

"It's really not popular at all," I say, truly surprised by the Garrett connection. "How did you end up renting a lake house there?"

Garrett cocks his head. "Funny connection, right? It started with my brother Jack. He rented it as a prank, pretending he'd bought his girlfriend a house, and then turned it into a proposal in front of the whole family."

I stare at him, jaw dropped. "A prank proposal?"

"I like your family," Wyatt says. "Brilliant."

Garret smiles. "I could ask Jack how he found Summerdale if you want. He probably just searched the internet for a nice house to rent that would fit all of us and be far enough away from the city to surprise his girlfriend, but not too far that it would be hard for the rest of us to get there. Jack's king of the pranksters. He'll put a lot of thought into planning out the perfect one."

I'm still stuck on the reason for the rental. "A prank proposal? Did she say yes?"

He chuckles. "Yeah, she did. They prank each other. Now they're happily married with a baby on the way."

"And your family keeps going back to Summerdale?" I ask.

"Yeah, Jack wanted to keep up the tradition to remember the happy occasion, so now we spend every Labor Day there."

"Which house do you rent?"

He shrugs. "Jack handles all that. I don't keep track of the address. This last time we rented a different house with a large second-floor deck overlooking the lake." He turns to Wyatt. "Worth a trip out there to check it out. Lots of trees, the lake, of course, houses tucked away around the lake and up the hill. There's this one huge house at the top of the hill and, for some reason, there's a lighthouse on the property. Right in the middle of open land."

"Obviously it's for the giant ships approaching by lake," Wyatt says.

I shake my head. "The lake can only accommodate rowboats and canoes. It's not that big."

Garrett squeezes my shoulder, sending a rush of heat through me. The amused look in his eyes tells me Wyatt was joking. I'm not used to so much joking around.

I continue sharing about my hometown in the hopes that Wyatt will be intrigued. "An eccentric recluse used to live at the top of the hill. He died before I was born, and nobody bought the property. People say it's haunted. I'm sure it's just overrun by raccoons and other critters, but it always gave me a creepy feeling."

Wyatt wiggles his fingers. "Ooh, sounds like a Scooby-Doo episode with old man Jenkins."

"Zoinks!" Josie exclaims, popping up suddenly and putting her arms around Wyatt and Garrett. "You two planning on solving a mystery?"

"Yeah, the mystery of the landlocked lighthouse," Wyatt says.

"Oh, are you talking about Summerdale?" Josie asks. "We were there a few weeks ago for my brother and sister-in-law's wedding reenactment. Love it there."

"Wedding reenactment?" I echo.

"This family is nuts," Josie says happily. "I fit right in."

Sean appears by her side, and they take their seats at the table.

Wyatt gestures to them. "Now why couldn't I have been born into a nutso family? I would've fit in so much better."

Sean smiles. "It can be fun and also aggravating. Everyone's high energy and hardheaded." He knocks on his head.

"That's just because of the high testosterone levels with so many men," Josie says with a laugh. "It's all evening out now that more women have joined the family."

"I'm thrilled you did," Sean says, giving her a kiss.

I sigh. I've seen Sean and Josie together these last five weeks at work, and they seem so perfect together. Always laughing, talking, and being affectionate with each other. I envy her the easy confidence and trust she has in Sean. They met before she was famous, and she knows he loves her for her, not for what he can get from her. I guess if I married my boyfriend from when I was fourteen—Levi did a fine job escorting me to the eighth-grade dance while following all the rules General Joan laid out—I could have the same. Ha. Funny but not. I don't wish away my success, but it would be nice to be able to trust in a guy like that, knowing we had something real.

I'm pulled from my angsty thoughts by Josie's unexpected question. "Harp, you want to do our song after dinner is served? This crowd would appreciate it."

I freeze. Josie and I both like musicals—her voice is like a dream—and sometimes we sing "For Good" from *Wicked*, a beautiful song between sisters. But that's just when we're hanging in one of our trailers. I need to prepare for a performance. And my voice can't come close to hers. There's a reason I never auditioned for the New York theater scene. I love musicals, but I know I'm not at the top tier of professional singers.

"Harp?" Josie asks, waving a hand in front of my face.

"Maybe just you," I say. "Your voice is so beautiful."

She cocks her head. "But it's a duet. And you sound good too. It'll be fun."

I lick my dry lips. "No, thanks."

"Come on, you'll be great," Josie coaxes.

Garrett pipes up, "My friend here is a hard no on the after-dinner show tunes."

I turn to him, surprised he spoke on my behalf. His hand

goes to my throat, his smoldering gaze sending a rush of heat from my throat all the way to my toes. "Terrible case of laryngitis."

I'm so enthralled I'm speechless, gazing into his eyes.

He drops his hand. I swallow and stare at the table, shaken by how much I want him. I didn't know how much until he touched me. What could've felt like a vulnerable position—his hand at my throat—turned me on. No warning sign of danger flashed through me. Only raw lust.

"Smoking heat stole your voice," Josie quips. "Got it. Carry on!"

Dinner arrives, and I belatedly put my napkin in my lap in a daze.

Garrett's voice rumbles in my ear, sending tingles down my spine. "Okay there, lamb chop?"

I nod woodenly, not willing to risk another look at the enticing man.

"She means well," he whispers.

I turn, and we're so close I see his eyes dilate. My voice comes out breathy. "I know."

"I mean well too. Just so you know."

My gaze drops to his sensual lips, a longing to get closer drawing me in.

"Would you mind passing the butter?" Wyatt asks.

Garrett straightens and passes it to him. Moment over. Was I about to kiss him at a table full of people? I know better than to add to the gossip about me and the secret prince of Brooklyn. What happened to all my good defenses? My gut check? The warning signs fizzled in the rush of lust.

I'm in trouble.

10

———————

Harper

At the end of the night, Garrett walks me out. It's just the two of us with Joe trailing a few feet behind. We stayed for a while, talking to Sean and Josie, so we're one of the last to leave. The museum is quiet and nearly empty.

"This place reminds me of Amalie Palace," he says. That's his family's palace in Villroy. I may have looked into the royal stuff.

"Do you visit often?"

"Not a lot. The reconciliation between our families is pretty recent. I've been there for two weddings and the last two Christmases. They have a Regency-themed Christmas ball. You probably would like it. Kinda like a historical movie set."

Sign me up! I would love to visit a palace and go to a ball. "Do they regularly hold themed balls there?"

"I dunno. They do for Christmas. It's because of my cousin's wife Alice. She's a Regency romance author."

I suck in air. "Alice Segal?"

"Yeah." He shakes his head, his lips twisting into a wry smile. "She even gave us a recommended reading list, heavy on the Jane Austen. *Pride and Prejudice* wasn't bad, actually. I caught the movie." At my silence, he turns to me. "Harper?"

I shut my gaping jaw. "You're related to the author of *The Scoundrel and the Governess*? *The Duke's Dare*? *The Viscount's Victory*? I love that trilogy, but especially the scoundrel book. Seriously, I have it in eBook, paperback, and audio, so I always have it handy for a pick-me-up."

He grins. "I'm sensing you're a megafan."

"Uh, yeah! Wow. I can't believe you're related to Alice Segal. Do you think she'd sign my copy of *The Scoundrel and the Governess*?"

His eyes sparkle as he takes me in. "Harper Ellis, secret romantic."

"I just like a happy ending."

He lifts his brows, his voice husky. "Who doesn't?"

I cock my head. Did he mean that in the *happy ending* way? Oh, he's good with the double entendre. I need to be extra cautious with this guy.

He smirks. "Now who has the connections?"

"Yeah, yeah."

"So you're into books and music, what else? Besides me, obviously."

Is it that obvious?

I fight back a blush. "There's not a lot of time for much else between work, fitness training, and nights out like this." It's a necessity for me to work out. Part of the acting gig, maintaining my looks for the camera and ensuring my wardrobe fits.

"Harper," he drawls.

"What?"

"Look at me. I work and keep fit. I still have other interests."

I lift my chin. "Like what?"

He gives me a slow sexy smile that makes my stomach flutter. "Like cooking. I'm an excellent chef."

I blink, surprised. Looking at this beast of a man with his hard square jaw and massive biceps, the last thing I thought he'd say was that he could cook. I expected him to say boxing or pounding nails. Something macho like that.

"You don't believe me?" he asks.

I recover myself. "No, I do. That's great. I don't enjoy cooking, so it's hard for me to wrap my head around." *Good save.*

"You'd like my cooking. Stop by my place for dinner sometime."

"It'd be easier if you came to my place. I mean, security wise." *Wait, did I just invite him over?*

"No problem. Just tell me when."

I swallow hard, suddenly wary. "This is just a friends thing, right?"

"If that's what you want," he says easily.

"Is that what you want?"

He gazes into my eyes, his voice gentle. "I want you to be comfortable."

I look away, checking in with my gut. I'm both nervous and excited about spending time with him. Nervous because I was just recently dumped. The last thing I need is Garrett and me blowing up in a public way. And we already did have a falling-out after our first friends date. Somehow I think he'd be insulted if I asked him to sign a nondisclosure at this point. I don't want to be *that* person.

His deep voice rumbles in my ear, sending a delicious shiver down my spine. "It's just dinner."

Be smart. Defenses up. Don't be taken in by his sexy everything!

"Okay."

He smiles, his aquamarine eyes warm on mine. "Great. What do you like to eat? I can make anything with a recipe on the internet."

"I'm flexible."

"I'll make this spicy shrimp and cauliflower mash dish. You bring the beer."

I make a face. "Beer doesn't go with that."

"Course it does."

"I don't have any beer."

"Fine. I'll bring the beer too. You bring your sweet self."

"I'm not sweet." I was raised to be tough and strong, never soft and sweet. *Chin up. I didn't raise a wimp!*

Get out of my head, Grandmom!

"Yeah, okay," he says.

"I'm not."

He stops walking and frowns. "I was really pissed when the paparazzi showed up on my doorstep."

I cringe. "I'm so sorry."

He slowly leans in, and my heart races. His gaze drops to my lips before he shifts to speak near my ear. "Sweet. Told ya."

I swallow hard. Somehow he sees past the toughness people know me for from my Amanda character, but also from the thick skin I've worked hard to develop. It's how I got through my strict upbringing, how I managed rejection after rejection, how I deal with getting fired and shows getting cancelled. Yet, deep down, I've always known it was a false front to protect my sensitive self. I don't know how he saw that about me so soon. An alarm goes off in my mind. This is a man who could get in close enough to do serious damage.

I keep walking, my mind whirling, my heart pounding.

He shoots me an amused look. "Relax. You're with the secret prince. What's he been up to all these years anyway? Polishing his mountain of gold coins? Strutting around in his royal velvet cape? Bonking his brothers on the head with the royal scepter?"

I bite back a smile. "Arrogant much?"

"Are you saying I have a big ego?"

"Yes!"

"Can't help it. It's in my genes. All the men in my family do."

"Sean doesn't seem that way."

"Sean is the worst! My God, it's like you can barely breathe with all the hot air he's putting out in the room."

I stifle a laugh as Sean comes up behind him. "What else does he do?"

"Back in the day, he'd strut around with his tool belt like he was *the man*, ya know?" He straightens at my amused look. "He's right behind me, isn't he?"

I nod.

He turns. "Hey, Sean, just singing your praises."

"Nice save, jackass."

He looks around. "Did Jack show up to this thing too?"

Sean claps a hand on his shoulder and turns to me. "Jack's our brother. This guy bothering you?"

"Little bit," I say.

"Hey!" Garrett protests. "I'm her friend date. That is an official title granted by her. How could I be bothering her when she bestowed the honor herself?"

Sean grins. "Indeed."

Garrett points to Sean. "Indeed!"

I lift my palms, laughing. "Okay, okay. You're both ridiculous. Is this how they talk in Villroy?"

"More like—" Garrett shakes out his shoulders and stands like he has a stick up his ass. "By order of the king, this date is official."

"Smooth," Sean mutters.

"And you're the king?" I ask.

One corner of his mouth curves up in an endearing smile. "Well, you wouldn't call me lamb chop."

11

—————

Garrett

I am *pumped*. I just filmed my first commercial. *Ka-ching!* Thirty grand in the bank. Mark Perlman knows his shit. That's my new agent. He got me in for the audition on Tuesday for the aftershave commercial he told me about, and two days later, I filmed it. He says it doesn't usually happen that quickly. I just got lucky with the timing. Anyway, all I had to do was fake shave in front of a mirror, shirtless; then I rubbed my jaw, pretended to put on aftershave, and smoldered into the camera, saying, "Ready for my woman." Then I held up Axel aftershave. I pictured Harper when I smoldered. It must've worked too because, after it wrapped, the director yelled, "Yes! Bring the thunder!"

I nearly bust a gut trying not to laugh. He was so thrilled he thanked me profusely because, apparently, it's unusual to get it in one take. All in all, a great first experience. Pretty fun just to do fake stuff as work. Mark says I'll get a SAG card for it, which is the union card for actors, and that means he can get me even better, higher-paying gigs only open to union actors. He wants me to audition for a sports car commercial next week and says my rate just went up. What a rush! I never thought I'd be able to afford a house, not for years and years. And now, if I get this next commercial, I could have a down payment. Unbelievable.

I can't wait to tell Josie. I ride my Harley through the streets of Manhattan, heading for the studio on Chelsea Piers where they film *Living Gold*. She got me on the list to get in, excited to hear about my experience. Today they're having a run-through without the studio audience, but she's on an hour lunch break. The timing worked out perfect. Funny they call it lunch, even when it's near dinnertime. It has to do with which meal number it is, related to union rules on number of hours worked and meals allotted.

Not gonna lie, the best part in all this is that it puts me and Harper on even footing. I proved myself with that commercial, which will lead to the next. No way she can feel like I used her for a leg up. This side gig is completely different from what she does. That means she can relax her defenses around me. I've missed her this week. I wear my heart on my sleeve and make no apologies for it.

After I give the guard at the gate my name and show him ID, I pull into the lot and park. Josie's trailer is the biggest one. She says you always know where you stand on the job hierarchy by the size of your trailer and whether or not you have to share it with someone. She's big time now, our Josie girl.

I tuck my helmet under one arm and knock on the metal door.

Sean answers. "Beast! I heard you're our new star."

I shake my head. "It was just a commercial. One line."

Josie pops up behind him, beaming. "Come in and tell me everything!"

I join her and Sean at a square table, where they were eating lunch, and set my helmet on the floor. "Okay, first of all, I had no idea it took so many people to make a two-minute commercial."

"Oh, yeah," Josie says. "It's an expensive production. Now multiply that by a gazillion for a movie. That's why the studios are always expanding well-known franchises and doing reboots. They want a sure thing to recoup their investment." She leans forward, her blue eyes gleaming. "So give us the play-by-play from the moment you arrived on set to now."

I glance at Sean, who looks amused. That sounds like too much detail. I give her the highlights and confess the one uncomfortable part—I had to wear makeup. I never knew guys wore makeup on camera. Small price to pay for a fun paycheck.

She claps. "Do the line."

I hold up a finger, conjuring Harper in my mind with her classic beauty—her mass of dark curls, the vulnerability lurking in her eyes, her soft-looking pink lips. Damn, I want her bad. I look at Josie and say my line, "Ready for my woman."

She squeaks. "Oh my God, he's a natural. That was *amazing*."

I look away, embarrassed but happy too. "Mark's getting me a personal acting coach."

Josie squeezes my arm. "That'll help broaden your skills, but, Garrett, you've already got the instincts." She turns to Sean. "Didn't that just give you chills?"

"No, actually," he says dryly.

She pats his shoulder. "Well, you're not a woman. The women will love this commercial, and the men will want to be him. What'd you wear?"

"I was supposed to be shaving, so I was shirtless."

"Now *that* gives me chills," Sean says with a straight face.

Josie covers Sean's ears while she speaks in a stage whisper that's loud enough for any audience. Sean rolls his eyes. "I saw you shirtless at the lake. You are one gorgeous man. The camera will eat you up." She takes her hands off Sean's ears and gives him an impish smile.

I rub the back of my neck. "Thanks."

"Are ya done ogling my baby brother?" Sean asks in an aggrieved tone.

"I'm giving him my objective professional point of view!" Josie exclaims. "Now, if I had met Garrett before I met you, I would've asked him if he had a grumpy older brother and ended up with you anyway, so you can just take it down a notch, mister."

Sean chuckles, holds her by the chin and kisses her.

I look away. Only so many ridiculously happy-in-love couples a guy can take.

"Is Harper in her trailer?" I ask.

Josie smiles widely. "I'll text her to see." She grabs her phone off the table and texts way too long for a simple question. *When will I learn?*

I stifle a groan. I thought Josie would know where she is. "What did ya say this time?"

She grins. "I just told her you're here and you'd like to see her. Oh, and also that you did a commercial because I was so excited for you. She says to stop by on your way out."

I grab my helmet and stand. "Did she sound upset or happy I did a commercial?"

Josie shrugs. "She didn't comment either way."

I exhale sharply. "I wanted to be the one to tell her."

She grimaces. "I'm sorry. I got excited. Next time I'll keep my mouth shut about your commercial work." She mimes zipping her lips.

I soften. "Sure. I'll see ya." I turn and head for the door.

"Break a leg!" Josie calls after me.

I turn back. "For my next audition or with Harper?"

Her eyes dart to Sean, who raises his brows. She gives me a weak smile. "Yes." She gives me directions to find Harper's trailer from here.

"Thanks." I head out the door. It's sweet that Josie wants us to get together, but it's best if she stays out of it. I don't need to deal with her disappointment on top of my own. Harper and I are far from a sure thing.

I find my way through the rows of trailers to Harper's. Joe's sitting on the steps of it, eating a sandwich. "Hey, Joe, how's the bodyguard gig?"

"Sweet. I get an apartment in Gramercy Park next to hers. Only a few guys I've had to scare off with a glare. No weapons or shit like that."

My chest tightens. I hate that she has strange men harassing her. "Glad she has you."

He steps down, getting out of my way. "She's real salt of the earth. Some of these actresses can be full of themselves, ya know?" He looks side to side. "Not naming names, but my last client was a doozy."

"I can imagine. I'm just gonna—" I point to the door.

"Sure, sure. She's on call in fifteen minutes."

I knock on her door. "Hey, it's Garrett."

"Come in!"

I open the door to find her on the floor, wearing a V-neck white sweater and a long ruffly black skirt. She's in the lotus position, her hands resting palm up on her knees.

"Yoga?" I ask.

"I do yoga, but just now I was doing my mindfulness meditation. It helps center me and get me ready to go back to work." She takes a deep breath and lets it out before rising gracefully to her feet. She smells sweet like flowers. Jasmine, maybe? One of my ex-girlfriends was into essential oils and used to have lots of different scents she experimented with in homemade cosmetics.

She looks up at me, a wry expression on her face. "So Josie tells me you're one of us now. SAG card in hand, ready to take the world by storm."

"Josie exaggerates. You know how excited she gets about stuff, right? She's like a puppy, bouncing around full of enthusiasm."

She inclines her head and goes to her mini-fridge for a bottled water. She holds it up for me.

I take it. "Thanks."

She takes a bottled water for herself and gestures for me to take a seat on the sofa. I do, setting my helmet on the floor. She joins me, tucking a leg under her and shifting to face me. "Sean dropped off the shelf pegs you sent, and I fixed the other shelf myself. Felt very handy. Thanks for remembering to do that."

I bite back a smile at the idea that pushing pegs into a predrilled hole makes her handy. "No problem."

She glances at my helmet. "Let me guess, you ride a Harley."

"Yup. I was so excited to share my news I forgot to fasten the helmet to the back. Why, do I look the type?"

"Burly tough-looking guy, uh, yeah."

I smile. "I traded my oldest brother for it when he decided he needed a car for his kid. He's got my black Mazda outfitted with an awesome stereo system. Totally wasted on kiddie songs."

She presses her lips together, an amused look on her beautiful face. "A motorcycle and a sporty car. Kinda cliché."

"And what do you drive?"

"When I'm in LA, I drive a Prius."

"Electric cars are cool."

She gives me a sheepish look. "It's kinda the LA actor cliché."

"Ha! Dissing my Harley cliché when you're talking about yourself. You forget I'm fluent in woman speak."

She rolls her eyes. "Because of your long line of girlfriends, I suppose."

I sip my water, considering how to answer. I know better than to talk about an ex to a woman I'm currently interested in. "I'm a serial monogamist, so I get to know women well enough to understand their language." Now I sound like a woke guy instead of a womanizer. "And I never cheat," I add. *Unlike your ex.*

She shifts uneasily. "Well. Huh. So, how did you like acting?"

I can't tell if she's happy for me or not. Her tone and expression are bland now. The last thing I want her to think is that I was using her as an in. "It's not like it's a profession for me. Just one commercial. One line."

"You didn't answer my question."

"It was fun," I admit. *A blast, and I can't wait to do more.* I keep that to myself, guilt tempering my happiness. I don't want her to take it wrong, and some part of me feels like I shouldn't enjoy doing something that could take me away from the family business.

She smiles. "Yeah, it can be fun. When I first discovered theater as a kid, it felt like I'd come home. Like I could finally express myself."

"By playing someone else?"

She leans closer, her eyes bright. "You always bring a part of yourself to a role. And sometimes it's the ugly parts you can't show the world. It's cathartic to get that out."

"I seriously doubt you have any ugly parts."

She hides a smile behind her bottled water and takes a sip. "Thank you. But do you get what I mean? Everyone has a dark shadow side they don't express. Humans are complicated and capable of a spectrum from the purest of goodness to the darkest of evil."

I shake my head. "Not me. I'm not that complicated. And I'm definitely one of the good guys."

She relaxes, leaning back on the sofa. "Maybe that's okay for you to feel that way. Sometimes all it takes is the right look for a guy's career to take off. It's much harder for a woman in Hollywood."

I snort. "I'm not in Hollywood. It was one commercial. Though I admit I'm thrilled with the money. I'm going for another commercial next week. I mean, I never thought I'd be able to afford a house so soon. It's mind-boggling how much you get paid for doing something fun."

She tilts her head. "There is that."

"It was kind of funny to be fake shaving, putting on fake aftershave, while all these serious people are working around me. I mean, the whole thing was funny in a surreal way."

She plays with the label on her bottled water, murmuring, "I'm glad you like where you landed."

The unsaid words hang in the air: *because of me*. I need to be sure she knows where I'm at.

I lean back on the sofa and turn my head toward hers. "Lamb chop."

She lifts her gaze to mine, a small smile playing over her lips. "Yes?"

"I don't see this as a career path. It's a side gig. I'm only working with an acting coach so I don't embarrass myself at an audition. This commercial was just one line, but if it gets more complicated, like, who knows, 'feed your dog the kibble that will give him well-formed crap,' well, I need to be prepared for that."

She bursts out laughing.

I relax and grin. "I do want to thank you for your part in opening up this opportunity. I know it was pretending to be your boyfriend at the gala that got me noticed by my agent."

She stops smiling, mumbling, "Your agent. Right."

I can almost see her defenses going up. "This isn't something I ever considered or wanted for myself, but it's here, and it seems stupid to throw away such a lucrative job. You know how much I make in construction?"

She shakes her head. "I don't need to know." She lifts her chin. "We're even, right? I used you for the good PR at the gala, and you got your start. Quid pro quo."

I take her hand, and she stares at it, but she doesn't pull away. "Now we're both in a better place. We don't need to fake anything for PR to help you save face, and I don't need anything from you but you."

She meets my eyes with a wary look. "What exactly do you mean?"

"I don't care about being seen with you in public. We'll do that only if you want it. I want the private part."

She smiles a little. "Private part sounds dirty."

For once I wasn't sneaking in a double meaning to flirt. "Harper, I'm not looking to get laid here. I can get that anywhere."

"I bet."

I cradle her jaw in one hand and gaze into her eyes. "I'll see you on Saturday for dinner at your place. Is there anything else you want to do?"

She blinks a few times, looking a bit like a deer caught in the headlights.

I wait her out, stroking the side of her neck with my thumb. Her skin is so soft.

She swallows. "My publicist can get me tickets to *Wicked*. It's my favorite musical."

"I'm there."

"Garrett?"

I push a lock of hair behind her ear and lean close to whisper, "Yeah, lamb chop?"

Her voice comes out soft, vulnerable. "I don't know if I'm ready for a relationship."

I kiss her cheek, so glad she's telling me what's up with her instead of putting up walls. "One date at a time. That's all. Date number one Saturday night." I grab my helmet and stand.

She stares at my helmet tucked under one arm. "Are we riding your Harley to the theater to see *Wicked*?"

"Depends how far your place is from the theater. Do you want to go for a ride on it? We could go out of the city on a different day for a joyride."

She wags a finger at me. "I'm on to your sneaky flirty language."

I scrunch my brows together like I'm confused. I do love to tease in a sexy way.

She presses her lips together, her eyes dancing with amusement. "You're good. That was great fake confusion, but now you're in professional actor territory here." She draws a circle around herself. "I'm all over those tells."

I take a bow. "Then I'll leave it to the expert. The queen of Summerdale, my favorite watering hole." I waggle my brows.

She huffs. "You are a beast!"

I wink and let myself out. She's so fun.

12

———

Harper

I pace my apartment, consider opening the wine early, and dismiss the thought. It's Saturday night—date number one with Garrett—and he's on his way over. Why did he number the date? How many does he expect to have? What happens when we hit a certain number? Do I unlock a new level of intimacy? I've never had a guy be so straightforward about what's going on between us. Most guys won't even say *relationship* let alone bring it up before the first date. He's almost too good to be true. He's cooking for me and going to see *Wicked* on Broadway. How many guys would do that?

I go back to my bedroom and check myself again in the full-length mirror. Is this outfit too much? I usually dress up for the theater, and I always have to look made-up and put together when I go out in public, but does it send the wrong message to Garrett? Do I look too eager? I'm wearing a sheer black blouse with a gold and black full skirt. It's a little retro looking. I kept the accessories simple—gold hoop earrings, black patent leather heels. A spritz of my favorite jasmine perfume. My hair's back in a loose bun. It's wholesome with a touch of sexy. I want to take it slow with Garrett because, well, part of me hopes this might be the start of something special. I need to know on a gut-deep level if he's worth risking my vulnerable heart. I've never been as tough as I wanted to be. I used to cry at everything and thought it was a failing. Turns out it's useful in my profession because I can cry on cue. My emotions are intense, my sensitivity high, thus, my defense system.

I remind myself to be wary. He's in the industry now, and that means he could still want a boost up the next rung of the ladder. I hope he wouldn't use me like that, but it's happened too many times for me to completely dismiss the possibility. I'm trying to be happy for him because he's excited. It seems he's mostly into it so he can afford to buy a house. That's a great thing that many people aspire to. Nothing wrong with that.

A small part of me can't help resenting how easy it was for him. Because of his looks, he sailed on in there. I had to deal with relentless auditions and rejections. *Hundreds* before I got a part. When I was fourteen, I commuted back and forth to Manhattan for a year, solo, to go on auditions. A fourteen-year-old girl riding the train and navigating the city to find audition spaces! Looking back, it actually sounds lenient on my grandmother's part. She probably figured the grueling commute and rejections would end my aspirations quickly. I was fortunate to get a part after a year. He walked in and got a commercial the same week.

Life's unfair. Sooner you learn it, the better.

Thanks, General Joan! My grandmother's voice never leaves my head. She was that strong an influence. I owe her a visit. She's eighty-seven years old, and I don't know how much time I have left with her. Though she's still strong and fiery as ever. I'm twenty-eight. She took on raising me at the age most women are done with babies, fifty-nine, rather than let my mother put me up for adoption. We're family and that's that, as she says.

I lean close to the mirror, checking my mascara. All set. I head back to the living room and take a seat in the corner of my cushy pale green sofa. Everything in my apartment is done in soft pastels. The living room is all about comfort—sofa with two matching cushy chairs, lots of throw pillows I knitted myself, and a soft geometric-patterned area rug. It's my haven where I can snuggle in.

I check my phone. Maybe he'll text he's going to be late, or that he can't make it after all. I've heard all the excuses from guys who find a better invitation come up on our date night. No text. A rush of excited nerves goes through me. It's a point in his favor. He's not bailing. *God, it's sad how low the bar is set.*

I pull up Alice Segal's *The Scoundrel and the Governess* on my phone. Nothing relaxes me more than getting lost in the funny banter of this long-ago time. Oh! I should get my paperback to give to Garrett. He said he'd have Alice sign it for me. What if he invites me to the palace where she lives? I feel like Alice and I could be best friends. At least the version of her I know through her stories. Silly, I know. She's no more her characters than I'm one of the characters I play. Though I did hear that the scoundrel was based on her real-life husband, Prince Lucas Rourke. (I should've made the connection from Lucas to Alice to Garrett earlier. The royal Rourkes are Garrett's cousins, of course.) At one point Lucas was the world's most eligible royal bachelor and totally fit her scoundrel description. Now he's hopelessly besotted with her. (One of her heroine's favorite ways to describe him.)

I pluck the paperback off my bookshelf and hug it to my chest. I should get all of her books to be signed. I gather them up and put them in a canvas tote bag for Garrett.

The intercom buzzes, and my heart races. *Calm down.* He's a nice guy. My brain knows that; I just need to convince my heart. Josie sings his praises all the time. She even told me his mom used to call him her teddy bear. I was a little embarrassed for him that she shared that, but I can see it. A big muscled teddy bear.

I hit the intercom button. "Yes?"

"Your date is here," Joe says. My new bodyguard insists my visitors go through him so no one sneaks past with a fake identity.

"The hot one," Garrett puts in.

I laugh and open the door. "Hi, come in."

He's carrying an insulated bag over one shoulder and a

brown bag tucked in his other arm. "I had some time, so I whipped up dinner ahead of time."

"Oh, cool." I direct him toward the kitchen.

He sets it down on the counter. "I made enchiladas because they travel better." One corner of his mouth curves up. "Truth is, I didn't want to be cooking here and get something on my suit before we go to the theater."

"It's a very nice suit." He's in a black suit, open white dress shirt, no tie. It's the open white dress shirt that has my attention, exposing tanned manly chest. I'm dying to see more. Josie told me he was shirtless for his commercial and that he's gorgeous. How unfair is it that the rest of the world gets to see that and I don't?

"Thanks. You look beautiful."

I take a deep breath, looking away. "Wine?"

"The proper response is thank you."

I flutter a hand in the air. "I'm not good with compliments. Thank you for saying that."

"I mean it."

I bite my lower lip, a fluttery feeling bouncing around inside me. Excitement? Nerves? Lust? I'm all over the place. "I'll get some wine."

He grins. He has the perfect amount of scruff, so sexy. "I brought beer. Mind if I put it in your fridge?"

"Sure."

He sets a six-pack in there. Is he going to drink all that, or will he be returning for date two or three or…I break out into a cold sweat. Why does a six-pack of beer feel like a commitment? And why am I so terrified? It's not like I've never had a relationship before or been in love. It's just that I've had so many bad experiences, I'm finding it hard to try again. *Perfectly normal*, I assure myself. It was only three weeks ago I found out Colton had cheated on me. I'm just being cautious.

Garrett takes a sip of beer, eying me over the bottle. "Need help uncorking the wine?"

"Sorry, I got distracted. I've got it." I head for the kitchen drawer, where I keep the corkscrew, but he's partially blocking it with his body. "Could you shift a little to the side so I can open the drawer?"

"There's a tax."

I lift wary eyes to him. "What kind of tax?"

"You have to make eye contact for more than three seconds so I don't feel like you're terrified of me."

I force myself to keep my eyes on his, channeling my tough persona. "I'm not terrified of you. Don't be ridiculous."

"I'd never hurt you."

"I know that. Move, please."

He pinches my chin. "In any way. Okay? You can relax."

My heart beats double time. "I'm very relaxed."

"Okay, lamb chop." He drops his hand and steps out of the way. "Tell that to the pulse point in your neck beating like a trapped rabbit."

I grab the corkscrew. "Ha! First I'm a lamb; then I'm a rabbit. Someone's quite the carnivore." I retrieve the wine from the refrigerator and remove the cork with efficient movements. "Could a terrified rabbit do this?"

He presses his lips together, his eyes dancing with amusement. "I doubt it. No opposable thumbs."

I'm tempted to chug straight from the bottle. Now that he's called out my nerves, they're worse. "Go ahead and take a seat at the dining room table. I'll serve up dinner." I indicate the light wood table in the open living area.

He smirks before heading over there. It's a little disconcerting the way he sees past my acting skills. Most guys can't. Hmm…this is a guy my fake orgasm cry will *not* work for. *Whoa, back it up.* I retrieve a wineglass, accidentally fill it nearly to the top, and take a healthy swallow with my back to him. He doesn't need to know how much I poured. And drank.

"Your place is exactly as I pictured," he says.

"Really?"

"Yup. Soft and feminine. Ever live with a guy?"

"Once. His stuff clashed. It was ugly too. He brought over a black leather recliner and a glass coffee table with sharp edges."

I leave my wineglass at the place setting across from him, gather our plates, and turn back to the kitchen. There's a half wall separating the kitchen from the living area, so I can see him checking out my apartment.

"If you ever make it to my place, I've got a sofa kinda like yours," he says. "Except the pillows came with it, and it's beige. Did you make those yourself?"

"Yeah." I glance over at the pale blue, white, and yellow knitted pillows in an assortment of Gaelic patterns. I was experimenting, but I like the way they came out. "I picked up knitting on the set of my first show from the actress who played my mom. She says it keeps you from grazing at craft services all day long. They keep snacks out for us and serve up meals. It definitely helped me not binge on M&Ms every day."

"There are worse vices."

"True." I've seen it happen. Drugs lead to a crash and burn. A lot of actresses smoke too, partly to keep from eating, partly from nerves. I knit and read mostly. Guess I'm kinda a homebody.

I take the lid off the enchiladas and put my hand over them. "Still warm. These look so good." He even sprinkled chopped scallions on top. I serve up a large portion for him, figuring he eats a lot since he's so big, and take a smaller portion for myself.

I return to the table with the food and take a seat, tucking my napkin on my lap. "I'd better be careful not to spill."

"Me too." He stands and removes his blazer, the play of his muscular arms catching my attention as he sets the blazer over the back of his chair. Then he sits, tucking his napkin into the top of his shirt.

He flashes a grin. "Why aren't ya eating, lamb chop?"

Busted. He knows I was checking him out. *Must be more subtle.* "I was being polite, waiting for you."

He winks. "Sweet." He cuts into his enchilada and takes a bite.

So I do the same. The combination of flavors melts in my

mouth, spicy goodness with melted cheese. "This is incredible!"

"Thanks. I can follow a recipe."

"What else can you make?"

He gazes into my eyes. "Anything you desire." His voice is gravelly, scraping against my insides.

I flush with heat, my pulse thrumming through my veins. I open my mouth and then close it again.

He smirks and goes back to eating. The man knows exactly what he does to me.

Yet somehow I can't return fire. It'll get out of hand. I'll end up grabbing his shirt and dragging him across the table to have my way with him. I'm not great at self-control once I get into the physical. Then sex and my emotions mess with my head, and I can't see the situation with any kind of objectivity. Probably why I'm blindsided by betrayal so often. I want to believe the best in a guy, but they always disappoint me in the end.

He lifts his beer to me. "Let's have a toast."

I lift my wineglass, which I completely forgot to drink. "Sure."

"To our first date. May it be less awkward than other firsts."

I narrow my eyes at the innuendo there, and he grins. I clink his glass. "I'm all for less awkward."

"Good." He takes a sip of beer, sets it down, and removes the napkin from his shirt. "Then let's get this out of the way."

"What?"

He pushes our plates to the side and crooks his finger at me. "The goodnight kiss. That way there's no awkward tension at the end of the night."

I stare at him, completely thrown. Who does that? Actually talks about it and puts it out there?

"Would you prefer I come to you?" he asks.

He assumes I'm okay with a kiss. It's just a matter of how.

"Harper, our food's getting cold." He crooks his finger again. "And we don't want to miss the show."

It's suddenly urgent that I lean toward him. He cups my

jaw and gives me a gentle kiss. A rush of sensation goes through me like a shot of whiskey, powerful and heated from the smallest sip, warming me all the way to my toes.

He draws back, his gaze intent on mine. "You okay?"

"Yeah," I say softly.

He shifts my dinner back in front of me. "No more awkward moment to worry about. Tell me how your taping went yesterday."

My gaze jerks to his. He sounds so casual and comfortable. Didn't he feel that chemistry? He nods for me to go ahead, his eyes smoldering. He *did* feel it.

I let out a small sigh of happiness. You know what? He's right. It's better to get the awkward out of the way. So I go ahead and tell him about the taping and how the comedian who was supposed to warm up the crowd called out sick at the last minute, so Josie went out there and entertained them just by having a conversation. I could never do that, but she's had lots of improv training and does standup comedy for fun. *Shudder.*

The rest of the meal passes in such a relaxed way I'm surprised when he asks if I'd like to take a walk before the show or just hang out here.

He sets his napkin on the table and stands. "We've got a little time since I prepared the meal ahead."

He sounds super casual. Too casual. It makes me think he cooked it ahead just so we'd have more time together the two of us. He's clever, finding ways to connect with me. And is that really such a bad thing? He seems sincere.

His lips curve up, a bemused expression on his gorgeous face. "You're thinking awfully hard."

"It's probably best if we stay here. Joe will have to tail us out there." I point toward the door.

"Okay." He stands there, hands in his pockets, looking at me expectantly.

"I'll clean up since you cooked, and meet you on the sofa."

"I'll help."

It's weird to have a guy willing to pitch in. I guess I'm used to spoiled guys with staff to handle the mundane.

Garrett rolls up his sleeves before gathering our plates. His forearms are tanned and corded with muscle. I'm dying to stroke the contour of muscle there and so many other places. I join him at the sink, where he's rinsing dishes and putting them in the dishwasher. He barely gave me a chance to do anything besides put our glasses away. We're finished in no time. There's still leftovers, so I put the lid back on the glass dish and transfer it to the refrigerator.

"Do you mind if I leave the dish and beer here?" he asks.

"Of course. Not like you can take it to the theater. I'll get it back to you through Josie."

"Or I could pick it up."

"Sure. Whatever works." My voice hits a high pitch. I feel like I'm already committing to date two at my place. I'm not sure how much longer I can resist temptation.

He smiles, his eyes soft. "For once I'm not adding flirty meaning. It's just a casserole dish, bag, and five beers. You can keep them, or I can get them later. Just stuff, yeah?"

I stare at him. "How do you do that? How do you know what I'm thinking?"

"You're sensitive, right?"

I clamp my mouth shut. That's a major flaw of mine I've worked my whole life to hide.

He gives my arm a squeeze. "I know you are. It's in your eyes. It shines through on *Living Gold*. I am too. So I can read you just like you can read me. If you tried to read me, that is. I can tell you're not trying too hard, or you never would've been a scared rabbit earlier."

"I was *not* a scared rabbit," I say through my teeth.

He leans toward my ear, and I wait for his whispered comeback that I'm sure will throw me off, but instead his lips graze my neck. My knees go weak.

He meets my eyes and brushes his thumb over my lower lip. "That's right. You're my lamb chop."

I'm speechless. He takes my hand and guides me toward the sofa. I follow blindly, anticipation racing through me. Maybe I am his lamb chop.

I halt, nerves racing through me. I'd better stall, shorten

the window of opportunity from kissing to naked. "I need to freshen up."

"Sure." He takes a seat on the sofa, leaning back and pulling his phone out.

I blow out a breath and head to the bathroom. After several minutes, I emerge with a minty clean mouth, fresh makeup, and a new determination. I will take charge of the evening. I'm not going to sit there, a bundle of nerves, trying to restrain myself. There's something very specific I want from him.

I return to the living room, standing across from the sofa, leaving a coffee table between us. "We still have some time."

"Yup."

I gird my loins. "I'd like to see you shirtless."

13

───────

He flashes a smile that he quickly covers. "And why is that?"

I gesture toward him. "Because everyone else gets to see you shirtless in that commercial. It seems only fair."

He stands, his eyes burning into mine as he closes the distance. "I dunno, Harper," he drawls.

"It's up to you, of course. No pressure." *Wow.* I feel like the guy here, orchestrating the journey into the physical.

He stops just out of reach, and I stare at the exposed tanned skin at the top of his shirt. He left the top two buttons undone. I'm so tempted to unbutton it myself, but I want him to feel comfortable with it. *Of course he's comfortable with it! He took off his shirt in front of total strangers!*

He waits until I meet his eyes before saying in a teasing voice, "It seems a little fast for a first date." He unbuttons the third button, giving me a glimpse of his pecs. "Not sure how I feel about it."

Another button.

I close the distance, fascinated. I've seen muscular man chest before, but nothing like his. He looks like a warrior—wide shoulders and broad barrel chest. I could totally picture him wielding a sword.

"Keep going," I whisper.

"Enjoying the view?" he asks in a husky voice, undoing another button. His rippling abs appear in front of my hungry eyes.

"More," I say.

"I'm running out of buttons." He finishes the last one, the shirt gaping wide open, but still tucked into his dress pants, obstructing my view.

I untuck the shirt and push it open. *Wow, just...wow.* There's ridges upon ridges. His abs lead to a deep V that disappears under the waistline of his pants. I'm torn between asking for the pants to come off or just exploring what he's offering.

He cups my jaw, bringing my gaze to his. "What's next?"

"I want to touch you, but I don't want you to move."

"Go for it."

I peel his shirt off, my fingers brushing his heated skin. I fold the shirt neatly in half and drop it on the coffee table before turning back to him. Now he's all mine. I place my palms on his chest and then roam, enjoying the play of hard muscle. His breath comes harder as I get bolder, flicking my fingers over his flat nipples, sliding down his sides, tracing the deep V I'm dying to follow all the way down. I glance at the bulge in his pants before lifting my gaze back to his.

"You're every bit as gorgeous as Josie said," I say, letting my hands roam back up and over his massive shoulders.

He closes his eyes, a strained expression on his face. "Please don't bring up Josie. She's like a sister to me. It fucks with my head."

I wrap my arms around him, enjoying the hard planes of muscle on his back. "Sorry. You feel like a warrior, strong and sturdy. I could see you slaying a dragon."

His eyes are intent on mine. "I'd slay a dragon for you, Harper."

I get chills, some primal part of me loving that he'd be that protector for me. "I believe you would."

"You know it's torture just standing still while you feel me up. Shirt's going back on."

"No, not yet!" I throw my arms around his neck, pressing my entire body against him. His arms wrap around me, holding me close, one arm banded around my waist, his other hand cupping the back of my neck. It seems as natural as breathing to lift my head and press my lips to his.

He groans and takes over the kiss, his lips demanding, his tongue delving into my mouth. Desire spears through me with startling intensity. This is nothing like his gentle good-night kiss across the table. It's hot and hungry. Suddenly I can't get enough, straining to get closer, wanting to merge with him. My hands go to his ass, and I press him firmly against me. His large hand slides down my spine to cup my ass, keeping us fused together. Oh, God. The need is over-whelming. The kiss never ending.

Long moments later, I tear my mouth away, breathing hard. "Do you have a condom?"

He stares at my mouth. "No."

"It's okay. I'm on the pill."

He turns away. "Gimme a few minutes."

I stare at his wide back, and then I can't help but touch it and kiss and taste. His shoulder blades are a work of art. Warrior man for sure.

"Harp, we need to slow it down." His voice sounds strangled.

I slide around to his front. "I don't think I've ever wanted someone as much as I want you."

He pulls me in for a tight hug, holding my head to his chest. His heart thumps hard under my ear. I can't do much but hug him back the way he's holding me. I want him fiercely, but there's something really nice about being held in his strong arms. Still doesn't quell the inferno raging inside me.

After a few minutes he frames my face in his hands, resting his forehead against mine. "I don't want our first time to be rushed."

"We can skip the show."

"We're having our date," he says firmly. "I want to know you trust me enough to give me more than just your body."

I squirm against him, needing him too much for rational talk. "Please?"

He chuckles. "Shirtless really got you going, huh?"

"Yes."

"Take off your panties."

I strip them off immediately, already soaked with desire.

He turns me so my back is against his front, slowly sliding my skirt up past my hips. His lips press against my neck, kissing a hot trail along the column of my throat. I tilt my head, giving him better access. His teeth scrape against me as his fingers slide toward the inside of my thigh. My entire body tenses, dying for his fingers to reach pleasure central. His other hand does the same, slowly tracing my inner thigh.

"Garrett, you're torturing me."

"Ah, now you know how I feel."

"Please," I whisper.

"Would you really have skipped the condom for me? Do you do that a lot?"

"Never. But I've never wanted someone so badly before."

He groans. "You have no idea how hot that makes me." He resumes his slow torture, his fingers trailing lazily along my inner thigh, skirting off to the side and up my hip, back and forth, stroking closer and closer, but never quite reaching where I need him most.

I grab his hand and place it firmly where I want it.

He chuckles. "Not one for slow, are ya?"

He traces me, circling, teasing, driving me insane. Then he just cups me, held in his large hand, completely still.

I grit my teeth. *I want to kill him. Slowly.* That's what he's doing to me. Killing me with frustration.

I grab his wrist and squeeze, hoping that will make some movement happen. "We're running out of time, and it always takes me a while."

He gives my earlobe a tug between his teeth. "You're soaked, nearly there. You're going to go off like a firecracker with me."

I huff, about to say *if you actually do anything about it in this century!* Except my breath catches as he sucks the cord of my neck at the same time as his fingers delve between my legs, stroking in a rhythm that has my hips moving in time. I close my eyes and completely let go in a way I never have before, my mind blank, my body nearly limp. The solid strength and heat of him, the firm hold on my neck, his sure fingers, all of it lets me relax. I'm rewarded instantly by a spiraling pleasure, my insides coiling tight.

He shifts from my neck to speak close to my ear as his fingers slide inside me in slow deep thrusts. Intense pleasure radiates through me as the tension rises. "So beautiful, so sexy. I love to feel you letting go."

"I'm close," I gasp out, shocked at how quickly I got there.

He slides his fingers out. "I know. Next time I'll be inside you."

A rush of desire floods me, the ache to be filled overwhelming. I push back against him instinctively, his massive erection pressing against my ass.

He shifts, not allowing me to seek him out. "Just take what I give." His fingers feather lightly over me, and when I relax against him, he increases the rhythm, stroking more firmly.

My head arches back. "Oh God! Garrett!"

His deep voice holds the sharp edge of authority. "Let go."

I explode, my hips rocking helplessly, the rush of sensation stealing my breath. Wave after wave of pleasure. I pant as he stays with me, his fingers guiding me through more and more, until I'm spent. He cups me firmly between the legs and nips my neck. I jolt, electrified and caught in his hold. I don't know if he's going to give me more or let me go. I'm not sure I can take more, but somehow I think he'd get me there.

He slides his hand away, and I let out a breath, clutching his arm as I lean back against him. He's quiet.

With great effort I straighten and turn to face him. "How are you?"

"I'm great," he says, pulling my skirt back into place.

I glance toward the bulge in his pants. "Can I help you out?"

"Another time."

"Why?"

"Because I want you to know I can give without asking for anything in return."

My lips part. It's like he both knows my fears and how to deal with them. I don't think anyone has ever read me so well. "You're a good man."

He pinches my chin and kisses me tenderly. A surge of affection goes through me, and I throw my arms around him.

He holds my gaze, still holding me by the chin. His voice is gruff. "I'm glad you think so."

I kiss him again, this time slow and easy, lingering in my afterglow.

He breaks the kiss and flashes a smile. "We should get going. I'll be in the hallway, trying to cool down."

"Oh, I know a better place. We could go on the roof. I have private access to a small garden with a view." I grab my panties. "Let me just freshen up."

"Careful. Remember what happened last time you freshened up. You attacked me. What's next?" He gestures toward his pants, frowning. "A guy can only take so much being on display. I'm not your personal stripper, ya know."

I laugh. "I really like you, Garret. You're not like most guys I date."

He smiles. "Back at ya. And I'm glad we're done pretending we only want each other as friends." He turns me and gives my ass a light pat. I squeak in surprise. "Now get in there before I go out of my mind from wanting you."

I practically float on my way into my room.

Garrett

Harper and I went up to the roof for some fresh air, and I finally got comfortable again. I didn't dare touch her or kiss her. A guy can only take so much temptation. Fortunately, it's time to go. I really do want to see *Wicked* with her, mostly because I want to see her favorite thing. I want to know everything about her. She's strong and vulnerable at the same time. I want to protect her, keep her, have her under me.

Yeah, so, slow is out. I know what she sounds like when she comes, what she feels like, her sexy scent. That's why I need to make sure we fit dates in too. I don't want this to be just a flash of heat that fizzles out. It's going to be tricky because that slow simmer I was going for is out the window. The woman can't resist me.

We make our way to the front door. I lean forward to open the door for her when she grabs me suddenly by the shirt, pulls my head down, and kisses me. Instinct takes over and I pin her against the door, pressing my body against her as my mouth crashes over hers. She makes this mewling sound in the back of her throat that makes me rock hard. Her fingers are tangled in my hair, her leg wrapping around me, her hips arching, seeking more. I push her leg down, knowing what she needs. I slide my hand between her legs, feeling hot wet flesh. I tear my mouth from hers.

"No panties," I gasp out.

"I need you inside me so bad," she says urgently, sliding her skirt up over her hips.

I take one look at what she's offering, and the thin line of control snaps. I lift her, and she wraps her legs around me eagerly. I shift us back to the wall, our mouths fused together, as I free myself. Her hands are all over me, her kisses frantic, eager. I shift her leg up, opening her wider, and press at her entrance. Oh God. With my last ounce of willpower, I break the kiss to check in with her.

"Sure?"

"Yes!" She grabs my ass and pulls me against her. "I *ache* for you."

I thrust deep, the sensation of her tight body gripping me nearly making me finish before we've got started. I take a breath, counting backward, trying to hang on.

Her nails dig into my shoulders. "Yesss," she hisses on a long breath. "Oh my God. You feel amazing."

I kiss her. "*You* feel amazing."

"Fuck me."

I thrust hard and fast, driven out of my mind by her soft moans of pleasure. She lifts her hips, meeting each thrust, taking me deeper. On and on in a feverish rush of pleasure. Her body clamps down around me, and then she cries out, going off. I let go, pounding into her until I explode, the intensity sharp enough to steal my breath and make my vision dim. *Jesus.* I collapse against her, breathing hard and slick with sweat.

Long moments later, she lifts her head. "I think you just ruined me for other men."

I chuckle and kiss her. "Good. Cuz I don't want you with any other man."

"Exclusive, huh?"

"All the way."

She beams a smile. "I'm glad we went for it. I couldn't sit through an entire Broadway show with the ache to have you inside me."

I stroke a lock of dark hair back from her face. "I ached to fill you. I still do. Crazy, right?"

"Not at all."

I withdraw and set her on her feet. Her legs wobble, and she grabs for me. "All those Pilates and I still wobble."

"You're not used to wrapping them around a beast like me. I should be part of your Pilates routine." I hitch up my pants and fasten them. "Stretch those legs, tighten, and thrust."

"A dirty workout routine. Now that I could get into." Her skin glows, her eyes promising more. "Are you sure you still want to go to the show?"

I can't resist her. I scoop her up, cradled in my arms. She licks my pec. "We'll be there by intermission." *Can't go wrong thinking with my dick, right?*

"Or another night altogether," she purrs.

I can't deny her, even though I had the best of intentions for tonight. The pull to join with her is too strong. We'll build up trust in bed. Plenty of time for talking after.

14

Garrett

"When's date two?" she asks, climbing up my body and stretching like a cat on top of me.

I stroke her back. "Next Saturday, sweetheart. We'll go to *Wicked*."

She smiles, her eyes sparkling. "You're wicked."

"You're mine."

She looks down and then quickly rolls off me.

I catch her in my arms, spooning her from behind before whispering in her ear, "I'll be good to you."

She laughs uneasily. "I'm not used to all these pretty words."

I let out a breath. "Ya see, this is exactly why I wanted to take it slow. If we had a real date, you'd have time to see you could trust me through my actions."

"So this is my fault?"

"Yeah."

"How is it my fault?" She sounds pissed.

I nuzzle her neck. "You made me strip, felt me up, and begged me to fuck you."

She wiggles her ass back into me. "I did do that, didn't I?"

"And I loved every minute of it. Now I'm gonna spend the night. I'll probably spoon you for a bit, fuck you a lot, and then tomorrow we'll do something more date like. So next Saturday will count as date three."

"You've got it all figured out." She sounds happy with my plan, but she's trying not to show it.

"Yup."

"I'm supposed to visit my grandmother tomorrow."

"Then I'll meet your grandmother."

She looks back over her shoulder at me, her eyes wide. "Seriously?"

"Why not? Women of all ages like me."

She snuggles back into me. "Cocky."

"You like that about me."

"I have to warn you, she's tough. I call her General Joan. Secretly. Don't you call her that."

I chuckle. "I know how to handle tough."

"Because of me?"

I give her a squeeze. *Adorable.* "I told you from day one you're sweet. This tough thing is an act."

"Most people don't see that."

I push her to her back, stroke her soft cheek, and kiss her. "I see you just as you are."

She opens her arms to me, and I join her, in our own private cocoon of warmth, affection, and maybe more. Definitely more.

Harper

So here I am on the back of Garrett's Harley, riding to Summerdale to visit General Joan. I left my guard behind because no one ever bothers me in Summerdale. Besides, we couldn't fit him on the bike. Ha-ha. Garrett's big enough to scare away most men. The fresh air whipping by, the speed, and the man I'm hugging make me feel like all is right in the world. It's the last weekend of September, a gorgeous fall day, and the leaves are just starting to turn gold, orange, and red along the highway.

I'm glad for the buffer of Garrett joining me today for my

visit, but I feel bad for him. He has no idea what he's getting into. When you think eighty-seven-year-old grandmother, you think warm and fuzzy. I know Garrett looks tough, but from what I've gotten to know of him, he really is a big teddy bear. I still can't believe he thinks I'm sweet. How Grandmom would cackle at that description! But Garrett insists on calling me sweetheart, and the warm way he says it makes me melt.

He already knew the way to Summerdale since his family comes here for Labor Day weekend. He slows as we turn onto Lakeshore Drive and points out the two houses his family has rented on different occasions.

He pulls up in front of a large two-story. "This is the one we just recently stayed at."

I lean forward so he can hear me. "I don't know who lives here now. Take your second left up ahead. My grandmother's house is the last on the street."

He continues on. Summerdale is a planned community, founded in the sixties by a group of hippies who saw it as their own utopia. The lake is at the center of town, with homes with large decks built around it. Tall trees surround the lake. The town is laid out like a bicycle wheel with spokes radiating out from the lake. There's a main street on one spoke with a café, a small grocery store, a restaurant with a popular bar, and a yoga studio. Other spokes lead to the churches, schools, town hall, and more homes like where I grew up. Those homes were added in the seventies. Bike paths connect everything together.

It's the kind of place where a kid can ride around town on their own with no restrictions. Crime is low and quality of life is high. The founders are mostly retired and moved away. Housing value has gone way up as more young professionals from the city settle here with their kids. Still, there's a good number of people who grew up here and moved back to raise their kids, or just never left. My three closest friends are back in town now, and I hope to see them during this visit too.

Soon the white two-story colonial home I grew up in comes into view. I'm glad to see the yard looks neat and the house in good condition. I pay for a landscape service and have a running tab with the local handyman. Grandmom insists on seeing to her flower beds herself, even though she has a bad hip.

He parks the bike in the street and takes off his helmet, looking over his shoulder at me. "You get off first." His lips twitch.

"None of that sexy talk here." I climb off, my legs feeling wobbly after the powerful vibration of the bike under me. I take off my helmet. Everything sounds so quiet now without the roar of the motor. Slowly, the familiar sounds of home reach me as a light breeze rustles through the trees and the birds whistle their jaunty tunes.

I smooth my curly hair down as best I can. "How do I look?"

"Beautiful as always." He gets off the bike, secures our helmets to the back, and returns to me, kissing my cheek.

"Do I have helmet head?"

He strokes my hair down with both hands. "Looks good to me." I definitely have helmet head. There's no hope for it with these unruly curls.

I glance down at my pale blue peasant blouse, jeans, and black ankle boots. Grandmom doesn't approve of "racy" clothes that expose too much cleavage. Everything's covered. I take off my jean jacket, a favorite of mine I don't get to wear often. It's warm now that we're not riding with the wind whipping past us.

"Ready?" I ask him.

"I feel like we're preparing for an ambush."

"Close." He's in a black leather jacket, faded jeans, and black motorcycle boots. Sexy as hell. I wasn't about to tell him to change, but I know what my grandmother will think. That's her problem.

He starts toward the front door. I grab the sleeve of his jacket. He stops and turns, his brows lifting in question.

I go on tiptoe to whisper in his ear, "Don't take offense at anything she says, and please don't judge me by what she says either. We don't see eye-to-eye on most things."

He glances at my hand clutching his sleeve. "Anything else?"

"She doesn't approve of motorcycles. Says they're a quick trip to the morgue. Sorry. I'm sure you're very experienced and only take planned trips to grandmothers' houses, not the morgue."

He chuckles. "Yeah. Would you have preferred we rented a car?"

"Oh no, I loved it. I've ridden a Vespa in Italy before. Tons of fun."

He takes my hand and walks me down the driveway to the front door. "You did not just compare my Harley to a Vespa."

I smile. "Your bike is much more powerful."

"Uh, yeah, and way cooler. You basically rode a scooter."

"It was not a scooter."

"Top speed was probably thirty miles per hour."

"Ha! I'm pretty sure I hit forty-five."

"In kilometers?"

I purse my lips, thinking that over. We were in Italy. Hmm…

We step onto the concrete front porch, and I stare at the doorbell. I told her to expect us between two and two thirty, and we're on time. She should be awake. She eats meals on the early side and takes a nap two hours after her early lunch.

"Are ya ever gonna ring the bell?" he asks.

"You rang my bell earlier," I say, stalling with some of his innuendo stuff. Anything to delay.

"You want me to do it?" he asks gently.

"I'm perfectly capable of pressing a doorbell. Oh, and you should call her Mrs. Ellis." I press the bell and steel myself. I refuse to rise to the bait or let anything she says hurt me. We've always been opposites. I'm sensitive; she's tough. Therefore, she had to make me tough.

The door opens a few moments later, and my grandmother appears, staring at us through the glass of the storm door. She looks put together as usual, with a turquoise scarf tied around her neck, a long-sleeved pale yellow cotton shirt, and black pants. Her hair is white, short, and parted to the side with a small wave; her brown eyes are sharp, her cheekbones sharper. She glances at me before staring at Garrett, making no move to open the storm door.

"Hello, ma'am," Garrett says through the door.

She turns to me and shouts through the glass, "He looks like a hoodlum!"

"Grandmom! He is *not* a hoodlum. Can you please let us in?"

She arches a brow, unlocks the storm door, and limps her way back to her favorite chair in the living room. It's a light blue wingback chair with a small ottoman. That chair is older than me. I've tried to upgrade the furniture around here, but she doesn't want me "throwing my money away" on unnecessary things.

I take a seat across from her on the lumpy floral sofa with its plastic slipcover. Garrett sits next to me, and the plastic squeaks loudly with his movement.

My grandmother's attention turns to me as she says with her trademark General Joan piercing stare, "Been in town for six weeks and finally made it out here. 'Bout time."

"I'm overdue for a visit, I know," I say. "My schedule is packed with work."

She sniffs. "Had time to dally with a man." She turns to Garrett. "Always take my granddaughter around on your crotch rocket? That's how it goes in the hood, huh?"

I choke on my own spit, mortified at her take on Garrett, who's one of the nicest guys I've met in a really long time. I turn to him, about to apologize for her, but the deranged man is smiling.

He rests his elbows on his knees, leaning toward her. "I live in a nice neighborhood in Brooklyn, ma'am. I work in construction at my family's business. This is the first time I've taken Harper on my bike, but if she's not comfortable, of course I'll find an alternate way to get us where we aim to go."

My grandmother blinks a few times, probably trying to decide if she's been bested or if he's being sincere. After all, he didn't say he'd never take me on his bike. He said he'd do what I'm comfortable with. And he neatly sidestepped the crotch reference. *Points for Garrett!*

"Grandmom, would you like me to make tea or fetch a drink for anyone?" I don't expect her to wait on us with the pain in her hip. She says pain is easy to deal with, and she doesn't trust a doctor to make her "bionic" with a hip replacement.

"I'll get it," she says, getting up from her chair after a bit of struggle. She should use a cane, but sees it as a sign of weakness. She refuses to believe she's old and rejects the senior-citizen label and all available discounts that go with it. Hardheaded to her own detriment.

I check in with Garrett to see what he'd like to drink and follow her through the archway into the kitchen to help. He can't see us in here, but I'm sure he can hear us since we're right next to the living room. I just pray my grandmother doesn't say anything insulting about him.

"It's good to see you," I say, reaching out for a hug.

She gives me a one-armed pat-on-the-back hug and murmurs, "Been too long. I know it's no fun to hang out with your old granny."

I get out two teacups and a glass for Garrett while she fills the kettle with water. "I thought you weren't old, just mature."

"Just an expression to make my point. I've still got all my marbles." She turns on the flame under the kettle, presses the button for the noisy stovetop vent over it, and faces me, arms crossed. "How long have you been seeing this guy?" She pitches her voice over the noise.

I'd love to turn off the vent so she'd keep her voice down, but I know she'd freak out that the propane gas will lead to an explosion if it's not vented properly. I decide to answer quickly and honestly without revealing too much to Garrett's ears. "Not long. We just met three weeks ago."

"Is he really in construction?"

"Yes. Why do you ask?"

She gestures toward the living room. "How could you

have met when you're working on a TV show and he's on a construction site? Something doesn't add up."

I fill her in on the Josie connection.

She nods once. "Construction is better than acting." She goes for her tin of tea bags. "All those actors you date are just full of themselves."

I clench my teeth. It might be true that I've dated some guys with big egos, but I'm also an actor, and there's a jab in there at me too. She thinks it's ridiculous that I get treated special and paid a lot to pretend to be someone else. She never understood it's a craft. Besides, people need entertainment.

"Garrett respects acting," I say. "In fact, he just did a commercial."

Her eyes narrow as she glares in the direction of the living room. "After he met you?"

"Yeah," I say with a sinking feeling.

"That's worse," she says. "Cut him loose before he rides your coattails to the top. You won't be smiling when he surpasses you."

"Why would he surpass me?"

"Have you looked at him? He reminds me of Gary Cooper, movie-star potential with that swagger and handsome looks. You know, Gary Cooper started as a stunt rider like your motorcycle man." I'm well versed in the old-time movie stars she likes. Gary had the handsome, everyman appeal.

I take a deep breath, reaching for patience. "He's not my motorcycle man."

"Whatever you call it. God forbid anyone commit to each other or say out loud that they're boyfriend and girlfriend. You kids make everything so complicated."

I fill the water glass, needing to check in on poor Garrett. "Be right back." I step out to offer him the drink.

He takes it with a grin. "Thanks. Who's Gary Cooper?"

"An actor most famous in the golden age of Hollywood, circa nineteen forties." I lower my voice. "Seriously, don't listen to a word she says."

He hides a smile behind the rim of his glass. "Now I see where you get your paranoia."

"I'm not paranoid."

He gets serious. "You weren't happy to hear I got an agent."

"I'm over it. Besides, it's not like I haven't had a long line of users before you. There's some basis in fact. I'm trying to be more trusting for you."

He takes my hand and brushes a kiss over my knuckles. A rush of tingles race up my arm.

"Harper!" General Joan barks. "What are you two doing out there unchaperoned?"

I roll my eyes as he chuckles. Like we're making out on her old slip-covered sofa.

I join her in the kitchen. "How've you been feeling?"

She waves that away. "Fine. You won't be inheriting the house anytime soon."

I grin. "How's the water pressure? I'd love to have a shower installed with multiple sprays."

She narrows her eyes. "Ha! Just as bad as always. Can't run the washing machine and take a shower at the same time."

"I can get a plumber in—"

"Bah."

I sigh. Never show weakness, never ask for help. She's always been so prickly. Her husband, my grandfather, died when I was five. I don't remember him well, but he was always smiling in pictures, his arm around her. She smiled just for him. I've always wondered if losing him was what made her tough or if she always was. Her daughter, my mother, had me and never returned. It's always been just me and the General. I have a few older uncles, her sons, as well as their wives and my cousins, but they don't live nearby. One of my uncles is the reason I first got involved in Best Friends Care.

A few minutes later, we're settled in her living room with our Earl Grey tea. Garrett puts his phone away when we return.

"Don't be posting pictures on the internet of my place," my grandmother tells him.

I close my eyes. I'm sure everyone is dying to see a nineteen seventies home with the original furniture and a chairlift. I had the motorized chairlift installed on the stairs last year when I saw how slowly she took the stairs because of her hip. She grumbled about it, but she uses it.

"No, ma'am," Garrett says. "Just checking the score on the Giants game."

"Men and their balls," she huffs.

Garrett fights back a smile and shoots me a look. I shake my head. She did *not* mean that in a dirty way.

"Have you watched *Living Gold*?" I ask her. She hasn't said a word about it in our phone conversations, and I've been waiting for her verdict.

"Course I did," she replies indignantly.

Part of me wants to know if she liked it, and the wiser part says not to ask questions I don't want honest answers to.

"Harper is fantastic," Garrett says.

My grandmother eyes him before saying, "It's on too late. Nine o'clock. I can barely keep my eyes open."

"I told you we can record it for you to watch later." I got her cable after some arguing over the unnecessary channels. I wanted her to be able to see my work.

She waves toward the TV and the cable box on top of it. "Too many buttons on the damn remote. I'd as soon erase it as get to watch it."

"I'll show you, ma'am. It's only tricky the first time." Garrett doesn't wait for an answer. Just hands me his water glass, gets up, and goes for the remote on the end table next to her chair.

My grandmother's eyes are huge. "Excuse me, that's my remote."

"I know, Mrs. Ellis. Watch." Garrett kneels at her side, pressing buttons as he explains each one.

"I'm not going to remember all that nonsense." She shakes her head and sips her tea, done with the whole thing.

After he gets it set up, he points out the buttons again.

"It's just here and then play. I set it to never erase, but you can change it when you want. Do you have a phone?"

"In the kitchen." She means the phone attached to the wall in there.

Garrett sends me an amused look.

I lift a palm. "I tried to get her a cell phone, but she refused."

"Don't need that thing beeping at me all the time," she says. "Everyone's a slave to their cell phones nowadays. Not me."

Garrett rises to his feet, goes to the kitchen, and returns a moment later with a small piece of folded paper. He hands it to her. "This is my phone number, ma'am. Call me if you have any trouble watching the recording. I'll walk you through it."

She takes the paper gingerly and sets it on the end table before returning her steely gaze to his. Most people would back off. Not Garrett.

"Anything else I can do for you, ma'am?" he asks.

"You can take a seat is what you can do," she says.

"Yes, ma'am." He takes a seat next to me. I hand him his glass, stunned by his composure in light of the prickly woman.

"Your construction worker is handy," my grandmother tells me. "Maybe he could take a look at the back gate. The latch is loose, and every gust of wind makes the thing slam open and closed, open and closed."

Garrett stands. "Happy to take a look, ma'am. Where're the tools?"

"In the garage," she says. "Through there." She points toward the kitchen.

I watch in astonishment as he disappears through the kitchen. First of all, my grandmother never asks for help from anyone. Second, he doesn't have to do work here. I brought him as a guest. There's a handyman in town who could do this for her.

She blithely sips her tea.

"Why didn't you have Frank take care of the back gate?" I ask.

"Frank hurt his back."

"What about Adam?" He's a master carpenter in town.

"I don't trust him to do the job right. He only works with cutting and sawing."

"But you trust Garrett?"

"Have you noticed how close his name is to Gary? Gary Cooper, now that was a real man." She nods once and then leans forward. "Your boyfriend has fine manners."

"Yes, he does." I smile to myself, bemused at the turn of events. That was a rare General Joan compliment.

"Still don't like his motorcycle," she adds. "Don't let me see you riding that again."

"How do you expect me to get back to the city?"

"Not too good to ride public transit, are you?"

I grit my teeth. I haven't shared about some of the hazards of fame, particularly the way some creeper men react to seeing me out and about, but there's no way I'm riding the train back to the city when I've got a perfectly fine mode of transportation right here.

"I don't know why you continue to imply I'm above it all," I say. "I'm still the same person I always was."

"No, you're not. No use pretending otherwise."

I blow out a breath. "I thought we'd take you to dinner. Then I'm going to visit with Sydney, Audrey, and Jenna before heading back."

She harrumphs. "I don't think your new boyfriend will be wanting the diner's early bird special. You go when you see fit. I just want to say one thing." She pauses, her gaze intent on mine. "Be careful with him. I see the appeal, but never forget the draw of money in your profession. I don't imagine construction workers make a lot."

My chest tightens. "He hasn't asked for any help from me."

"Be smart, Harper. What have I taught you?"

I grind my teeth. "Never show weakness."

"That's right. If you do, others will take advantage. Like all your sorry exes. You keep getting taken in by a pretty face. That is *not* what makes a man. I blame myself for not having a male role model around here for you." She blinks a few times and looks away. "Your grandfather could've been that for you. He was a real man."

I have only vague memories of him. He seemed big and bold to little me, with a great booming laugh. "Sorry. I know you miss him." I leave out any mention of my exes. I know my history with men isn't stellar. I'm too trusting, and I mostly meet people connected to the industry in some way.

She waves away my sympathy and purses her lips. "I hope I'm wrong about Gary."

I don't bother to correct her on his name. I hope so too.

15

Harper

After our visit with Grandmom, Garrett pulls into the parking lot of an old white clapboard house with a wooden sign hanging out front that reads The Horseman Inn. Under that it says 1788. It's my friend's place now, a restaurant and bar. It was only an inn in the olden days. I seriously thought we'd never get out of my grandmother's house. She had him fix the gate, open a painted-shut window in her sewing room, and then proceeded to interrogate him about his intentions toward me. She actually asked him if he was the play-the-field type or the marrying type!

And he said the marrying type!

Grandmom was not impressed. Me, I nearly swooned. He's like something out of one of Alice Segal's romances, only he's real. I can't stop hugging him around the middle. We're still on his bike in the parking lot.

He turns off the bike, takes off his helmet, and looks at me over his shoulder. "This town must have a long history."

I smile dreamily. "The inn predates the town from when it was a stagecoach stop. Now it's a restaurant with a bar tucked in back. My friend Sydney owns it."

"Should we, uh, go in, or do ya wanna keep sitting here hugging me?"

I loosen my grip and take off my helmet. "I can't believe you called my grandmother Queen Joan."

"She really does remind me of my dad with her voice of authority. She could have royal blood."

I shake my head, smiling. "She ate it up." I was shocked. My grandmother preened.

He grins. "I told ya women of all ages love me."

"I know you said that, but she's in a whole different cranky category."

"People are all the same. They just want to be recognized and treated with kindness."

My throat tightens with emotion. He's just so…perfect. Can anyone be that perfect? It's scary, but I want to believe in him.

"Ready to get off?" he asks with a wink.

I laugh and get off his bike. He's always sexy flirting.

A few moments later, he opens the wooden front door of the restaurant for me, and I step into the warm and inviting space. There's a hostess desk up front, empty now, and just past it is a huge stone hearth that was used for cooking back in the old days. The front dining room is empty since it's late afternoon. The bar is in the back, along with a large room added on in the seventies. It's the only bar for miles around, and locals often gather just to watch the game on the three flat-screen TVs behind the bar.

A young man I don't know is setting the tables for the dinner service in the front dining room. "Hi," he says. "We're not open for dinner until five, but you can help yourself to the bar."

I nod. "Thanks. I'm friends with Sydney. She's expecting me."

I take Garrett's hand and guide him through the maze of dark wood tables. Looks like Sydney's attempting to make it more upscale. I wonder if the menu changed too. Used to be home-style comfort food—meatloaf, fried chicken, burgers. Most every dish came with a baked potato or French fries.

I peek around the corner. "Hi!"

Sydney's working behind the bar, her auburn hair up in a

messy bun. She drops her rag and throws her hands in the air. "Oh my God! It's Harper Ellis!"

I laugh. She likes to pretend she's a fangirl. A few people at the bar watching the football game turn to look. I don't know them, some men in their thirties. They glance at Garrett and turn back to the game.

Sydney takes off her apron and rushes around the bar to hug me. "The famous Harper Ellis! And is this the secret prince of Brooklyn?" She grins at Garrett. "I have a Google alert on her name since she can't be bothered to keep me updated on her career highs."

Garrett smiles and offers his hand. "That's me, though the secret's out on being a prince. Garrett Rourke."

"Sydney Robinson. I own this beautiful mess." She plants her hands on her hips and looks around the historic restaurant she inherited from her dad. Her pink T-shirt with a rhinestone heart, black skinny jeans, and high-heeled boots look out of place in the dim historic setting. Not that I'd expect her to wear an old colonial dress.

"It's nice," Garrett says, rocking back and forth on his heels. "The floors are a little wavy."

"Ah, yes," she says. "Sloping floors, low ceiling, original post and beam." She gestures around. "We've got all the cool historic touches and all the modern headaches. Let me get a replacement behind the bar, and we'll take a seat."

She gets the guy we saw in the front room to take her place. Then she pulls her phone from her back jeans pocket, tapping away. "I'm letting Jenna and Audrey know you're here. They're around. Jenna just opened a bakery in the old café."

"Wait, the café closed?" I ask.

She lifts her brows. "Ah, yeah, last year. Keep up with the times. Summerdale moves fast."

"What about Rainbow?" She was one of the last original hippie founders and the owner of the café.

She gestures for us to join her at a table for four. "She retired to Florida like all the senior citizens. Your grandmother being the exception." After we're all seated, she props her chin on her hand and asks brightly, "How'd it go with her?" She knows exactly how difficult the General can be.

"Like expected with me," I say. "She had Garrett running around fixing everything she can't trust Adam to do, because how could she trust a master carpenter with a small job?"

Garrett puffs his chest out. "Takes a skilled construction worker to fix the back gate latch."

Sydney grins.

"I put my foot down when she wanted him to fill a hole a woodchuck dug under her fence," I say. "Of course she still warned me to be careful. She thinks all men have an agenda."

Sydney purses her lips, thinking that over. "You know, I can't say she's wrong. Some are better at hiding it than others. Look at my dad, a decent guy. Nobody knew he ran this place into the ground before he died."

I shoot her a sympathetic look. She was close to her dad. Her mom died when we were twelve. After her dad died, Sydney's oldest brother took over the restaurant. Last year he said it was a lost cause and wanted to sell it. Sydney moved home, determined to continue the town's legacy and her father's.

Sydney continues. "I've got a marketing background, so I figured all it takes is some good word of mouth and advertising. Welp, it also takes money. I'm having no luck with the banks with the debt we're in."

"How much?" I ask.

She holds up a palm. "Nope, not going to ask my uber-successful friend for a handout."

"You could pay me back."

"This is a hometown deal. Local investment for the locals. You keep giving to Best Friends Care. Your reach is global now, lady."

We chat for a bit, catching up on old times.

She waves over my shoulder. "She's here, and she brought her secret prince!"

Garrett turns, smiling at my friends. "Just Garrett."

I stand to greet Jenna and Audrey. "It's been too long."

Jenna is long and lean, surprising for someone who loves

to bake. You'd think she'd have love handles. She's wearing a black turtleneck with jeans and black boots. Audrey is more understated in a beige tunic over beige yoga pants. Her black hair stands out in stark contrast. She runs the local library.

I hug them both.

Audrey glances over at the bar area and quickly faces front again. I hadn't noticed him when we first came in, since Sydney distracted me with all her enthusiasm and big hugs. Her oldest brother, Drew, is sitting in the corner, nursing a beer, his gaze on the game. He's as dark as Sydney is light. Hard to blame him after serving as an Army Ranger on multiple deployments. Not that he was ever Mr. Sunny. He's five years older than us, and rarely acknowledged his little sister's friends. Audrey has had a secret crush on him for as long as I can remember. She even wrote him regularly when he was deployed, but, apparently, none of her emails ever let him know how she feels about him.

After we're all seated at a larger round table with ice water and a bowl of pretzels, Sydney announces, "Garrett is much nicer than Nick." That's my ex from a few years back. She met him when she visited me in LA.

Jenna checks Garrett out. "It doesn't hold true that the more gorgeous they are, the more of an asshole they are, huh?"

"Uh, thanks?" Garrett says.

"We could tell you're not an a-hole right away," Sydney says, leaning around me to speak directly to Garrett. "First off, you took Harper to her benefit when she was suddenly single."

"That sounds like a sitcom right there," I say. "*Suddenly Single.*"

"Speaking of, we love *Living Gold*," Audrey says. "We had a watch party when it aired for the first time here at the bar."

"Aww, thanks, guys." They say they love everything I'm in.

Garrett puts his arm around the back of my chair, resting his hand on my shoulder. It warms at the spot. "We had a watch party at my parents' house too since my sister-in-law Josie Abbott is in it."

"Oh my God, I love her!" Sydney exclaims.

"What's she like?" Jenna asks.

They all turn to Garrett, excited to hear about Josie.

I wave in front of their faces. "Uh, guys, I've only worked with her for the past seven weeks."

"Yeah, yeah," Sydney says, looking at Garrett expectantly.

Garrett smiles. "She's great. Really bubbly and outgoing."

"I could see that about her," Sydney says. "Unlike our Harp, who only comes out of her shell onstage." She elbows me.

"Sydney used to be my costar in our school's drama club," I tell Garrett.

"That's right," Sydney says. "But Harp was always the star."

"Sydney can sing and she's funny," I say.

She pulls her hair band out and shakes out her long auburn hair dramatically. "And you'd think that Broadway would've called after our freshman production of *Grease*." She sticks her tongue out at me. "Harper abandoned us for Hollywood after freshman year."

"We're so proud of her!" Jenna exclaims. Audrey nods vigorously.

"Wish I could've seen it," Garrett says. "I've only had one line ever."

I hitch a thumb at him. "Garrett just filmed his first commercial."

My friends stop smiling. I know I've bitched about my exes using me, but Garrett's different. The man did chores for my grandmother on his day off.

He cooked for me.

He's the *marrying* type.

It hits me in a dizzying rush—I'm falling for him. It's a too fast, scary, out-of-control feeling, but there it is. In that moment, my defenses completely crumble. I can't fight this thing. It's too powerful, unlike anything I've ever felt before.

"Oh, you're in the business too?" Sydney asks him in a terse tone.

"Just got in, actually," he says. "After the gala, I got an agent. I'm really in construction with some acting on the side. I had my first session with my personal acting coach, and there's more to acting than I realized." He squeezes my shoulder. "The more I learn, the more I admire Harper and what she does with a role."

I smile what I'm sure is a dreamy smile. "Thanks."

Sydney shoots me a questioning look, checking if I'm okay with the commercial thing.

I send back the all-clear signal with a small nod.

The guy behind the bar calls over to us, "Anything else I can get you?"

Sydney pops up. "I'll get us some champagne to celebrate Harper's new show." She leans forward, smiling. "The good stuff."

"I'll chip in," I say.

"Get out, lady! I own the damn place. It's like, a write-off."

"Tax-deductible champagne?" I ask in a teasing voice. "Who's doing your books?"

"Ha!"

As soon as she's out of hearing range, I turn to my friends and lower my voice. "How's she doing here, really? Is she going to be able to keep the place open?"

Jenna and Audrey exchange a look.

Audrey speaks first in a whisper. "She's working on a big New Year's Eve party with a silent auction as a fundraiser. After that, I'm not sure if there will be enough to keep the place open."

"Maybe it's best if it closes," Jenna whispers. "I know it's a piece of history, but if she sells, someone with money could come in and turn it into something new. Like I turned the café into a bakery."

"Weren't you working in IT?" I ask Jenna. "That was a good-paying job."

"My soul was dying," she replies.

"Oh."

She waves that away. "You don't know anything about that since you followed your heart from the beginning. The rest of us are looking around, saying, is this all there is?"

"You too, Audrey?" I ask.

"I'm happy running the library, but even I sometimes wonder if the grass is greener doing something else. Something exciting."

I stare at her. "Like what?" Audrey has always been about books, books, books.

"Pole dancing," Sydney says with a laugh, returning with the champagne. "Our little Audrey on the pole."

Audrey shakes her head, blushing and glancing at Garrett. He's smiling. "That's you, Syd."

"I'd pay to see that," I say.

Sydney holds her palm out for cash.

"Just Audrey," I say.

Audrey shakes her head vigorously, waving her hands back and forth. "No, no."

Everyone laughs.

Sydney pops the champagne, and we clap. Once everyone has a glass in hand, Sydney raises hers. "To Harper, our hometown girl gone big time!"

I lift my glass to them. "To you wonderful ladies. I've missed you. I swear I'm going to come back to visit more."

"I'll drink to that," Sydney says.

We all clink glasses and drink.

"You should stop by on Thursday nights," Sydney says. "We started a book club."

"You mean Audrey started it, right?"

Sydney inclines her head. "True, but we have it here. I renamed it the Thursday Night Wine Club because who are we kidding? Audrey's the only one who ever finishes the book. The rest of us just drink wine and gossip. Two birds, one stone this way—supporting The Horseman and feeling like we're more intellectual. The group's been growing and the wine's been flowing."

Audrey sighs and looks to the ceiling.

"I could get into a Thursday night wine club," I say. "Too

bad I can't make it. Dress rehearsal is on Thursdays, and then I have to be fresh and ready to go for Friday's taping. No late night wine drinking."

Sydney tosses her hair and bats her lashes at me. "One day when you get off the Hollywood treadmill, you'll have time for these more glamorous social events."

Garrett chuckles. He knows what a red-carpet event is like now.

We talk for a while. They're curious about Garrett's royal side, and he doesn't disappoint with the details on Villroy. Before we go, I try one last time to contribute toward The Horseman. Sydney won't have it. Finally, I say, "I'll be here for your fabulous New Year's Eve party, and you can't stop me from bidding on the auction items. In fact, I'll donate a few items too."

Her blue eyes light up. "Oh, Harp, that would be fantastic. I know you don't get rushed when you're in town by fans, but you're famous, and I know it'll draw a crowd to have you here."

I sigh dramatically. "Everyone's crazy about me but General Joan." *And I wish I didn't care so much about her approval.*

"You're invited too, Garrett," Sydney says.

He smiles. "Thanks."

I shake my head. "He'll probably escort my grandmother here. He called her Queen Joan, and she practically swooned." I leave out my own swooning moment.

Sydney slaps the table. "No! The general swooned?"

"She likes Garrett better than me. He taught her how to record *Living Gold*, fixed her back gate, and unstuck her painted-shut window."

Sydney eyes him. "I'm starting to like him better than you too. What can you fix around here?"

"What do you need?" he asks.

I put up a palm. "No, no, no. You call Adam or a local contractor. He is outta here."

She whips out a business card and hands it to him. He stands, tucking it into his back pocket. This guy. Too generous. My heart is officially melted. No walls could stand up around him.

I hug my friends goodbye and return to Garrett. He puts an arm around my waist and says to Sydney, "I'll be back to help you out with my toolbox. Maybe before your New Year's party."

"I love this guy!" Sydney exclaims. Then she jabs a finger at him. "Just don't hurt her. She's had enough of that shit."

"I'll treat her right," he says solemnly.

I give him a squeeze around the middle. *Melted.*

Sydney walks over, smiling, and punches his bicep playfully. She has brothers, so that's her friendly way. When she punched me in kindergarten, saying she wanted to be my friend, I went home and cried. I didn't want a friend who punched me. My grandmother told me to punch her back with equal force (which wasn't much, my feelings were hurt more than anything), and we've been friends ever since.

Garrett just smiles and waves bye. I guess he's used to punches with five older brothers.

We head out the door. I shouldn't have stayed away so long. I let the tension of visiting my grandmother keep me from my friends. There's nothing like having friends who've known you your whole life. I know they see the real me.

Garrett retrieves our helmets from the back of his bike. "So, think I'll be here on New Year's?"

"I hope so," I blurt. It's three months away. I don't usually admit my hopes for the future this early in a relationship, but it's true.

He kisses me. "I like that you're thinking that way about me. Now let's get back. I'm dying to have you again."

A thrill goes through me. I throw my arms around his neck and kiss him passionately.

"Harper Ellis!" a shrill old lady voice exclaims.

I jerk away, looking around wildly for my grandmother. Sydney peers at me through an open window of her restaurant. "Ha! I still got it." She's great at impressions.

I shake my head. "Very funny. Not!"

"Better make that business private," she says. "Tongues will wag, and you'll hear from the General!"

Garrett chuckles and hands me my helmet. "Small-town gossip, huh?"

"It's a little scary how quickly word spreads." I wave to Sydney as she slips back inside.

His phone rings, and he pulls it from his pocket. "Uh-oh. It's your grandmother. She probably wants to know why you're mauling me in a parking lot."

I gasp. "No! Don't answer."

He grins and gets on the bike. "It's my brother."

I smack his shoulder, climb on behind him, and press my burning cheek against his back. The hazards of going home again. Feeling like a teenager caught with the bad boy.

Except, this time, he's actually good.

16

———

Garrett

Tonight's our second date, and we're finally going to see *Wicked*. I can't wait to share all my big news with Harper. I knock on her apartment door. She's expecting me. I've already gone through building security, her guard was notified, and so was she. I don't mind the layers of protection. Anything to keep her safe. Joe waits by my side for her to answer.

She opens the door with a wide smile and steps back. "Come on in."

I nod at Joe and shut the door behind me. "Hello, beautiful."

She does a little hip pose in her sleeveless dark red dress, and then she throws her arms around me, kissing me with wild abandon. I wrap my arms around her, caught up in it like always. She grinds against me, and I slide my hand to her ass, cupping her. She moans into my mouth, and I'm ready to take her right now.

I break the kiss, determined to have this date with her. "Harp."

Her hazel eyes are bright, her cheeks flushed. "Quickie?"

I grin. "Come on, now. They're gonna be pissed that you keep taking those reserved seats and skipping out on them."

She pouts. "You're right. After."

I kiss her and nip her bottom lip. "Can't wait." I step away from her, working on cooling down.

"I'll just get my purse and let Joe know."

A few minutes later, we're heading downstairs in the elevator with her guard. It's only a fifteen-minute drive to the theater. She's wearing a white shawl around her shoulders that's lacy enough to hint at the bare skin underneath. So sexy. She catches me up on her week at work, and the excitement over a major movie star, Claire Jordan, visiting the set to see Josie, who somehow knows her through the Rourke family connection. First I'm hearing about it. Apparently, my cousin Princess Sylvia used an American wedding planner for her stateside wedding (she married an American), who's close friends with Claire. The connection started with Sean to Sylvia to wedding planner lady to Claire to Josie to Harper. Small world. Makes me think at some point I would've met Harper through one of those links. Fate at work here.

Harper continues. "The best part is—and I had no idea about this—but Claire has her own production company based in Connecticut."

"Cool."

"Yeah, I told her I was interested in directing, and she told me she'd love to meet with me about a project! She's got a lot in the pipeline—movies, TV shows, even some reality TV based around classic cars. Have you heard of *Hot Finds*? They go around looking for classic cars to—"

"Fix up. Yes, I love that show with Ty and Park."

She bounces on the balls of her feet. "I mean, I don't expect her to *hand* me a movie to direct, but directing an episode of an established show while I'm on hiatus from *Living Gold* could be a start. Our last episode is at the end of the month. Then we play the waiting game to see if we get picked up for more episodes." She smiles up at me. "It could mean I'd be local for a while."

"That sounds good to me."

The elevator doors open, and Joe goes ahead of us. He heads out the front door first and waits for her. I hold the front door open for her and follow behind. The car's right out front, a silver Mercedes.

"Amanda," a man yells, "take me with you."

Harper's eyes widen as she takes in the disheveled middle-aged man in a stained short-sleeve button-down shirt and jogging pants. Joe confronts the guy, telling him to back away. Harper hurries into the back seat of the car, and I follow her.

"That's the guy who broke into my apartment," she says, craning her neck to see where he went. "He wants tough Amanda to whip him."

Joe's heading this way, and I don't see the guy anymore.

I turn to her. "Joe scared him off."

She grabs my hand, clutching it tight. "He was arrested. I guess he's out of jail."

"Do you have a restraining order against him?"

"Yes."

"Report him."

Joe slips into the front seat. "Let's go." The driver pulls away from the curb. He turns to Harper. "I'm reporting him for violating the restraining order. He's got some mental issues. I told him you're not Amanda, and to leave Harper Ellis alone or he'd be arrested. He barked at me and ran away."

"You mean like a dog?" I ask.

"Yeah. Harper, I've got you covered. Don't let that ruin your night. He's misguided. I don't think he means to hurt you, so much as he's hoping you'll train him like a dog."

Harper lets out a shaky breath. "Yes, well, that's not happening."

"He can't get into the building either," Joe says. "Put him out of your mind." He shoots me a look that says *step up, man*.

I cup her jaw and kiss her. "Anyone who tries to get near you has to get through two manly beasts ready to kick ass."

She gives me a wobbly smile, resting her hand on my chest. "That reminds me of when I mistook you for my guard."

I place my hand over hers. "Best day ever."

She unbuttons my white dress shirt enough to slip her hand in, stroking my chest. "You're a great distraction," she purrs.

I stroke her hair back over her ear. *I hope I'm more than that.*

She removes her hand and buttons my shirt. "So I told you all about my week. How's things with you?"

"Well, first of all, I'm an uncle again." I can't help my wide smile as I pull out my phone to show off the picture of my twin nieces. "These are my oldest brother Dylan's girls, Maya and Eva. Fraternal twins, though it's hard to tell them apart at this point. Maya's wearing the striped yellow hat, and Eva's wearing the striped pink. Mom and babies are doing great."

"Congratulations! So that makes how many nieces and nephews for you?"

"Three nieces, all from Dylan's family, but there's more on the way. My brother Jack's wife is due the first week of November. Connor's wife is expecting too, but that's still a while away. Anyway, we're having a big-sister party at my parents' house tomorrow. It's family tradition to have a party for the older sibling before the baby comes home, to make them feel special. Each of my older brothers got one when the next kid came along to bump them out of baby-brother status, except yours truly since I'm the youngest. You wanna go?" I want to introduce her to my family because I have a good feeling about us.

Her eyes widen, her jaw dropping.

I press under her chin, closing her mouth, and kiss her. "Why so shocked?"

"You want me to meet your parents and, like, your whole family?"

"Yeah, it'll be fun."

She stares at me. "That sounds serious."

"I met your grandmother."

"That was more like…well, you offered…"

"I was a buffer?"

"Yeah."

I tuck my phone away, hiding my disappointment. "That's okay. You don't have to go."

"No, I will. I'm not used to meeting my boyfriend's parents. Now I'm nervous. Do I bring something?"

I smile. "Not necessary. And don't worry, Josie will be there too. My brothers are like me, only not as cool."

She laughs.

"And, in other good news, I booked a second commercial. I'm psyched. Filming is next Friday. It's for an electric car that I'm gonna make look cool just by fake driving it. The script says I park it in the city, plug it into a charging station, and then walk off with my beautiful girlfriend. No lines, so it's super easy. I asked if you could play my girlfriend, but they'd already cast it."

She bites her lower lip.

I meet her eyes. "Are you upset I asked for a part for you, or that I got the gig?"

She squeezes my arm. "Neither. It was nice of you to think of me."

"I'm psyched. After this, I'll have enough for a down payment on a house. It's a dream come true."

She leans her head against my shoulder, and I wrap an arm around her. "I'm happy for you." She doesn't sound enthusiastic, but she's trying. It'll take time for her to trust me. I get that, and I'm willing to put in the time. What I'm not willing to do is give up what's shaping up to be a lucrative new career. My agent is working hard to find me more and better work, and I love working with my acting coach, who's been very encouraging.

I'm starting to think acting could be a real possibility. For the first time in my life I've got ambition, something I'm willing to work really hard for. And it's all mine. I'm replaceable at my job. That's a fact. My brothers could always get another guy on crew. If they had really wanted me to stick around, they would've given me a title and position. I shouldn't feel so guilty about branching out on my own.

My family and Harper need to be on board with this new direction because, if something big comes along, I'm not giving it up.

Harper

I'm trying to wrap my mind around the whirlwind night so far. I was excited to see Garrett; then I had a reminder of why I have a guard in the first place when Walter approached me again, then Garrett sprang the *meet my parents* invitation on me, which is nerve-racking enough, and *then* he tells me he booked another commercial. I'm happy for him. Really. How could I not be when he's so excited? I can't help it if my first gut reaction is wariness. I'm working past that. I don't want to ruin a good thing just because my instincts shoot up warning signals. In this case, they're wrong. I have to believe that.

We're ushered into the theater through a back entrance and make our way to a side door, where we're escorted to our center seats. I try to relax. This is my favorite show, after all. I've seen it nine times. I love the music, but most of all I love the story of the misunderstood wicked witch, who everyone judges just because she looks different. She was born with green skin. It's a reminder to consider a person's character more than their appearance. As an actor I work hard to get to the essence of a character.

The show begins a short while later, and I catch myself watching Garrett out of the corner of my eye just as much as the action onstage. He seems to be soaking it in. I hope he likes it. I'd love to take him to more Broadway shows.

As soon as the curtains close for intermission and the house lights turn on, I ask, "What do you think so far?"

"Amazing. I'm really into live music, and this is an art form all on its own, the way they tell a story with it. And the pipes on those two lead actresses, incredible!"

I beam. He gets it. "Yes. Only the best of the best make it to Broadway. There's never a bad performance. At least I've never seen one."

He nudges my arm. "How many times have you seen this one?"

"Number ten tonight. And I'd see it weekly if I could.

Afterward, I'm supposed to meet some of the cast and get some pictures with them."

"You didn't tell me that part. I'll get them to sign my program."

"Sure." I lean close. "And then we can go back to my place and pick up where we left off earlier."

He grins and taps my nose. "Horny beast."

"Guilty." I laugh. No one's ever called me a beast.

After the show, which was incredible, we wait for the audience to clear out before slipping behind the curtains to meet the cast. They're pumped up after their performance, and it's great to see everyone again. I've seen this particular cast three times.

The actress who plays the good witch signs Garrett's program, and a photographer my publicist called gets a picture of them together. I join them, and they take more pictures. Next they get a shot of us with the wicked witch and then with the whole cast.

"We're going out after this," Glinda the good witch (aka Laurie) says. "You want to meet up?"

Garrett puts an arm around me. "Actually, Harper can't wait to get me back to her place."

I smack his chest playfully, secretly glad he's not diving into the party scene. I want him to want me for me, not the glitzy stuff around me.

"Ooh, Harp, looks like you got a real man on your hands." Laurie licks her finger and does a sizzling sound when she touches his shoulder.

Garrett laughs.

"So great to see you all. Fantastic performance," I say. "Have fun tonight!"

I head out but not before I hear her sing-song, "You too, sexy mama."

I laugh.

Garrett holds my hand, entwining his fingers with mine as we meet up with Joe and head out the back entrance. No creepers or paparazzi, and we make it safely into the car. I breathe a sigh of relief.

"I can see why you like the show," he says. "You're the wicked witch, and your grandmother is the good witch."

I suck in air. I cannot believe he saw that. It's true. Their lives are intertwined, at odds, one struggling, the other sailing through. I always felt wicked, unable to live up to her strict standards.

"What happened to your parents?" he asks gently.

Not only is he extremely intuitive and sensitive, but he also takes great care with me. It makes me want to share.

I whisper in his ear, "I'll tell you my story if you tell me yours. Not here."

"Sure. My story is boring though."

"Ha! Nothing boring about being born royalty. Are your sisters-in-law considered princesses?"

He lifts his brows. "As a matter of fact they are."

I don't say another word. We both know why I asked. If things keep going well between us, one day I could be a princess. I wouldn't say no to wearing a tiara and staying at the palace in Villroy.

"I want to go to that Regency-themed ball pretty badly," I confess.

"You only want me for Alice."

"It's a two-fer."

He laughs. "Last time she dressed her baby girl Sigourney in this little blue gown that matched hers. She goes all out. I'll take you next time on one condition."

"What?"

"You have to promise not to forget I exist once you meet your idol."

A bubble of pure happiness blooms inside me. "Yes." I flush with excitement, but then I remember my grandmother. "I can't, though. My grandmother expects me for Christmas, and she's getting up there. I don't know how many Christmases I have left with her."

"She's tough as an ox. She can come along on the royal jet. I bet she'd fit right in with my cousins. And really hit it off with my dad."

"Maybe." I can't ask her to travel for selfish reasons. What if she fell ill? It would be my fault.

"Sure, we'll see where we're at then."

Once we're back in the privacy of my apartment, he makes himself at home on my sofa and pats the space next to him. "Story time," he says. "You tell me yours, and I'll tell you mine."

I'm suddenly nervous. My grandmother's warning sounds in my head: never show weakness. And then my publicist's voice: every person you let in must sign a nondisclosure. I let myself be vulnerable with him. And I have to be brave and keep doing that. It's the only way to really connect with the man I'm beginning to suspect I love.

I join him on the sofa and take a deep breath. "Not much to tell. I never met my dad. He was married with a family of his own." I swallow hard, surprised it still bothers me after all these years that he never acknowledged me. "My mom had me very young and left me as a newborn in my grandmother's care. My grandmother is her mom."

"Did your biological mom visit?"

I smile a little. It's nice of him to refer to her that way. She never felt like a real mom. "No. I don't think she felt welcome. I think my grandmother scared her away."

"Did you ever try to get in touch with her?"

I hate to admit it because it just shows how little she cared. "No, I planned to as an adult, but...she got in touch with me when I got my first show at fifteen. We met up in LA. She asked me for money, and when I said no, she said my grandmother had tainted her against me. I was saving every paycheck at the time, terrified I'd get fired and never work again."

He kisses me. "I'm sorry."

A lump forms in my throat. "Don't share that with anyone, okay? Just between us."

"Of course. Who would I tell?"

"There's a lot of people who'd pay good money for dirt on me."

"Harp, don't you know me better than that by now?"

I blink back tears. "Sometimes it's hard to trust. I'm trying, okay?"

"Anything you tell me stops here. I'm not trying to gain anything from you besides your...company."

"What were you going to say?"

He shakes his head, smiling. "No. Not the time for dirty joking around. So my story is simple. I told ya how my father was banished. After that, it was a pretty normal life from my perspective. By the time I arrived, my dad was working for my uncle's construction company, handling the financial side, and my mom raised us six boys. They stopped having kids after perfection, as you can see." He gestures with both hands toward himself.

I laugh. "Obviously."

"Eventually, me and my brothers were brought into the company as our uncle taught us the trade. When he retired, he gave the company to me and my brothers. We're equal co-owners. My older brothers have worked out a niche in the new company we formed under it for real estate development, Rourke Management. I missed out on that. I'm still just working crew. They didn't think I was experienced enough for a high-level position at first, and now those positions are all filled." He sounds bitter.

"That's the second time you mentioned being passed over."

"Yeah, well, I guess it's been on my mind a lot lately. I'm suddenly ambitious for more."

"Like an acting career."

"Can't deny it would be awesome." He gives me a sexy smile, his big hands sliding my dress up. He lifts me to straddle him. "Now let's get to the important stuff."

I wrap my arms around his neck and kiss him, relieved all the intimate sharing is over. This is so much easier—only his mouth on mine, his hands roaming all over me.

He stands, keeping me wrapped around him, and walks into the bedroom. No more words. Just a passionate joining. I tell myself not to worry about his newly found ambition. I can't let that come between us.

17

———

Harper

I'm nervous, like, big-time nerves, approaching stage-fright levels as I wait on the front step of the brick rowhouse where Garrett grew up. Hard to believe six boys lived in this small house, especially if they're as big as he is. I can only imagine the teen years with all that testosterone—sweat, loud voices, eating everything in sight. I'm picturing his mom as an exhausted aged woman, so when the door pops open to a beautiful woman in her fifties with dark brown shoulder-length hair, bright blue eyes, and smooth fair skin, wearing a pale pink sweater and snug black trousers with black boots, you can color me shocked. She looks like she could be in a commercial for anti-wrinkle cream. I want all her beauty secrets. Dead serious.

"Hello, welcome!" she exclaims, stepping back to let us in. "So glad you could all make it for Olivia's special day." She says "Olivia" extra loud. That's Dylan's little girl. I memorized his family's names on the way over. Music plays in the background, something cheerful about a dolphin. Kid music?

I step inside, where an adorable toddler wearing a silver glitter tiara and a pink leotard with a matching tutu is twirling in the living room. She beams at her grandmother, spots us, and runs to grab an older man's pants leg. It has to be Garrett's dad; the resemblance is striking, though Garrett is thick with muscle. They have the same aquamarine eyes, sharp cheekbones, and square jaw.

Garrett makes the introductions. Mr. and Mrs. Rourke greet me warmly, as well as Joe. I brought my guard for my own peace of mind. I didn't want anyone following me here or showing up uninvited to their home. Garrett told me his parents wouldn't blink an eye about Joe since palace guards are the norm. His dad grew up with them.

"Dylan will stop by a little later in time for cake," Mrs. Rourke says. "Ariana is in the hospital with the twins for another day. So today is for the big sister."

Garrett gestures for me to follow, a present for Olivia tucked under one arm. He crouches in front of her, where she's still clutching her grandfather's leg. "Happy big-sister day, Olivia! This is my friend Harper." He sets the large present on the floor in front of her.

I bend down to her level. "Hi! You must be so excited to be a big sister."

She nods and stares at the present with its wrapping paper of brightly colored balloons.

Garrett gestures to it. "This is from me and Harper. Go ahead and open it."

She pulls at the paper, and a tiny piece comes off. Another rip for another tiny piece. This could take a while.

Garrett gets to his feet, and I join him.

Mr. Rourke remains standing behind Olivia, who's industriously unwrapping her gift, piece by tiny piece. "Dylan wants to talk to you later about the crew chief position."

"Whatta ya mean?" Garrett asks. "That's Jack's job."

"Jack's decided to stay home with the new baby for a couple of years while Riley works full time."

Garrett's eyes widen. "Seriously? And Dylan wants *me* to be crew chief?"

"Of course."

"But what about when Jack comes back?"

Mr. Rourke smiles. "If things keep going the way they are now, the business has room for you all to grow with it."

Garrett's brows furrow, looking deep in thought. I can read him now. It's the promotion he's always wanted, but he's also got this acting gig he's hoping will take off, which means he'd be leaving his family's business just when they need him most. He told me Jack's wife is due with the baby soon.

He exhales sharply and looks down at Olivia. "Want some help?"

She shakes her head, her tiara tipping forward. She pushes it out of her eyes and uses both hands to secure it on top of her head. Her hair is dark brown and wavy. I never had my hair down as a kid. General Joan felt my crazy curls needed to be tidy and secured at all times. Ponytail or braids.

"How old is she?" I ask.

"Twenty months," Mr. Rourke says. "My wife and I enjoy watching you on *Living Gold*. Actually, she was a big fan before that with *Capital Asset*."

"Thank you. I appreciate it." Garrett has trained me well on receiving compliments properly. Ha.

We all glance down at Olivia. She's got the wrapping paper off and is struggling to pull the cardboard away from her gift—a sports ball set with a foam soccer ball, basketball, and football.

"Open, please," she says, looking up at us adults.

Mr. Rourke picks up the box. "The packaging is tough to open. Let me get scissors and work on it."

Just then the front door opens to a handsome man in a black leather jacket and jeans. "Where's my girl?"

"Daddy!" Olivia shrieks and runs full speed to him. That must be Dylan.

My eyes sting at the reunion. He scoops her up and hugs her. She rests her head on his shoulder, holding him tight, her little face ecstatic. He tosses her in the air, catches her, and kisses her cheek. "I missed you the past couple of nights, pumpkin. Did you have fun with Grandmom and Grandpop?"

"Uh-huh," she says. "And Nonna and Nonno too."

"Wow, the whole gang got together just for you." He

hoists her onto his hip. "You must be one special kid." He lifts a hand in greeting to Garrett and walks over to give him a slap on the back.

"Yes," she says. "I'm a big sister. I help Maya and Eva." She crinkles her nose and sing-songs, "They're just babies." She speaks really well for a toddler. For some reason I thought kids didn't speak full sentences until at least two. Not that I have experience with little kids.

"They're so lucky to have you." Her dad sets her down, and she runs into the kitchen, where Mr. Rourke is struggling with the plastic ties holding the sports ball set together.

He thrusts his hand out to me. "Hey, I'm Dylan."

"Harper," I say, shaking his hand. "I recognize you from your Villroy wedding pictures. That was a major event."

He grins, his blue eyes sparkling. "Sure was. I'm the crown prince, until I wasn't. Anyway, we had a good reunion out there. And Josie tells me she loves working with you on *Living Gold*. Fun show."

"Thank you." I cross my fingers and hold them up. "Let's just hope enough people feel the same way." The ratings haven't been great, but, according to my agent, many viewers of our channel prefer to binge-watch when the whole season is out. "I'll know the first week of November if the show gets a second season."

Garrett's brows draw together. "Knock wood it does, but do you know what you'll do if it doesn't? Would you stay in the area?"

Dylan excuses himself and joins his daughter in the kitchen, giving his dad a shoulder squeeze before moving to the sink to prepare a sippy cup of water for his daughter. What a great dad. How different would my life have been if I had two loving parents like Olivia? Garrett had that too. Maybe I wouldn't have felt the need to escape into a character, or to travel so far away at a young age. I shake it off. I'm happy with my work. And my childhood gave me the drive to get where I am today. It's for the best.

Garrett takes my hand and leads me to a plush dark blue sofa. "Harp?"

I cross my legs and turn to him. "Yes?"

"You never answered my question. Would you stay in the area if *Living Gold* isn't picked up?"

"If there was work for me, yes. I hope something will work out with directing, but I don't know. I have to go where the work is. Well, you know from Josie."

"True. I house-sit for her enough." He squeezes my hand. "I hope we'll keep in touch if we have to be separated."

My chest tightens. He's just so expressive. I don't even know what to say. "Thank you."

Mrs. Rourke opens a door in the kitchen. "Get up here, everyone!" She looks over at me. "Has anyone offered you a drink?"

Garrett leaps up. "Got it."

I follow him into the kitchen. People pour out of the basement, crowding the kitchen as they gather around the island. What were they doing down there? I didn't hear anything. Of course, the children's music is loud, and I was distracted by the people I did meet.

Garrett works his way around the room, introducing me to his brothers and their wives, but there's one woman who needs no introduction.

"One of us, one of us," Josie chants, her blue eyes dancing before she throws her arms around me. "What's it been, two whole days since we've seen each other? What's new?"

I laugh. "Not much. We saw *Wicked* yesterday, and now here I am."

"Oh, I love *Wicked*. But my dream role is Dolly in *Hello, Dolly*. What's your dream Broadway role?"

"Elphaba in *Wicked*, but I don't have the pipes."

She tilts her head. "Really? I always pictured you as Marian the librarian in *The Music Man*." She turns to Garrett. "She has that sweet quality about her. Marian goes from uptight librarian all the way to a trusting happier woman."

"Why? Because I love books?" I ask.

Josie's eyes dance with amusement. "Mmm-hmm."

I fill in the blank. "Because I'm uptight and distrustful. Gee, thanks."

Garrett points at Josie. "Nailed it." He puts an arm around my waist. "You should try for that part."

I press my lips in a flat line. "I'll get right on that."

"Seriously," he says.

I turn to him, fighting to rein in my temper. "You don't just decide to take the part. It has to be in a current run, it has to work with my schedule, and they have to agree I can pull it off." *And I am not uptight and distrustful. Definitely not uptight, and I'm trying really hard not to be distrustful. Don't you know how vulnerable I've let myself be with you?*

His brows draw together. I keep forgetting how in tune he is to me.

"Make it happen," Josie says. "If you want it, that is. I just pictured you that way. So…" She grimaces. "*Living Gold* is looking dicey. I thought it was so good, but maybe it's not striking the right note with the audience. Ratings are declining week by week."

My gut does a slow roll, but I put on a positive face. "My agent says just wait and see if it builds. Binge-watching could save it."

"I'm looking over some scripts Claire sent my way," she says.

"Cool." *I didn't get any scripts.*

She immediately senses my discomfort. "She's like a mentor to me. Hey, I could be your mentor. Would you like that?"

How can I say no? Just because I'm older and have worked longer. She's had decent-sized roles in two movies, and I've only had bit parts. Maybe she *should* be my mentor. "Sure."

She squeezes my arm. "Oh, that sounded like I'm full of myself, didn't it?" She gestures for Garrett to back off and throws her arm around my shoulders. "Just know I'm here for whatever you need, okay?"

"Absolutely, thanks." My knee gives out suddenly, and I gasp. A soccer ball just hit the back of my knee.

Olivia zips by, following it, kicking it around the kitchen.

"Take it outside, young lady," Mr. Rourke barks. "Who wants to play soccer with Olivia?"

All the guys follow her out the door. Wow. A whole soccer team of manly men following a toddler around the backyard.

"It's a perfect fall day," Mrs. Rourke says. "Let's sit outside on the deck. I'll get the veggies."

Once I'm settled on the back deck with the ladies, I actually enjoy myself, chatting and eating veggies dipped in ranch sauce. It's me, Mrs. Rourke, Josie, and the wives. Becca and Riley are both pregnant and chatting about that. Riley's due at the end of the month. Becca's not even showing yet. She's tall and thin, so I guess the baby has room to stretch out in there at this point.

We chat and watch as seven grown men, including Joe, follow a toddler around with a foam soccer ball, cheering when she kicks it toward a small net someone found in the storage area. She's winning.

The neighbors stop by, the Bianchis, who it turns out are the grandparents of Olivia. Dylan married the girl next door. I'm so curious to meet his wife. Her mom is brassy and outspoken, her face dominated by dark brown bangs and large glasses. Her dad is quiet and smiles a lot.

Mrs. Rourke introduces me to them.

"The superstar actress," Mrs. Bianchi says. "Two in the family now. Next thing you'll all be moving to Hollywood."

"I'm not a superstar," I say, secretly thrilled she thinks so. Hollywood hasn't granted me that status.

"Course you are," she says. "I've seen you on two popular TV shows. Now can you help me carry in the manicotti?" She's balancing two covered trays.

"Sure," I say, surprised she asked me since we just met. Her husband carries in a covered pitcher of clear water with fruit slices floating in it.

I follow her inside the house.

She speaks over her shoulder to me. "I brought the healthy water. Gotta sneak in some extra vitamins for all the pregnant women here. My daughter says the twins are her last, but there's no shortage of grandbabies for me to spoil now that the younger Rourke sons are settling down. We're all family here."

"That's really nice."

I set the still-warm tray on the island.

She gathers up some plastic plates and starts serving with a large spatula. "So is it serious with you and Garrett?"

I nearly choke on my spit. This is the kind of thing I expected to hear from Garrett's mother not his neighbor. "I don't know." *Where is Garrett?*

"Mmm-hmm. How long have ya been dating?"

I glance toward the back door, willing Garrett to notice I'm getting the third degree from his neighbor. "Uh, we met a month ago, but I guess you could say we've been officially dating for…" I trail off, unsure how to say we had "friend" dates that, in hindsight, were real dates minus the hooking-up part.

She pins me with a knowing look. "I'm up to speed on modern dating. My own daughter lived in sin before Dylan made an honest woman of her. It worked out, so who's to say it's wrong? Unless you ask Father Richards." She expertly scoops up a large helping of manicotti and sets it on a plate. "Now Josie, she moves around a lot for work. Have you talked about what that will mean for you and Garrett?"

I gulp. *Is she going to share all this with Mrs. Rourke?* "Uh, he says he hopes we'll stay in touch."

She smiles. "He's a sweetheart. You know that, right?" She waits for my nod before continuing. "He always was, even though he tries to cover it up with his big muscles and tough expression. He's the only one who texts his mother regularly, keeping her up to date. We knew the moment he met you."

My cheeks warm. "Oh. That's nice." *I can't believe he told his mother about meeting me! So sweet.*

She points her spatula at me. "If you're not serious, you should cut him loose. He's looking to settle down like his brothers. Twenty-six is plenty old to settle down. How old are you?" She lifts her head, her dark brown eyes shining with bright curiosity through her glasses.

"Twenty-eight," I reply automatically, though I don't like to share my age. It can be limiting for an actress.

"Are you hoping to have kids?"

I glance toward the back door. *Garrett!!! SOS!* "I don't know," I mumble.

"Don't wait too long. Ariana didn't get started until thirty-one. Now she was smart, using those new ovulation tests and timing everything just right. Course it helps the Rourke men are virile."

I almost blurt that I'm on the pill when I realize it's none of her business. *Why is this woman interrogating me? Mayday! I'm bailing any minute now.*

Mrs. Rourke rushes in. "I'm here to help."

I let out a breath. The rest of the family files in after her. My interrogation is over, thank goodness. I help hand out the plates of manicotti, and people start heading to the dining room table. I follow last with Mrs. Rourke.

"Do you like modern art?" she asks me, gesturing toward a painting on the wall. It's really ugly—purple and red scribbles with a bright yellow splotch of paint in the middle. "Garrett gave it to us."

Garrett calls over from the table, "It was a birthday gift Jack gave to Con, who left it at my place. I'm not into modern art."

"It's unusual," I say diplomatically.

Mrs. Rourke smiles, admiring it. "A famous artist made it. Who knows, one day it could be worth something."

Mrs. Bianchi comes up behind us, peering at the painting. "Frankly, I don't see the appeal. I wouldn't pay a dime for it."

Mrs. Rourke purses her lips and continues on to the dining room table.

I join them. Everyone's talking and laughing, except Jack, who looks sullen and keeps shooting glances at the painting. He was the original owner of the painting, buying it for Con. After I finish my manicotti, curiosity gets the better of me.

"Jack, did you want the painting back?" I ask. "You gifted it to someone, and then it was regifted, so maybe you were hoping…"

He scowls, brushing his tousled dark hair back. "I'm not hoping."

"Who's the artist again, honey?" Riley asks. His pregnant

wife's eyes narrow, almost daring him to say. There's a definite tension in the air.

"You wouldn't know him," he mumbles.

"I'd like to hear," Mrs. Rourke says. "Garrett didn't know. Who is it, Jack?"

"I could look him up," Mr. Rourke says. "Maybe we should donate it to a museum."

Mr. and Mrs. Rourke walk over to the art on the living room wall, tilting their head this way and that.

"It's not signed," Mr. Rourke says. "Maybe it's on the back." He goes to lift the painting off the wall when Jack stops him, rushing over.

"Don't touch it!"

"What's the matter?" Mr. Rourke asks.

"Do ya think it'll affect the value?" Mrs. Rourke asks.

Mrs. Bianchi joins them, shaking her head. "I don't think anything could make it less valuable. This looks like someone spilled paint on it from a better piece they were working on. Either that or a toddler did it. No offense, Olivia."

Olivia runs over at her name, and her dad follows.

Soon everyone's settled in the living room, staring at the painting. Riley takes a seat on the sofa and sighs. "Jack, just tell them. It's gone on long enough."

He rubs the back of his neck and glances over at her. "Ry, come on."

"What, Jack?" Mrs. Rourke asks with a smile. "Did you pay a lot for it? I'll give it back to you if you'd like."

"He dug deep for that one," Riley says.

Jack shoots her a dark look.

"Oh, Jack, I had no idea," Mrs. Rourke says. "Gosh. Maybe we should sell it and then give the proceeds to your child's education."

Jack closes his eyes. "It's garbage, okay?" He opens his eyes, his expression pure misery. "I pulled it out of the garbage and gave it to Con as a birthday gift. Just a prank. He took it as truth and hung it on his wall."

"Bastard," Con says with a note of amusement. "I had to stare at that hideous thing for years on the living room wall."

Jack laughs and stops abruptly at his mom's glare. "So then Con left it with Garrett, who dumped it on you."

Mrs. Rourke speaks through her teeth. "I thought they just didn't have an appreciation for art. Was it at least in the trash of an artist?"

Jack lifts one shoulder. "I dunno. I found it on the street. I doubt it. Sorry. I'll put it in the trash where it belongs." He takes it off the wall and heads out the back door with it.

Garrett leans over to me. "Jack is king of the pranksters. I don't think I've ever heard him apologize for one."

"I knew it!" Mrs. Bianchi crows in the tense silence. "Didn't I say it was garbage?"

"No, you didn't say garbage," Mrs. Rourke huffs.

Mrs. Bianchi gestures broadly. "I said it wasn't worth much. Like a toddler spilled their juice on it and then peed."

"You did *not* say that," Mrs. Rourke says hotly.

"I know art, Tara," Mrs. Bianchi says smugly. "Ya know, everyone *thinks* they have good taste, but only a select few actually do."

Mrs. Rourke lifts her chin. "I studied art history in college, you know."

Mrs. Bianchi waves that away. "I'm sure those old pieces are easy to value. Modern art takes a special eye." She taps the side of her glasses.

The two women bicker louder and louder about who knows more about art, and somehow veer off into who is the superior contributor to the church's Thanksgiving dinner for the homeless.

Jack returns just as their bickering hits a high note over the value of street art, which Mrs. Rourke says still qualifies as art, and Mrs. Bianchi says is a crime plain and simple. Boy, it didn't take much to get these two going. I exchange a look with Garrett, who shrugs and then whispers in my ear, "There was a feud. I'll explain later."

Jack rushes over to the women still standing near where the painting was on the wall, and holds up his palms. "Please tell me I didn't restart the war over this painting."

"What war?" Mrs. Bianchi throws her hands up. "There

never was a war. There was only *some* people, who were falsely accused, and *some* people, who did the accusing."

Mr. Rourke speaks up in a commanding voice. "Ladies, I don't think we need to rehash old grievances."

Mrs. Bianchi gestures to Mrs. Rourke. "I gave her a serving spoon to make up for it." She crosses her arms and nods once. "The moment I knew we'd be tied forever through our children, I did the honorable thing. I bought and wrapped the spoon she claimed I stole and mended that fence." She shoots Mrs. Rourke a dark look. "It was met with less than stellar enthusiasm." She pats her hair. "Enough said."

"You complimented the pattern!" Mrs. Rourke exclaims. "I know you know which spoon I'm talking about—"

"Mom," Jack says loudly.

"What?"

"It was me."

Her brows knit together. "What was you?"

He sighs. "I stole the serving spoon."

Mrs. Rourke shakes her head. "Jack, that was so long ago you couldn't have been more than—"

"Five," he says.

Mrs. Bianchi smiles smugly. "I'm not surprised at all. I told you I wasn't a thief."

Mrs. Rourke tilts her head, still confused, as she stares at Jack. "So you're saying when you were five years old, you stole my serving spoon from the potluck at the Bianchis'? That was a big spoon. How come I never saw you with it?"

He scrubs a hand over his face. "I hid it in a box in the storage area of their basement. I thought it was funny watching everyone wonder where it was. How was I to know it would lead to decades of war between you two?"

His wife, Riley, pipes up. "He was too chicken to speak up after all that time. Keep in mind he was thinking with an immature five-year-old brain."

Mrs. Rourke scowls. "And secretly howling with laughter for years. Oh, Jack." She turns to Mrs. Bianchi. "I had no idea. I don't even know what to say. All this time—"

Mrs. Bianchi gives her shoulder a squeeze. "No need to

say anything. We're family now." She holds out her hand, and Mrs. Rourke takes it. "Now let's go get your serving spoon back." She glances at Jack. "Come on, you dig it out, you trickster. And then you can clean out my whole storage area next weekend to make it up to me."

"Mine too," Mrs. Rourke says.

Jack's shoulders slump, but then he brightens. "I can't. I've got a baby on the way. Riley needs me."

Riley smiles widely. "We've got a few weeks, babe. I can spare you."

Jack jabs a finger at her before accepting his fate and following the two women out the front door.

As soon as the door shuts behind them, Garrett quips, "Classic Jack," and everyone laughs.

A short while later, Mrs. Rourke returns, triumphantly holding the serving spoon in the air.

"It's a beautiful Gaelic pattern," Mrs. Bianchi says.

Mrs. Rourke washes it and puts it in the drawer, closing it with a sigh. She turns to us. "Time for big-sister cake!"

18

———————

Garrett

I'm spent, lying in Harper's bed, trying to catch my breath. She threw herself at me as soon as we got back to her place, and now in the happy aftermath, I'm feeling pretty good about how things are going between us. She seemed to find my family amusing, which is better than thinking they're nuts. Since she seemed comfortable, we stayed late, hanging with everyone. I think my family approves, which is important in a family like mine since we spend so much time together at work and just about any occasion.

And Dylan took me aside to offer me a promotion to crew chief with a salary bump too. He said it was long overdue, and he'd been hoping to pull Jack to a project manager position and me up sooner, but they just couldn't make the numbers work before. It means a lot to me. I should've spoken up about feeling passed over, but, once I had more experience, I kept telling myself it was because they needed someone like me they could count on in crew to do the job right. It seems my big brother was looking out for me like always. I accepted the position, of course. Acting is still a side gig. But if it comes down to accepting a major acting role or sticking by my family, it'll be hard for me to choose. My loyalty to my family runs deep and, for once, I know they really need me.

Harper stirs by my side. Sweet Harper. Maybe it's a good time to tell her how much I care about her.

I roll to my side and stroke her hair back from her face. "Harp, I just wanted to tell—"

She jackknifes upright and slaps a hand over her mouth.

"Harp?"

She races to the bathroom, slamming the door behind her. The distinct sounds of retching follow. My own stomach churns in sympathy.

I give her a few minutes before getting out of bed, pulling on my boxer briefs, and knocking on the door. "You okay?"

"Fine," she says. More retching.

I grimace. See? Fine is never fine.

I hear the toilet flush and then water running. She opens the door, her skin chalk white, her eyes glassy. "I might have food poisoning. That manicotti."

"I had the manicotti too, and I feel fine."

She pats my arm and brushes by me. "Going to bed."

I follow her, going back to what I was about to say. "Tonight was special—"

"Oh God." She races by me on her way to the bathroom, slamming the door, locking it, and turning on the fan.

This is concerning. What if she passes out in there? Would she even let me help her? The lock looks like one of those pinhole kind. I could open it with a piece of wire or a paperclip if I had to.

"Call out if you need me," I say through the door.

"Please go away. In fact, go home. I don't need any witnesses. It's going to get ugly."

"I can take care of you."

"I can take care of myself."

"I'm staying."

Silence.

I head back to bed. But I don't sleep. I listen for her collapse or her calling out to me. Maybe she'll just stumble out and come back to bed.

Finally, after a quick doze, I wake at three a.m. and knock on the bathroom door. No response.

I search for something to jimmy the lock open. I find a paperclip on a script sitting on top of her dresser. That'll do. I straighten it, pop the lock, and slowly open the door.

She's asleep on the floor in front of the toilet on a large bath towel. Poor thing.

I scoop her up, and she moans in her sleep. I settle her back in bed. Her skin is clammy. I cover her with the blanket and pull a small trash can to her side of the bed in case she needs it.

She's up again at six, retching into the trash can. She collapses onto the mattress afterward. I get up and take the trash can to empty it in the toilet.

"What are you still doing here?" she croaks when I get back. "If it's not food poisoning, you're going to get whatever this is. Some kind of stomach virus."

"I'm sure if it's a virus, you already gave it to me." I set the trash can back in place with a new liner I found under the bathroom sink. It smells like lemon.

She waves me away weakly. "I don't want you to see me like this."

"You're just sick. Same old Harp."

"Saint Garrett," she mumbles before falling asleep.

I pull my phone out and Google what to do for a stomach virus and food poisoning too, just to be safe. Normally I'd get in touch with my mom, but it's too early to call. Knowing my mom, she'd want to come over and take care of Harper herself. She's very hands on and doesn't flinch at the tough stuff. She's gone through plenty of illnesses, broken bones, and bloody wounds with me and my brothers. Sometimes I think she would've made a good emergency room doctor. Nothing fazes her.

The alarm on Harper's nightstand goes off an hour later, and she jerks awake, sitting up and then moaning. "The room's spinning."

I help her lie down again. "You got up too fast."

She moans. "Turn it off."

I reach over her and turn off the alarm.

"I have to go to work," she says.

"You're sick."

"No, I'm feeling better." But she doesn't move.

"You're still weak. You were up all night puking up your guts."

"Not just that. I think I lost ten pounds last night. I need to brush my teeth at least."

"I'll help you to the bathroom. Take it nice and slow."

I walk around to help her slowly move to a sitting position. "Let me know when you're good. I don't want you to pass out."

A few moments later, she says, "I'm good." I help her stand and walk her to the bathroom. She gets her toothbrush and toothpaste out of the medicine cabinet, but before it even gets to her mouth, she's retching in the sink.

I hold her hair back and put a hand on her forehead so she doesn't crash into the faucet.

She finishes and rinses the sink. Then she rinses her mouth.

"You're not going to work," I say. "Call in sick."

"I can't take a sick day. People depend on me. The cast, the crew, the writers. It's the read-through."

I guide her back to bed. "What happens at the read-through?"

"Everyone gathers to read through the script. The crew takes notes on the tech side; the writers take notes on what worked and didn't. They revise the script right after. They need me." She collapses into bed.

"I'll call Josie and she'll explain."

"Just give me half an hour," she says weakly. "I'm tough. I'll power through."

"Has anyone ever told you to stop acting tough?"

"No. I'm so tired." She rolls to her side.

"Do you want to give the entire cast, crew, and writers this virus you've got?"

She sighs. "No."

"I'm calling you in sick. It's probably a twenty-four-hour thing. Most stomach viruses are, according to the internet."

"'K."

I leave her to rest in bed, adjusting the bedroom curtains to keep out the light. Then I go to the living room to call Josie and explain.

"Oh no, that's terrible," she says. "Should I send chicken soup?"

"I'll get some for her. I'm sure she'll be okay by tomorrow."

"Okay, keep me posted. And if you get sick, let me know. I'll get your mom over there."

I smile. Notice how she didn't volunteer. "Thanks."

Once Harper's awake, I'll change the sheets and clean up the bathroom for her. In the meantime, I help myself to coffee and a piece of toast. Then I remember her guard. I'll stop by his apartment in a bit and let him know what's up.

She might not want me to take care of her, but I'm not leaving until she's better.

～

Harper

I'm sitting at the breakfast bar in my kitchen with Garrett, slurping down chicken soup. I feel like I got run over by a truck, but at least the virus seems to be done with me. About twenty hours of wretchedness. It's late Monday night now, and I'm hoping, after a good night's sleep, I'll be able to go to work tomorrow.

"I can't believe you stuck around," I say. "And you cleaned. That's saint territory. Really, you didn't have to do all that."

"I take care of those I love."

My head whips toward his, my heart pounding.

He smiles. "Why do you look so surprised?"

"We haven't been dating that long."

"Little over a month, but I feel like we've really gotten to know each other."

I stare at the counter, checking in with my gut. No warning flags go up. *I do love him.* My throat clogs with emotion, and I can't seem to get the words out.

"You don't have to say anything back," he says.

I lift my head and clear my throat. "I do feel something for you. It's just hard for me."

"Sure, I understand. Just baggage. Your exes. Men, in general."

"I'll get there. Don't you have any baggage?"

"Not really. Things have always been clear to me. It's either working or it's not. This right here feels like it's working. More than that, it's special. You think I clean just anyone's bathroom?"

"No." My voice comes out small.

"It wasn't pretty."

"I know. God, I'm so sorry. You didn't have to do that."

"You think you'll make it to work tomorrow?"

"I have to. Besides, I'm better."

"You've barely eaten your soup. You look like a strong breeze would knock you over."

"I'll power through." I kiss him. "Thank you for everything."

He smiles, his eyes warm on mine. "You're welcome."

After our meal, which was just soup and crackers for me (he had grilled chicken and vegetables), we settle on the sofa to watch a movie. I let him pick, and I'm surprised he puts on a Star Trek movie.

"You're a Trekkie?" I ask.

"I like space movies, all kinds. It's like the last place you see a renegade hero. Everywhere else is just same old."

"Sort of like westerns used to be with the rugged cowboy living life on his own terms."

"Exactly."

I snuggle up against his side, feeling more content than I can remember. "I think I love you too," I whisper.

He kisses my hair. "I know it."

I'm too tired to worry about what this all means for our future, so I let myself lean on him and soak in the moment.

I'm getting ready for bed later that night when Garrett rushes into the bathroom. "Out!" he barks, rushing to the toilet.

I don't make it all the way out the door before he pukes up his dinner. Oh God. I rush back to the sink and throw up mine. The sound of his retching triggered my gag reflex. I quickly rinse and rush out of the room, shutting the door behind me.

I can still hear him in there, and nausea rises in my throat. I escape to the living room. I'm not sick. It's empathy vomit. This is bad. Now if I try to take care of him the way he took care of me, I'll just make it worse.

I wait until I hear him stumbling into the bedroom. I hope he doesn't collapse. There's no way I can lift him.

He climbs into bed. "Definitely a virus. Otherwise, mine wouldn't have been so delayed. Put the trash can by my side."

I quickly do as he says. "I'm sorry, but I can't hear you get sick because it triggers me to get sick. I'll sleep in the living room, but call out if you need me. I'll try to help."

He grunts.

It's a long night. I can hear him stumbling to the bathroom and staying there for a long time. I listen for a crash. If he goes down, it's going to be loud. But he doesn't. He just lumbers back and forth all night. Hopefully, he'll be better by tomorrow, and I'll order him chicken soup just like he did for me. I've never had to take care of someone before. My grandmother never got sick when I was a kid. At least not that I ever knew about. Maybe she hid it well. And I've never lived with someone who was sick before either.

He rises at noon and makes his way to the living room. "I'm starting to feel human again. Did you miss another day of work?"

"Yes. I didn't want to leave in case you needed me."

He collapses on the sofa next to me. "Nasty virus. I just hope we didn't give it to anyone at the party."

"It's possible we got it from someone at the party."

"Or it could've been from someone in the cast of *Wicked*. I shook a lot of hands. Who knows? I'm gonna check in with my family." He pulls out his phone, sends a few texts, and leans his head back on the sofa a few moments later. "Everyone's fine."

"How did you find out so fast?"

"It's lunch hour at work. I've got my brothers on a group text. Then I just checked in with my mom. Thank God. I didn't want the newborn twins to be exposed. They're home now."

"Do you want to watch TV?" I ask.

"Sure, I could use a distraction."

I hand him the remote, and he switches it to a car channel, where the mechanics are fixing up a car and telling the viewer how to do it. Such a guy way to relax.

He slides an arm around my shoulders.

I feel so close to him. No one has ever taken care of me like he did. Except my grandmother, but she had to. She loves me in her way. It's just not the way I needed. I need to forgive her for that. We're like oil and water. Just the way we're made.

But, Garrett, we're like mud, sticking together. *How romantic, Harp!*

"You were so good at taking care of me," I say.

He gives me a wry smile. "You're a shitty nurse."

"I know. I'm sorry. Empathy nausea was too much for me to function."

"It's okay. I survived. I'm used to my mom, who's like an ER doc and Florence Nightingale wrapped in one."

"Would you have preferred your mom?"

"Nah. I prefer a shitty, sexy nurse any day." He kisses me and slides a hand under my shirt.

I push him away with a laugh. "Next weekend. No way I can manage sex after what I've been through. You too. Aren't you feeling exhausted and weak?"

"I'll make you do all the work." He lifts me to straddle his lap and kisses me tenderly. "You can nurse me back to health this way."

Who would've guessed? I'm a fantastic nurse after all.

19

––––––––––

Harper

The next three weeks are a blur of work and seeing Garrett every chance I get. I'm on a roller coaster of emotion like I've never felt before. I'm flying high when I'm with him and irritable when we're apart. It must be love—exhausting and exhilarating at the same time.

I finish filming *Living Gold* on Friday, our second to last taping, and drag myself back to my trailer, stretching out on the sofa. I should be getting home, but I need to lie down first. I can't remember ever feeling so exhausted before. It must be lingering fatigue from the stomach virus combined with truly being in love for the first time. Those other times were more about me telling myself I was in love. This is the real deal.

There's a knock on my trailer door.

"Come in," I call. Joe's out there, so he would've cleared anyone first.

The door pops open, and Josie steps inside. "Are you okay? You haven't seemed quite your usual energetic self."

I sit up. "I'm not, but it'll be okay. It's just lingering fatigue from that stomach virus. It took a lot out of me, and it takes time to build your strength back. I'm not even back to my full workout routine."

She sits next to me and squeezes my arm. "Maybe you should see a doctor. What if it's something more serious?"

"Garrett had the same thing, and he's fine. Last weekend he ran a 5K. For fun."

She shakes her head. "What a show-off. Did he tell you it was for fun?"

"Yes."

"He and his brothers are such athletes. They need to flex those muscles once in a while. Of course, your guy flexes all the time with his weight lifting. I bet he could lift both of us, one in each hand."

I laugh. "Like a circus guy."

"Right?" She gets serious. "Have you heard anything about the show getting picked up?"

"Nothing yet. All I know is it's not building in the ratings like they hoped."

She wrings her hands together. "I feel responsible. It's the first time I was the lead in a show. Maybe I'm not appealing enough."

"Josie, it's not you. You're fantastic. Really. Who knows why one show strikes a chord and another doesn't? It's out of our hands."

She nods, her expression somber. "What will you do if it doesn't?"

"I refuse to think about that until I know for sure."

She blows out a breath. "My agent sent me a pile of scripts to look over. I think that's a bad sign."

"Not necessarily. Maybe she's just thinking of work for your hiatus."

"Do you want me to put in a good word with Claire? You said you hoped to direct something for her."

"I have her info. I'll get in touch when the time is right."

"You're awfully calm about everything."

"Well, I have two advantages. One, this is my fourth show, so I know they don't last forever. And two, I can't even think about moving away for work. Things are really good with Garrett." My eyes water. I get so emotional whenever his name comes up. "He's coming over later to cook me dinner."

She claps and hugs me. "I'm so happy for you! Don't tell the others, but Garrett is my favorite of Sean's brothers. He just has such a good heart, ya know?"

I nod and a tear escapes.

"Oh no! Why're you crying? That's a good thing!"

I sniffle. "I know. I've never truly been in love before." I grab a tissue and wipe my eyes. "I thought I was before, but this is way more intense. I guess when someone gets in deep, it sort of loosens the defensive walls."

She smiles. "You're like Marian the librarian at the end of *The Music Man* when she's open and happier because of it. I'd better call Broadway and tell them to get you into a revival of that show. You're perfect for it."

"Was it like that for you and Sean?"

She looks thoughtful, her lips pursing in concentration. "Not exactly. I didn't have defensive walls around my emotions. It was more like, I needed him to take my work seriously, even though I was the one who really needed to own that. It was at a time when I got nothing but rejections. Fortunately, he's the steady sort, who never wavered in his feelings for me. Once he *finally* admitted he had them."

Her phone buzzes, and she checks the screen. "Speaking of my honey. I gotta go. Enjoy your dinner tonight. What's he making you?"

"Risotto, I think."

"Oh, I want to come with you! I've had his risotto. Did you know every time he house-sits for us, he leaves a dinner for our first night back?"

"I didn't know, but I'm not surprised at all." I hesitate. "You and Sean are welcome to join us."

"Ha, thanks. I can tell you want your honey all to yourself."

"I missed him this week."

"So sweet!" She stands and hugs herself, rocking side to side. "I remember that delicious falling-into-each-other feeling. Now it's all—" she imitates Sean's gruff voice "—I love you, now strip." She claps a hand over her mouth. "Oops! TMI. Gotta go!"

I laugh and see her to the door. Then I head out, Joe in tow, to meet my love.

Garrett

I knock on my love's door, freshly showered, two bags of groceries in hand.

She opens it. "I love you."

I smile widely. "I love you too, sweetheart." I set the bags down on the kitchen counter and turn to face her.

She launches herself into my arms. "I mean I really love you. I miss you terribly when we're apart, and I'm happy the moment I see your face again." She peppers my face with kisses.

She's the One. I finally found her. I do the only logical thing. I scoop her up, cradled in my arms, and carry her to the bedroom. "Dinner can wait."

"I want you so bad."

I strip her down the moment we get to her bedroom, and she helps take my clothes off. We slam together in a frenzy as the fire ignites between us. Then we tumble into bed, a tangle of arms and legs.

I cover her, holding my weight on my forearms.

Her fingers slide to the nape of my neck. "No matter what happens, let's never forget this moment."

I still. "What would happen?"

"Circumstances beyond our control. I don't know. Take me." She grabs my ass and pulls hard.

I thrust deep. It feels so good without the condom. She's the only woman I've ever had like this. Her trust in me was there from the beginning. It only needed time to surface beyond the physical.

I pump slowly, gazing into her eyes. "I could never forget a single moment."

"Me either," she whispers, her eyes shiny with unshed tears.

Something deep passes between us. Our emotions binding us together. Nothing could be better than this.

"More," she demands.

I give her what she needs, sliding a hand under her hip and angling her, taking her deep. The way we both need.

Her soft sounds of pleasure fuel my own. I rock into her faster and harder until we're both panting. She throws her head back, crying out with her release, and I let go with a harsh sound, pleasure flooding me. So damn good.

I collapse against her, and she holds me tight. She doesn't want to let me go. Neither do I.

Long moments later, she loosens her hold, and I roll off her. She wipes her cheeks.

"What's wrong?" I ask, propping up on an elbow.

"Nothing," she says with a laugh. "I've just been feeling everything really deeply lately. It's your fault, I'm sure. Making me love you so much."

"You sure that's all?" Josie told me they were all nervous about the show's ratings. If it gets cancelled, more than a hundred people are out of work. Including my love. I don't want her to move halfway around the world for work, but at the same time I could never hold her back. We'll figure something out.

"Yeah. I mean, my future job security is uncertain, but that's the life I signed up for. And I wouldn't want to be playing the same character the rest of my life anyway. That would get old."

I kiss her. "You hungry?"

She presses herself against my side. "Just hold me a little longer."

That's not like her. I'm the cuddler more than she is. I wrap an arm around her, concerned. "If you got a new job in LA or wherever, we could do the long-distance thing. You'd come back eventually, right? Josie's found more work in New York than she originally thought." Now that I'm taking Jack's place as crew chief, I'm staying rooted here. I can still take modeling and commercial gigs locally. That's a huge advantage of working for family. They're flexible and don't mind me taking a day off here and there.

"Let's not go there. I just want to enjoy now."

I wish I could, but her tears have me on edge. "Does it bother you that the press dubbed you Princess Harper?" The paparazzi have snapped photos of us in front of her building when we go out. They're calling us the royal duo. Almost sounds like we're superheroes, so I don't mind.

"It's better than having everyone think I'm the tough bitch I used to play on TV. Half the time they call me Amanda. Princess Harper sounds regal and softer too."

"Okay. But I'm all ears if anything's bothering you. I just don't remember you being so teary before."

She sighs. "I'm exhausted, to be honest, between work and recovering from that stomach virus."

My brows knit together. "It's been three weeks. I thought you'd bounce back like I did."

"Maybe it's the stress of knowing our show's ending soon. Next Friday is our last episode. Will you be there for the taping and the wrap party?"

I stroke her cheek and kiss her. "Absolutely."

She hugs my middle. "It'll be a little subdued since we don't know if it's goodbye forever or for the season."

"That's fine. As long as it's not *our* goodbye forever."

Her eyes widen. "Why would you say that?"

"Uh, because I don't want to say goodbye."

"Me either."

"Good."

"Fine," she says, rolling to her back. "It just sounded like you were implying something."

"You're so touchy lately." I'm about to ask if she has PMS, but then think better of it. I've had my head ripped off for that question before. Instead I tuck her close. She burrows into my chest and sighs.

∼

Harper

So *Living Gold* was cancelled yesterday. I've mourned, cried my eyes out, bitched to Josie and Garrett, and now I'm trying to be fine with it. It's been twenty-four hours, and my agent is putting out feelers for my next gig. I'm not just upset because it ended after one season, it's because I fear what this means for my future with Garrett. I should get in touch with Claire about directing, though it doesn't necessarily mean I'll be local. Most work is still in LA. I can't seem to muster enthusiasm for anything. I'm not myself—restless, agitated, nothing appeals, whether it's food or books or TV. I'm about to jump out of my skin.

Garrett's stopping by tonight. He was here last night, too, to comfort me about the show's demise.

The moment he arrives, I know something's up. He's pumped full of energy and bounds inside, hugging me and kissing me soundly on the mouth.

"What's going on?" Maybe he found a house he liked. After his two commercials, he can afford it.

"Guess," he says, bouncing a bit.

"Did you buy a house?"

One corner of his mouth lifts. "No, sweetheart, I'd want your input on that."

My heart squeezes, my throat tight. He makes it sound like we have a definite future together. I'd like that. "Did you book another commercial?"

"Better. My agent got me a part in a prequel to *Journey to the Galaxy*." He rubs his hands together. "Someone dropped out, and he got me in. Can you believe it? I'm going to play Drake's dad in a flashback. Me, part of the *Journey to the Galaxy* franchise!"

My lips part, momentarily speechless. That is a *major* movie franchise. After only two months of acting lessons and two commercials. I know the industry isn't fair, I know beautiful people have an advantage, but I'm still...stunned.

His eyes sparkle with happiness. "Say something."

"What about your job?"

"I'll only be away for six weeks. I leave this Sunday, and I'll be back in time for Christmas." He smiles widely. "My brothers are willing to pitch in during my absence. They're psyched for me. We're all big fans of *Journey to the Galaxy*."

"Congratulations," I force out.

He gets serious. "Are you mad?"

My mind boggles with everything I'm feeling. He's leaving. He's surpassing me. I just lost my job and feel shitty all the time, and he's on top of the world. Every fear and worry I've suppressed bubbles to the surface.

I keep my tone even. "It's hard to get over how easy it is for you to get gigs. I paid my dues. You didn't."

"Who knows, maybe this is the end of the road for me. I don't pretend to have your skills. You're a true artist. But I'm willing to work hard to get there."

I tell myself to swallow the bitterness, but what comes out is exactly how I feel. "That all sounds great, but the fact is, all of this industry work was so damn easy for you. And it's because of me. You never would've had an 'in' if I hadn't gotten you in the spotlight. My grandmother warned me you'd use me and surpass me. Hell, it's not like it's never happened before, so what did I expect, right? Why should I be blindsided once again by the person I thought loved me stepping over me on his way to better things?" At his silence, I throw my hands up. "See, it's true! You have nothing to say to that."

He clenches his jaw. "I can't believe you think that about me. I am *not* like your user exes."

I cock my head. "I'm sorry, did you get a modeling gig before the press went nuts over us walking the red carpet together?"

"I could've done that without you."

"But you never did. You were industry adjacent. You knew people in it—your mom modeling, Josie acting—but it's not until you met me that you went for it. And that's because my spotlight shone on you. Now I'm out of work, and it's all you, you, you." My voice cracks.

"Ya know, Harp. I don't like your tone here."

I straighten my spine. "Oh, so sorry I have a tone."

He jabs a finger at me. "Haven't I been good to you?"

I cross my arms, hugging myself. My throat is so tight I can barely speak. "That's what hurts the most. I let you in. I trusted you. You didn't even talk to me about taking this job in LA. Just told me after the fact. Couples are supposed to talk about stuff ahead of time if their relationship is the most important thing. Obviously for you, it isn't."

"Because I thought it was a no-brainer." He frowns. "I didn't think you'd resent me for taking the opportunity of a lifetime. Just to be on set would be an honor, but to actually play Drake's father? That's major. I can't turn it down. I'm committed and they need me."

I need you. I keep that to myself. It sounds weak. I'm strong and stand on my own two feet. I never ask anyone for anything. That's not how I was raised.

He plants his hands on his hips and lets out a long breath like he's frustrated with me. I'm the one who's frustrated with him. Here I am, putting us first, thinking of every next step with the two of us in mind, and he just goes out and does this. My eyes get hot.

"Do you want me to get you a part?" he asks. "Maybe there's still a role you could step in for."

I wipe away tears. "Don't do me any favors."

He steps closer, his tone gentling. "I'm sure you'll find something soon. Hey, why don't you come with me since you're not working at the moment?"

"They always keep the script and filming locked up tight because of the huge fan base. That means you're going to be spending all your time on a closed set." My gut churns, nausea rising in my throat. "You won't have time for me. Besides, I told my grandmother I'd go home for Thanksgiving and Christmas. So you do your thing. Have fun."

"Do you not want me to take this job?" he barks, and I jump, my hand flying to my throat. "Am I supposed to choose to stay here with you and turn down the opportunity that takes me away? I said you could come with me!"

I seriously feel like I'm going to be sick. "I'm not going with you."

"And you're okay with me taking the job?"

I breathe in deep, trying to keep the nausea at bay. "Garrett, you already told them yes. What does it matter what I say at this point? You've got the fabulous acting career you wanted. Enjoy it."

He scowls. "You know what? I thought we were past this bullshit. I thought you trusted me. I thought you loved me."

I suck in air. "I do love you."

"No," he snaps. "If you really loved me, you'd support me. You'd be happy when I'm happy and root for me all the way." He slices a hand through the air. "You're too tangled up in your own ego and ambition to give me this. You'll always resent that I have something the camera likes, that an audience will like."

"You're twisting this all around. You're the one who's leaving me behind for better things. Just like everyone in my life." I turn away. "I don't know why I thought you'd be different."

He shifts, standing in front of me. "Maybe I got lucky, having the right look, being at the right place at the right time, but I know I also have good instincts. Everyone says I have huge potential."

I press my lips together, fighting tears, and nod.

"Everyone but you." He shakes his head. "Life's hard enough without the person who's supposed to be closest to you resenting your success."

"I don't resent it. I'm hurt."

"Yeah, well, so am I." He takes a step back. "I don't want to be with someone who can't root for me. Goodbye, Harper."

I gasp. "What?"

"It's over."

I can't find my voice. I'm too shocked.

He turns and walks out the door.

I stumble back to the sofa, curl my knees up, and burst into tears. God, could things suck any worse? Here I was worried about my future job prospects and how to keep him in my life, and he just walked out for his own job. It was so easy for him too. He didn't hesitate, just walked out. Another wrenching sob escapes. Everything that held me back from investing fully in this relationship was peeled away by his warmth and affection, and then he took it all away.

I lost him.

Oh God. Why did I say those hurtful things? I should've kept my cool. But I couldn't. Even now, my emotions are overwhelming me, making me feel sick and shaky.

I slap a hand over my mouth and run to the bathroom to puke up my guts. God, on top of everything else—my job ending, my relationship crumbling, and I'm still sick? I'm falling apart physically and emotionally, and I don't have the strength to deal with it all. I'm so damn tired. I clean up and stumble to my bed, flopping down on it.

What is wrong with me? I've always been sensitive, my emotions close to the surface, but I've never felt so out of control. I don't even truly believe he used me. Not anymore. I lashed out with all those old fears when I should've pulled him in close. That's all I wanted was for him to stay close. To put us first the way I was trying to do.

I curl up on my side and let the tears fall. The best part of my life just walked out the door, and I have no idea how to get him back.

20

———

Harper

It's Thanksgiving Day, and I'm back in Summerdale at my grandmother's house. I tried to get in touch with Garrett, but he won't take my calls or respond to my texts. He's ghosting me or maybe he's just caught up in his exciting new work, but he's going to have to deal with me when he gets home for Christmas because—

I'm pregnant.

I found out two weeks ago. I finally went to the doctor because I just didn't seem to be getting better, and that's when I got the big news. In hindsight, the symptoms were all there, but I was fooled by the fact that I'd taken an early pregnancy test that came out negative. I'd noticed I was three days late and still hadn't bounced back from the stomach virus. With the negative results, I'd figured my cycle was just off from being sick.

Turns out things did get screwed up from my stomach virus. I missed a day of taking the pill when I first got sick, and the next night I took it and then threw it up a few minutes later when Garrett threw up. So two nights without the pill gave my body a brief window of opportunity for conception. I was so caught up in a roller coaster of emotions with the show ending and then Garrett ending us, plus hormones, that, well, it wasn't easy to think clearly for a while there.

Now I am. I'm keeping this baby, already very much in love with the life stirring inside me. I'm twenty-eight with the means to care for a child. I'll do everything I can for Garrett to be part of the baby's life, even if he doesn't want to be part of mine. I plan to tell him in person when he returns.

I still haven't told anyone. My secret joy is mixed with shame and fear. I was an accidental pregnancy. I swore I would never do that to my child. My grandmother never bothered to disguise her disappointment in my mother. How can I tell her I've done the same thing? She'll judge me, maybe even tell me never to come back the way she told my mother.

I'll be a disappointment to my grandmother all over again. The only mother I've ever known.

I blink back tears as I baste the small Cornish hen in the oven. Grandmom is too practical to waste a big turkey on the two of us. I break off part of a roll and chew. Bland food is my friend now, keeping the nausea at bay. I glance over to where she's sitting at the small Formica-topped kitchen table, peeling potatoes.

"How's your Gary?" she asks. "Thought he might come with you today."

I turn, my jaw tight. "It's Garrett."

She nods. "That was a reference to Gary Cooper."

"He's in LA filming a movie."

She peels more furiously. "I see."

I join her at the table. "He broke up with me. I wasn't too happy with him leaving me for better things, and I said some things I regret. Now he won't talk to me."

"Have I taught you nothing?"

"I know. Life's unfair."

She gives me a sideways look. "If you regret what you said, you should go to him and say so. Chin up. Use that strength I drilled into you."

"I wanted to be here for Thanksgiving with you."

"Hogwash." She picks up another potato, peeling efficiently.

"I did. You're getting up there in maturity."

She eyes me. "You resent him."

I sigh. "I don't. Not anymore. It was the heat of the moment, and I didn't know…" I stop myself and stand, not ready to share my big news yet. "I had a lot of stuff going on at the time."

She grabs my arm in a tight grip. "I thought he was more than a user."

"You did?"

She looks up at me. "How many young men do chores for their girlfriend's grandmother? None of your past boyfriends gave me the time of day, let alone offered to do work for me."

My eyes sting with hot tears. "I don't know what to tell you. He doesn't want to be with me. He left, and I haven't heard from him since. He doesn't respond to my calls or texts."

"So go to him."

"You don't understand. It's a closed set. He wouldn't have time for me." *And I'm not ready.* I pull away and get the cranberries out, rinsing them at the sink. She doesn't say another word. My thoughts tumble over each other, replaying the last time I saw Garrett, and all my worries and fears about the future for me and my baby. I can manage on my own if I have to. I know I can. But it won't be easy. I have to tell him, and I have to tell my grandmother too. No one else needs to know the particulars.

Once we're settled for Thanksgiving dinner, my grandmother asks me about my future job prospects.

"I don't know. I might have a lead on directing something." I still need to set up a meeting with Claire Jordan. Hopefully, something will come through. It's been difficult to think of anything beyond my pregnancy. It was such a shock. And now a secret joy.

"What about movies? I know you want to do them."

"My agent takes care of that. If something comes up I'm right for, he'll let me know."

She sets her fork down and wipes her mouth with a napkin. "So no more Princess Harper, huh?"

I stare at the table. "No."

"Didn't suit you anyway. You're much stronger than any wimpy princess flaunting their silly gowns."

I'm not so strong. I'm afraid to tell you about the baby. My eyes get hot, and I will myself not to cry. Grandmom could never stand the sight of tears.

"If you miss him so much, call him." She jabs her finger toward the phone on the wall. "Go ahead and use my phone. I'll pay for the long distance." She must sense I'm near tears if she's willing to cover the long distance.

I want to laugh and cry at the same time. As if everything could be fixed with a phone call. He'd probably answer, thinking it was my grandmother, and then hang up on me. I know our next conversation has to be face-to-face. "It's complicated."

She harrumphs. "Doesn't have to be. Tell him what's what. You want him back. You can both be actors. The world is big enough for the two of you."

I take a deep breath and blurt it out. "The three of us."

"What?"

I look down at my stomach. "I'm pregnant." I risk a look at her, expecting judgment. Instead she just looks shocked, her hand over her mouth.

My gut churns. "I know my mother sprang the same news on you in the same stupid accidental way—"

She drops her hand. "This is nothing like your mom. She was a rebellious teen. You're nothing like her." She takes my hand. "I'll help you raise the child. You'll stay here."

Tears leak out. "I thought you'd be mad or disappointed or something."

"Honey, this is a much different situation. You're mature with a good head on your shoulders. You can handle this. Your mother, well, that was my fault. I failed her."

"What?"

She shakes her head, her lips twisting. "She was the last of my four kids, a surprise baby at forty, and my only girl. I spoiled her, we all did. She became ungrateful and entitled. And when she was a teen, rebellious. We let her think she could do no wrong. But then she did. She got together with an older man she met at a bar, getting in with a fake ID." She exhales sharply. "When I think of what could've happened to her going around bars. Turned out she'd been doing that since she was seventeen. No matter what your grandfather and I did, we couldn't get her under control. Anyway, your father never knew about you. I tried off and on over the years to track him down based on the information she gave me, and finally found out he died when you were five. That was the year your grandfather died, and I was too caught up in mourning to say anything about it. Ultimately, I decided it was better if you thought he had another family and that's why he couldn't be in your life."

My jaw drops. "My dad never knew about me?" That's so much better than thinking he didn't care. Not that it matters now since he died.

"I'm sorry, Harper. I did what I thought was best at the time. I should've told you the truth."

That makes me wonder if she lied about my mom too. "You always said my mom dropped me off after she had me and took off. Is that true? Why wouldn't she come back to visit? Did you tell her not to?"

She closes her eyes for a moment, a pained expression on her face. "She planned to give you up for adoption. When I found out, I pressed her for the details. Her plan was to leave you bundled on the doorstep of a childless couple in town. Like a present. Well, I was having none of that. You're my granddaughter. I told her I'd adopt you and that was the end of it. I was fifty-nine at the time, and my only goal was to stay alive long enough to see you launched into the world. And here we are. Who knew I'd live this long?"

I stare at her, my mind whirling at all this unexpected news. Everything is so different than I thought it was growing up.

"I never told her not to visit," she says. "That was her choice."

I nod, my throat tight. After meeting my biological mother briefly when she asked me for money, well, I can't say I missed out on much. She never loved me, not like my grandmother did.

I give her a watery smile. "It's hard to imagine you spoiling your daughter. You've always been so strict."

She takes my hand and gives it a squeeze. "With you it was only because I was trying not to make the same mistake I made with her. I was tough because I wanted you to be strong and sure of yourself. I wanted you to stand on your own two feet. She got too much outside validation. It made her weak and susceptible to others."

I press my lips together. "You were too hard on me."

"Because I loved you, dear girl." Tears shine in her eyes.

And now I'm crying. "I always felt like I couldn't live up to your standards. I'm not naturally tough. I'm sensitive."

"I saw that in you, and I tried to make you more, to protect you. It seems I screwed up both my daughters."

I laugh through my tears. "You did. But I don't think I could have the job I do now without that strength and toughness, so I guess I owe you a thank-you for that."

She gestures me over and hugs me. "I'm sorry I was hard on you. I love you. I know I don't say it much, but I do."

I kiss her papery thin cheek. "I love you too."

She pushes me away. "Now eat. You have to keep up your strength for the baby. I'm going to get you some prenatal vitamins, and I want you to make an appointment with a doctor right away."

I sniffle and take my seat. "I am taking vitamins, and I already found a doctor."

"My girl." She pats my hand. "You have to tell him, you know."

"I know but not yet. When he gets back, I will, face-to-face."

"You do what you think is right."

I slice a piece of chicken, my appetite returning. "Always do."

She laughs. "You're a lot more like me than you realize. We're both badass women."

My head jerks up. "Grandmom!" She never uses foul language.

"Own it," she says.

I laugh. "Always."

Garrett

I'm back from LA after six weeks and three days away, and I'm man enough to admit it—cutting ties with Harper was a huge mistake. I couldn't enjoy myself in LA because I missed her too much. I get that she's sensitive about being used for her celebrity, and I should've stuck it out. Instead, my own sensitivity kicked in, making me defensive and cut ties. And for what? Who knows if I'll get another job again in the movie industry. It depends if the movie takes off, if casting directors like what they saw from me, on so many factors out of my control.

I don't kid myself that I'm a great talent like Harper, though my acting coach is pleased with my progress and says if I keep working at it, I can get to a professional level. Right now, let's face it, I'm mostly eye candy with a bonus of having royal blood. Audiences like that. I'm like a curious exhibit at the zoo, and that's not something you can build a career on. I guess my own ego got in the way this time.

Pride held me back from getting in touch with her. Stupid, I know. Now that I'm back home, it feels urgent to see her. It's Christmas Eve. She's not home, and she's not answering my texts. My calls went to voicemail. I can only hope she's at her grandmother's house. I want to spend Christmas with her. My family is in Villroy again to celebrate the holidays, and I had to miss it because of my work schedule. I miss everybody, but mostly I miss Harper.

Only one way to find out. I call her grandmother. She actually called me the day after Thanksgiving to ask when I'd be back because she needed some boxes moved out of the attic. And then she gave me her number so I'd let her know. She must really like me. Harper said she has a handyman on retainer to do any odd jobs her grandmother needs, so it's not like I'm the only one who could help her move boxes.

The phone rings five times before she picks up. "Hello?"

"Hi, Mrs. Ellis. It's Garrett. I'm back in town. Is Harper with you?"

"Yes." The phone sounds muffled. "Harper! Go check the mailbox for me. I'm waiting on some Christmas cards to make sure my cousins haven't kicked the bucket."

I hear Harper muttering something in the background. *My love.*

"Ma'am—" I start.

"Tsk," she says, then a moment later, "She's gone to get the mail. How soon can you get here?"

Hope fires through me. "Hour and a half, two tops."

"Okay, I know she's anxious to visit her friends, but I'll keep her here for you. She has something to tell you."

My mind races. *Did she meet someone else? Is she moving to LA for a job? London?* "What?"

"Not for me to say. Now don't go speeding to get here. I know how to keep the girl busy."

"I'm sure you do. Thank you, ma'am."

"See you soon but not too soon. Bye."

Thankfully, the roads are clear as I ride my Harley to her grandmother's house. It was too hard to rent a car at the last minute around the holidays, and I don't like to ride my bike on icy roads. I take this as a good sign. I was meant to get to her today. I really hope it's not bad news. If she met someone, I'll win her back. If she's working thousands of miles away, I'll visit. As long as we don't have to completely end.

By the time I turn down her street, I realize I should've brought a present for her and her grandmother. It's Christmas. I was so focused on seeing Harper, I completely forgot. I turn and go around the lake to a small grocery store I passed on the way. It's afternoon on Christmas Eve, so I'm hoping it's still open.

I park and go to the door just as a guy puts the closed sign up. They close at four p.m. on Christmas Eve. "Wait!" I say through the glass door. "Can I just get two things?" I stare for a moment, struck by the store employee's resemblance to Santa Claus. He's got white wavy hair, a long white beard, and black suspenders over a red shirt covering a round belly.

"It's Christmas Eve," he says. "We're closed."

"Sir, I need a present for my girl and her grandmother. I need to win her back. Do you have flowers, candy, or Christmas cookies? Anything that would help a foolish man get back in the good graces of the only woman he's ever truly loved?" *Heart on my sleeve with nothing to lose. That's me.*

He unlocks the door. "Who's the girl and grandmother?"

"Harper and Joan Ellis."

"Joan Ellis, hmm? I might have something she likes." He winks and turns, gesturing for me to follow. "She's a tough one, but if anything's going to win her over, it's this."

I follow him to the holiday section. He points out a red wooden soldier nutcracker. "Seems appropriate, huh, sonny?"

I shake my head. The meaning is not lost on me. Guess she's hard on everyone. I grab a stuffed reindeer and a stuffed Santa. At least they're cute. "Do you have any flowers or candy?"

"No flowers this time of year. Candy's up front by the register."

I take my gifts to the front register and scan the offerings. It's just candy bars and gum. I push my plush presents forward and pull out my wallet. "This'll do. Thanks so much."

"You one of Harper's Hollywood friends?" he asks.

"No. My sister-in-law's an actress. We met through her."

He rings it up. "Well, we've always been rooting for her here in town. Let her know I tune into *Living Gold* every week."

"I'm sure she'd like to hear that. I didn't catch your name."

"Nicholas."

St. Nicholas? I clamp my mouth shut over my little joke. "Thanks for your help today, Nicholas."

I pay for the items, stuff them safely into my leather jacket, and continue on my way. I park in the street in front of her grandmother's house and notice a dark blue Ford pickup truck in the driveway. Since I can't imagine Mrs. Ellis driving this huge thing, I'm hoping Harper rented it. Only my churning gut tells me it's a man's truck. All of my warm feelings take a dive. This is what Harper needs to talk to me about—she met someone. But why would Mrs. Ellis tell me to come over, then? To force a confrontation? I know she's not the cuddly grandmother type, but I didn't think she was deliberately mean.

I ring the bell, leaving my gifts tucked into my jacket. It makes me look like I gained fifty pounds, but I'm not facing her new boyfriend holding a stuffed reindeer and Santa.

Harper opens the door. "Garrett! I didn't know you'd be here." She looks amazing, her eyes bright, her skin glowing. She's wearing an oversized V-neck red sweater, black leggings, and black boots. I just want to scoop her up and carry her away.

"I called and texted you today, but you didn't answer. I'm sorry it took me so long to get in touch."

Her eyes go soft. "I turned my phone off at my grandmother's insistence. She wanted my full focus on helping her decorate the tree. Come in."

I step inside. A guy around my age is standing in the living room in a long-sleeved blue cotton shirt, jeans, and sneakers. Dammit, he's good looking. *Actor?*

Mrs. Ellis rises from her chair. "Garrett, this is Drew, a friend of Harper's. She's known him her whole life as someone to count on. Strong and a good provider." She smiles at him and then turns to Harper. "Special forces in the military, so he'll keep you safe too."

Red-hot jealousy spikes through me, and my hands form fists.

Garrett

"So this is your new guy?" I ask Harper. "Did you wait at all after we broke up, or did you just call him right away?"

Harper gasps and turns to her grandmother. "Are you trying to instigate something?"

The guy rubs the back of his neck. "I thought your heat wasn't working. It seems warm enough in here."

"Yeah, you're not needed here," I say. "You should go." I jerk my head toward the door.

He ambles closer and narrows his eyes at me.

Mrs. Ellis claps. "You two should take it outside."

The guy stares me down. "Who are you?"

I get into battle stance, legs wide, fists at the ready. "I'm the guy who's gonna be with Harper long term."

He shakes his head. "Fine by me. I'm here to fix the heat."

"I can do that," I say.

"There's nothing wrong with the heat," Harper says.

Mrs. Ellis plants her hands on her hips. "Well, if you're not going to fight, we should all have cocoa and cookies to catch up."

Harper goes to my side. "Drew, I'm so sorry she called you all the way over here for nothing."

His lips twitch. "I should've known she was up to something." He leans around her to address Mrs. Ellis. "Thanks for the offer of cocoa, but my family's expecting me for our own Christmas Eve celebration."

"Thanks for stopping by," she carols, taking her seat. "Merry Christmas."

"You too." He lets himself out.

The moment he does, Harper scowls at her grandmother. "What in the world are you doing? Dragging Drew out here for a false errand on Christmas Eve!"

She smiles serenely. "I wanted to see if Garrett would rise to the occasion. Jealous? Check. Tough enough to go toe-to-toe with an Army Ranger? Check. Men should be men. Thank God you got a real man this time."

Harper throws her hands up. "We broke up, Grandmom, you know that."

"Take off your jacket," Mrs. Ellis says to me. "Stay a while."

I unzip my jacket and pull out the stuffed reindeer and Santa, which seem utterly ridiculous in light of all the turmoil going through me now. I can't wait another minute to say what I have to say.

"Harper, we need to talk. Can we go outside?"

"It's freezing out there," Mrs. Ellis says. "Talk in here."

Harper turns to her and says in an even tone, "I'd like some privacy to talk to him, please."

Mrs. Ellis lets out a huge sigh and rises from her chair with some difficulty. "I'll go upstairs, but don't be doing anything inappropriate on my sofa."

"We'll try to restrain ourselves," Harper deadpans.

Mrs. Ellis slowly makes her way to her chairlift, and I just know this is going to take way too long for me and Harper to connect.

I follow her. "Ma'am, could I carry you upstairs? You look like you weigh one hundred pounds soaking wet. It's no problem." I hold my arms out to her.

Her face flushes, and she calls over to Harper, "Your fellow is ridiculous." She turns to me. "No, thank you, I can manage just fine."

I wink. "I'll get you in my arms one day, Queen Joan."

"Nonsense," she snaps, but I don't miss the twinkle in her eye.

I join Harper on the sofa, and we wait as the chairlift makes its slow humming way upstairs.

"You can start talking now," Mrs. Ellis says. "I can't hear a thing over the noise of this contraption."

"We can hear you," Harper says loudly.

"Harper has something to tell you," Mrs. Ellis says.

"I have something to tell her too," I say.

"Well, what are you waiting for?" Mrs. Ellis demands.

Harper turns to me with an apologetic smile. "Sorry. Let's just pretend to talk until she's in her room."

"Did you meet someone else? Just tell me. I can take it."

"Garrett, there's no one else. Drew is just a friend."

I relax. Everything else is fixable. I hope.

Finally, Mrs. Ellis makes it to a room upstairs and shuts the door.

Harper exhales sharply. "I never thought she'd get there."

"Harp, I've missed you." I go to hug her, but she pushes me away.

"Wait. I need to tell you something, and I want you to know I don't expect anything from you. Okay?"

"Are you moving to LA?" I ask.

"No, stop guessing. Just listen."

"Okay." I brace myself, praying it's not that bad. I want to be with her so much.

"I'm pregnant."

The breath leaves my body, my head spinning.

"Garrett, are you okay?"

I suck in air. "Yeah. I'm okay. You surprised me. I thought you were on the pill. It's mine, right?"

"Of course it's yours. I was only with you."

"Okay, sorry." I shove a hand through my hair. "I'm just so surprised. How did this happen?"

"I missed a dose of the pill when I got that stomach virus, and the next night I threw it up when you got sick, so there was a window. At first, I wasn't sure because the pregnancy test was negative, but then I went to the doctor later, and it was positive."

"When did you know?"

"Four days after you left. I tried calling and texting you, but you didn't respond."

I groan at my own stupidity. "I was mad. I wanted to be fine without you and I wasn't. God, I can't believe I didn't know all this time."

"It's okay. I knew you'd be back, and this was a conversation we needed to have in person." She smiles. "I'm happy about it."

"Me too."

She searches my expression. "You are?"

I take both her hands in mine. "Of course."

She sniffles. "I had all this shame at first. I was an unplanned pregnancy, and I didn't want to follow in my mother's footsteps. And then we broke up. I never expected it to happen this way. I swore my child would be born into the kind of two-parent family I always wanted as a kid. Now all that matters is that the baby is healthy."

I lean forward, elbows on my knees, still reeling. "I was an unplanned pregnancy too. My parents call me a happy accident. Family story goes, Connor was supposed to be the last, the fourth born, but he was such an angel, they decided to have another, and Brendan was such a mischievous devil they were shocked. I was an oops, and my dad got snipped right after, saying six kids was plenty."

"I sure wasn't a happy accident."

I straighten. "This baby is." I stare at her stomach covered by the large sweater. It still looks flat.

"I was going to call you tomorrow about meeting up over the holidays, but I'm so glad you're here now."

I can't take my eyes off her stomach. My daughter or son is in there. "Is everything…okay with it?"

"Yes. I'm eight weeks along, due next June. I want you to be part of the baby's life, but I don't want you to feel like we have to be together because of it."

I push a lock of her hair over her ear. "I'm thrilled to be a dad. I want to be part of this child's life in whatever way you need. And I hope we'll raise the baby together as a couple. And I'm not saying that because of the baby. I came here today to tell you I love you, and this time apart so I could work in a movie wasn't worth losing you. I'll do whatever I can to make sure we're together. I'll run projects by you before I accept. You were right about that. Couples should make these decisions together because it affects both of us. And if you'll have me back, I hope you'll do the same because we're more important than any job."

She throws her arms around me. "I'm sorry I said those hurtful things the last time we talked. I messed up. All I wanted was to keep you close. I'm okay with your acting career. I'm okay with anything you want to do. I'll root for you all the way."

I pull back and frame her face in my hands. Her lower lip wobbles, tears threatening. My own eyes sting too. "I believe we have a future together, Harper. I've waited for the One for a long time. My life started again in a new way the moment we met and for the better."

"Oh, Garrett." She kisses me and hugs me tight for a long moment.

"And now you give me this gift." My voice chokes. She pulls back and strokes my cheek. "A child. It's the best gift you could've given me." I gesture to where the stuffed reindeer and Santa are perched on the coffee table. "Better than my gift for you."

She laughs through tears. "Which one is mine?"

"Whatever one you want." I cradle her jaw and kiss her. Then I stare at her stomach. "Is it okay to touch it?"

"Of course. The baby's protected in there. You can touch." She lifts her sweater, and there's a slight rounding that wasn't there before. I place my hand over it, my throat clogged with emotion. "I don't feel any movement. Are you sure it's okay?"

"It's too tiny to feel yet. Soon."

"You are the One, you know. I want to marry you."

She looks away. "We don't have to be married just because I'm pregnant."

I cup her jaw and turn her back to me. "Don't you understand how much I feel for you? I never want us to be apart again. I knew that before you told me the baby news."

She worries her lower lip. "Maybe we should wait until after the baby's born. You might change your mind."

"Never doubt my word. I will stick with you and Garrett Junior for the rest of my years."

She smiles. "Garrett Junior? What if it's a girl?"

"Joan?"

Her jaw drops. "No, stop."

"What? Your grandmother would love it."

She smiles tenderly. "You actually like her."

"What's not to like? She raised my future wife, the mother of all my future children."

Tears leak out of her eyes, and I pull her close, hugging her.

After a bit, she lifts her head, wiping her tears and sniffling. I fetch her a tissue from her grandmother's side table.

"Thanks," she says. "And, as far as work goes, I'm going to be directing a few episodes of a new show through Claire Jordan's production company. It films in New York. I had a good meeting with her, and we talked about my future career. I'd like to do more behind-the-scenes work that would keep me local. At the time, I was thinking of visitation for you with the baby, but now it means so much more. The exciting part is, she asked me to pitch some show ideas. I like the idea of running a show because that gives me creative control, including where we film. So that means I'll be working closely with her, so I'll be near you. What do you think?"

"I think this is the best Christmas I've ever had. My love found a way to be with me and made us a family."

She smiles and kisses me. "Well, you helped."

"I sure did." I frown, thinking of my part in all this and future encounters. "Did the doctor say it's okay for us to…" I lower my voice, not trusting Mrs. Ellis. She could be eavesdropping. "Make love."

She laughs. "Yes, it's fine. But when I get bigger, it'll be tough to work around the bulge."

"I'm tough. I'll power through."

She beams at me, and my chest aches with all I feel for her, and now for this child. I didn't expect to be a dad, but I couldn't be happier. And I have the down payment on a house now for my new family. I can't wait to tell my parents they'll be grandparents again, but it's too late to call them in Villroy. They'll be in bed.

"Should we tell her she can come down now?" Harper asks.

"Yeah, we're good." Suddenly I know why Mrs. Ellis kept saying Harper had something to tell me. "She knows about the baby, doesn't she? I'm surprised she didn't beat me away with a stick."

"Ha! It wouldn't have done any good. You would've turned that stick into a cane for her with your mad skills and offered to make her another. Such a softie."

"I see past the prickly exterior. She's good people."

"She is. I'll go get her." She heads upstairs.

I lean back on the sofa, the plastic slipcover crinkling under my weight. Now if I could just get Harper to marry me, I could relax. I want the baby to have my name, no question who the father is. I want a solid foundation for him or her. I can't wait to find out what we're having.

A few minutes later, the chairlift makes its slow way down. Harper smiles at me from the landing above while she waits for her grandmother to finish her journey downstairs.

"Looks like we'll be family," Mrs. Ellis announces. "Soon as you marry her."

I go to the bottom of the stairs and pitch my voice over the hum of the chairlift motor. "That's the plan, Queen Joan. Harper will be a princess too." I wink at Harper, figuring she'll think that's funny, but she actually looks excited. "How do you like that?"

"I *so* want to visit the palace," Harper says.

Mrs. Ellis sniffs. "I wouldn't mind taking a look around."

"You're both invited. My family goes out every Christmas on the royal jet. What do you say next Christmas we go? The baby can meet his extended family."

"Or hers," Harper chimes in happily.

I grin at her. I catch Mrs. Ellis's scowl. "No?" I ask.

"I'm eighty-seven years old, young man. You think I can wait a year? I'll go next summer when the weather's nice enough for me to enjoy seeing an island."

Harper laughs. "Apparently, my grandmother researched your royal background after your first visit here."

Mrs. Ellis purses her lips. "It's my job to look into who you get serious about." She smiles at me. "I knew he was a keeper."

"Thank you, ma'am," I say, surprised.

She gets off her chairlift at the bottom of the stairs and gestures me closer. I lean down, and she pats my cheek. "You're a good man, Garrett."

I kiss her cheek. "And you're a good woman. I'll always honor and respect the woman who raised my amazing woman." I gesture to Harper, who walks downstairs, smiling with tears in her eyes.

Mrs. Ellis wipes her eyes. "Okay, enough of that mushy stuff. I need to go make the cocoa."

I can't help but tease her about earlier. "Sure you don't want to wait for a rival to come over and prove I'll rise to the occasion before cocoa?"

She cackles, making her slow way to the kitchen. "Have to keep you on your toes."

Harper wraps her arms around my neck and kisses me tenderly. "I love you, you wonderful man. I've never been so happy in my life."

"I love you too. So damn much. It almost feels too good to be true. I had no idea how it would go today, and now it's like—"

"The universe is smiling down on us."

"It's you." I kiss her again, overwhelmed with all I feel. "Always you."

She hugs me and goes up on tiptoe to whisper in my ear, "She goes to bed at seven. After that, we can go back to my place for our own celebration. Know what I mean?" She grabs my ass.

I cock my head. "Not sure. You'll have to explain a little better."

She slides a hand to my cock, and it rises to the occasion instantly.

"Do you like marshmallows, Garrett?" Mrs. Ellis calls from the kitchen.

I jerk away from Harper, my ears burning.

Harper cracks up. "She has radar for—" she finger quotes "—hanky-panky."

"Sure, thanks, I'll take marshmallows," I say.

"I'll need you to get some from the store," Mrs. Ellis says.

"I'm fine without."

Harper giggles.

Mrs. Ellis pokes her head in, smiling wickedly. "Sure?"

I'm onto her. That's her way of saying *keep your hands to yourself, mister. Except it was her granddaughter who got handsy!* "We're getting married as soon as I can convince her."

She narrows her eyes. "Before the baby's born."

I turn to Harper. "Valentine's Day wedding? Sean and Josie had one and it was great. We still have the arch of silk flowers. Actually, it's been used for a wedding re-enactment for my other brother, who had a courthouse ceremony. Third time would be good luck."

"I have got to meet this family of yours," Mrs. Ellis says.

I grin. "They're nuts in the best way. I'm sure they'd love you."

She pats her hair, pink rising in her cheeks. "Yes, well…" She shuffles back in the kitchen.

Harper wraps her arms around my waist. "If you're not careful, she's going to fall in love with you too. I really don't want to compete with my grandmother for my man."

I laugh and then get back to the important part. "So Valentine's Day? Hearts, cupids, and all the dark chocolate with cherry squares your heart desires. Wait." I go down on one knee. "Harper Ellis, will you marry me?"

"Yes!"

"Yes!" Mrs. Ellis exclaims a second later, beaming at us.

I hug Harper and smile over at Mrs. Ellis, who waves her dishrag at me before going back to the kitchen.

Harper beams at me. "I can't wait to be your wife."

"Me too." I kiss her tenderly, but then it flashes to heat, wild and out of control. God, I've missed her.

"Cocoa's just about ready," Mrs. Ellis calls.

We break apart, smiling. Time flies when you're making out with your future wife in her grandmother's living room.

We join Mrs. Ellis, gathered around the small kitchen table, the three of us planning a Valentine's wedding and a summer vacation together.

We leave Mrs. Ellis out of the honeymoon plans.

Harper

My grandmother insisted we drive her old Toyota back to the city instead of me riding on the back of Garrett's motorcycle since I'm pregnant. I have the sneaky feeling she's secretly hoping Garrett will return on Christmas to pick up his bike just so she can see him again. Truth is, seeing how well he treats my curmudgeonly grandmother is probably what made me fall so hard for him in the first place.

The moment we get inside my apartment, I throw myself into his arms. "I've missed you so much!" *Kiss. Longer kiss.* "I can't wait to get…" *Kiss.* "Naked."

He scoops me up and carries me into the bedroom, smiling big time. "You held out on me at your grandmother's place."

"Are you kidding me? I can't throw myself at you there. And she's always listening. Her hearing hasn't diminished at all, unfortunately."

"Now, sweetheart, that's uncharitable."

"Oh, Garrett, you have so much to learn."

He sets me down next to the bed and pulls my sweater over my head. He stares at my breasts. "Did your boobs get bigger?"

I look down at my newfound cleavage. "Yup. Pregnancy side effect."

"Nice," he says, sliding the straps of my bra down, his big hands running over my shoulders as he does. He takes off the bra, caressing my breasts with both hands. "I'm liking this pregnancy effect."

"You can say it. I was too small before."

He kisses me. "You were perfect before. You're perfect in every way." He grins, sits on the bed, and gives me a tug, pulling me closer. His mouth closes over my breast, suckling hard. It's a direct line of pure pleasure, making me ache with need. I slide my fingers into the hair at the nape of his neck and hold him to me. His hands roam over my ass and squeeze.

I sigh in pure bliss. He shifts, giving the other breast the same attention, making me moan. My knees grow weak.

"Garrett," I whisper.

"Too many clothes," he says, stripping me out of my leggings and panties.

I step out of them and help him undress, both of us admiring each other like it's the first time we've seen each other. It's been too long. We slam together the moment we're naked, kissing wildly. His hands are everywhere at once, and then he's lifting me. He breaks the kiss and sets me in the center of the bed.

I open my arms to him, and he joins me, resting his weight on his forearms. He strokes my hair back. "You sure this is okay with the baby?"

I smile at his concern. "Yes."

He pushes inside slowly, watching my expression the whole time, his brows knitted in concentration. I love this man.

I wrap my arms and legs around him. "Promise it'll be okay. Do what you want."

He thrusts slow and deep, his head dipping to nuzzle my neck. I stroke the broad planes of his back. All this muscle and power, yet he holds himself back, treating me with such care. Tears spring to my eyes.

He lifts his head, stilling. "What's wrong?"

"How did you know I was crying?"

"You felt far away."

I stare at him. "How do you feel that?"

"I dunno, Harp. We're connected. What's wrong?"

"I just love you so much, and you're so tender with me."

"Of course I'm tender. I love you."

I nod. "It's okay, I'm better now. Kiss me."

He does. I can feel him holding back this time, and I realize he's right about our connection. And that just makes me completely relax and let go. He responds instantly, his mouth hungry, his thrusts harder and faster. Pleasure cascades over me in waves, building and building.

He breaks the kiss, gazing deep into my eyes, and it's all there—the intense pleasure, the love, the care he takes with me. He shifts, hitting just the right angle, and I go off, pleasure bursting through me as I rock against him. He takes his own pleasure, thrusting deep over and over before his head throws back in ecstasy, the cords of his neck standing out.

I stroke his neck, and he grabs my hand and kisses it. "You good?" he asks. "Everything good with the baby?"

I beam. "We're both great."

He pulls out and rolls to my side. "Thank God. I don't think I could keep my hands off you for months."

I curl up against his side and stroke his chest. "Merry Christmas, Garrett."

He kisses me and tucks me close. "Merry Christmas and many more."

"You know my grandmother is hoping you'll go back tomorrow to get your motorcycle so she can see you for Christmas."

"I planned on it. Besides, my whole family's in Villroy. Time to spend Christmas with my new family."

My heart squeezes. I climb on top of him and pepper his face with kisses. "Wonderful, wonderful man."

He twines his fingers together and puts them under his head, a smug smile across his gorgeous face. "Got that right."

I nip his bottom lip. "Beast."

He arches his brows. "So you finally see it, huh? That's what my brothers call me because of these guns." He pulls his arms down and flexes for me.

"Beast on the inside."

"Round two, you say? That's what I'm hearing with your sexy talk." He rolls on top of me and nips along my neck.

I laugh and hug him tight. He's mine forever, and I'm so lucky to have a future with him. My beast, my teddy bear, my love.

EPILOGUE

Garrett

Two days before New Year's, I bring Harper to my parents' house. I was waiting for them to return from Villroy to share our big news in person.

Harper grabs my hand tightly as we walk up the front stoop. Joe's behind us. He sticks with us when Harper's in public, but here he doesn't need to go ahead to scout it out.

"Are you nervous?" I ask her.

She lifts our joined hands. "Was it my death grip that gave it away?"

"Hey, if Queen Joan is on board, King Daniel will be too. He's the one to watch. My mom just loves babies. She'll focus on that."

"Oh great, put it that way."

I ring the bell.

Harper takes an audible breath.

"Relax," I tell her.

"Garrett, this is big—"

"Hello!" My mom opens the door. "Come in. So good to see you both. Hi, Joe." She steps back. My dad is in the entryway to greet us too.

"We missed you at Christmas," my dad says.

"I know," I say. "Couldn't be helped this year. Maybe next year."

"Maybe?" he says. "Definitely. You're invited too, of course, Harper."

"Please join us in the living room," my mom says. "We got in yesterday, and we're still a little confused with the time zones."

"It's dinnertime to us," my dad puts in. We're here for lunch.

"Mind if I check out the pool table downstairs?" Joe asks my mom. "I'm only on duty for the transportation part of the day today."

"If you'd like," she says, sounding surprised. I told Joe our news and why we're here today. I also told him he could take a walk or play pool while we deliver the news. He heads down to the basement.

We all settle in the living room. The ugly painting I gave them from Jack's prank has been replaced with a beautiful landscape painting of Villroy.

I gesture to it. "That painting is so much better than the scribbles."

"Thanks," my mom says, glancing over at it. "It was commissioned by the king and queen as a Christmas gift for us."

"Oh, wow," Harper says, staring at it. "Villroy is so beautiful. I can see the palace at the top of the hill there. Like something out of a fairy tale."

"It's good to have the reminder of home," my dad says. "Now can we offer you a drink?"

My mom jumps up.

"I'll get it, Mom," I say.

She smiles her loving smile at me. "Thank you, my sweet teddy bear."

My ears burn. "Mom, please."

"He is," Harper says, leaning into my side. "Can I call you that too?"

I tap her nose. "No." I head over to the kitchen and open

the refrigerator. "Looks like bottled water and beer. What would everyone like?"

Harper says, "Water, please."

Everyone else follows suit. Guess it's early for a beer, though I suddenly want one. I never had to share such big news with my parents before, and if they don't respond positively to the surprise baby news, I know Harper will be upset. I'm too happy to worry about anyone's reaction. In any case, I'd better break the news gently.

After I pass out glasses of water, I sit on the love seat next to Harper. My parents are on the sofa across from us. "Harper and I have some news."

My parents look at us expectantly.

"So," I say, glancing at Harper. She's so tense she's not even blinking. I take her hand, and it's like ice. "We're engaged."

"Oh!" My mom throws her hands in the air. "Wonderful news! Oh, I'm so happy for you both." She rushes over to hug and kiss Harper and then me.

My dad joins her, slapping my shoulder and kissing Harper's cheek. "Welcome to the family, Harper."

My mom covers her cheeks as she smiles at me. "My baby, my last boy, getting married." She glances at Harper's hand and stops smiling. "No ring, Garrett."

"We'll shop for it later," I say. "It's only been a week."

"How did he propose?" my mom asks Harper.

"He went down on one knee on Christmas Eve," she says.

My mom sighs happily.

I take a deep breath and say the rest in a rush. "There's more good news. Harper is pregnant. Baby is due in June."

My dad's brows shoot up.

My mom stares at Harper's stomach. "That's not why you're getting married, is it?"

"No," I say, taking my love's hand, entwining our fingers together. "She's the One. You know how you said you knew right away with Dad? And, Dad, you said the same. You knew when it was the One for you. I knew with Harper."

"I love him so much," Harper says, her voice choking with

emotion. Her eyes water, and she brushes away a tear. She's been extra sensitive with the pregnancy hormones.

"Aww!" my mom exclaims, rushing over to hug Harper. She sits on the arm of the loveseat next to Harper. "I can tell you do, honey. I'm so happy for you both." She leans past Harper to give my shoulder a squeeze.

"Congratulations," my dad says stiffly. "Though I thought we had that talk about the order of things, son."

"Sometimes there's a happy accident," I say pointedly.

My dad walks over and kisses the top of my head. "More like a gift."

"You're so lucky to have loving parents like this," Harper says.

"What kind of parents are you used to?" my mom asks with real concern.

I jump in to explain because Harper's bottom lip is quivering. "She was raised by her grandmother. You'd like her, Dad, she's got that stiff-upper-lip toughness that queens have. I call her Queen Joan."

"I call her the General," Harper says with a laugh.

"We'd love to have her over," my mom says, putting her arm around Harper. "We're your family now, too, so you'll have all kinds of loving people around you—the royal pain-in-the-neck kind and the sweet loving kind. That's me, if you didn't know."

My dad harrumphs. "It's good to have a balance of parenting styles."

My mom smiles at him. "It is."

They take a seat on the sofa across from us again. My mom pulls out her phone. "Do you mind if I share the good news with a few people?"

"We're trying to keep it quiet since Harper is a public figure," I say.

"Only family, promise," my mom says.

"That's okay," Harper says.

My dad pulls out his phone too, and the two of them start texting like crazy.

I exchange an amused look with Harper.

My dad puts his phone down and turns to my mom. "We're going to need more food."

She nods. "I'll call for some."

He stands. "I'll go next door and see if the Bianchis want to join us. They always have plenty of food."

She jumps up. "Great idea!"

He grabs his jacket and goes out the door. My mom hustles to the kitchen to pull out a take-out menu.

"What's happening?" Harper asks me. "Is everyone coming over?"

"Seems that way. I did tell them we had big news before we got here. Maybe they were hoping it was an engagement and spread the word to my brothers that we might have a celebration. Baby was a bonus."

Her eyes widen. "They were that confident we were engaged?"

"I'm guessing, but..."

There's a knock at the door.

"That was fast," Harper says.

"Could you get that?" my mom asks, gesturing to me.

"Sure." I walk over and open the door. My oldest brother, Dylan, is standing there, holding my niece Olivia, who's holding a bouquet of congratulations balloons. His wife, Ariana, is behind him, with a double stroller for the twins.

"Is this where the party is?" he asks.

I laugh and let him in. "What did Mom and Dad tell you?"

"Mom said you were crazy about Harper, and she felt sure an engagement was in the works. So here we are for your engagement party. We were next door. Give him the balloons, Olivia."

She thrusts them at me, and I take them. "Thank you."

He sets her down, and she runs straight to my mom in the kitchen.

"Be right back," he says. "I'm gonna help Ariana with the twins and their gear. Congratulations, Harper."

"We're having a baby too!" Harper exclaims happily.

He smiles widely. "Double congratulations are in order

then. You'll love having kids. We do." He leaves to help his wife.

"Can you watch Olivia?" my mom asks us. "I'm going to the basement to get the decorations."

"Mom, how in the world did you know?"

She taps her heart. "Mom radar working better than ever! I know you, Garrett, and when I saw you two together for Olivia's big-sister party, I knew it was just a matter of time." She beams and rushes to hug me and then Harper. "Harper, any questions you have about pregnancy or birth, anything at all, I'm happy to share. I had six healthy boys."

"I'd love that," Harper says. "Thank you, Mrs. Rourke."

"You can call me Mom if you'd like, or Tara."

"Thank you, Mom."

"Aww!" She hugs Harper again and kisses her cheek. "What a wonderful way to start the new year! A new daughter! Gosh, I never thought I'd get one." She heads to the basement.

In no time there's a full house. All of my brothers are here with their wives, even Brendan, who lives up in Massachusetts. He stuck around for the holidays. My dad's back with the Bianchis—our neighbors and Dylan's in-laws—since he married the girl next door.

Josie and Harper are talking excitedly about our new house right across the street from them in Park Slope. Sean let us know it was going on the market, so we put in a preemptive bid yesterday, and we found out it was ours today. We're thrilled. The baby can get to know their aunt and uncle right across the street, and we'll watch each other's places when someone has to be away for work. Everything's falling into place in my life. A new house, a wife, a baby. I'm going to be a husband and dad, something I've always wanted, with the most amazing woman.

I join them, wrapping an arm around my future wife.

She smiles up at me. "Josie says there's a lot of new moms in the neighborhood."

"That's great. Our kid will have cousins and neighborhood friends to play with."

"I'm so excited for you both," Josie says. "I just knew right from the beginning that you two were a match." She calls over to the kitchen. "Didn't I say that, Sean?"

"What's that?" he asks.

"I said they were a match," she says.

He nods. "True. She desperately wanted Harper in the family."

Josie wags her finger at him. "That's not the only reason. I thought they were perfect for each other."

He laughs. "Glad to have you guys across the street."

"Thanks, bro," I say. "Can we count on you for babysitting?"

"We'd love to," Josie answers for him excitedly.

"We get first dibs," my mom pipes up.

"I'm here whenever you need me," Mrs. Bianchi says. And she's not even a grandmom to our kid!

"Thanks, Mrs. Bianchi. We really appreciate that."

She beams, walks over and pats my cheek. "We're family. Besides, I know a thing or two about raising strong daughters."

My mom joins us. "And I know about raising strong sons."

They lock eyes and then burst out laughing.

"You sure do, Tara," Mrs. Bianchi says.

"Oh, you too, Donna, you too," my mom says. "I'm so thankful to have Ariana in our lives. And you too, of course."

They hug and then break apart, smiling.

"Any other takers on the babysitting gig?" I ask jokingly.

A chorus of enthusiastic replies goes around the room. Wow, I didn't expect so many offers, even Jack and Riley with their two-month-old son, Aiden, chime in. Everyone except for Dylan.

"No?" I ask him, pretending offense.

He shrugs. "We've got three kids under two. We were kinda hoping you'd help us out."

"We'd love to," Harper says. "Olivia is darling, and I'm sure the twins will be just as wonderful."

Just then the twins burst into wails, waking from their naps in their infant car seats.

Olivia slaps her hands over her ears. "Take them back! Take them back!"

Dylan shakes his head as Ariana and Mrs. Bianchi go to pick the twins up from their car seats. "Olivia keeps asking us to return them to the store. Says they're too noisy."

"C'mere, Olivia," my mom says. "I've got a special job for you."

Olivia runs over, and my mom puts her on her hip, talking to her as she gathers napkins from a cabinet.

Harper turns to me. "Having a baby is going to be some ride. Are you sure you're ready for this?"

"Bring it on."

She winces. "My new sisters-in-law gave me some straight talk about the birth. Not pretty. I'm trying not to freak out."

I put an arm around her shoulders. "Hey, if I can stand watching it, you can stand doing it."

She laughs. "The good news is, they said they'd give me any baby gear they were done with." She goes up on tiptoe to whisper, "They must know I can afford to buy gear, but they're being so generous."

"Ya know, I'm starting to see what Josie was talking about with you being like Marian the librarian, emerging as the trusting happier person in the end."

"I am happy." She throws her arms around my neck and kisses me. "So, so happy."

"Eww," a little voice says. "Mommy and daddy kissing."

I look down at Olivia. She thrusts a napkin at me, clutched in her fist. "That's right. It means we're happy just like your mommy and daddy."

She sticks her tongue out like *blech* and skips away.

"Now where were we?" I say, pulling Harper close.

She smiles against my lips. "Mommy and daddy kissing. *Eww.*"

"That's right." I kiss her again and smile.

We join my family gathered in the kitchen once more to celebrate. I look around at all my brothers with their wives, my nieces and nephew, and it hits me how lucky our child will be. Our baby will grow up with lots of uncles, aunts, and cousins, two fantastic grandparents, honorary grandparents (thanks, Mrs. Bianchi!), a one-of-a-kind great-grandmother, and us, two loving parents. I was the last born, last for everything, but I'm the one who brings the most important piece of the puzzle. With me and Harper getting married, the Rourke family is now complete.

And it all started when this beast finally met his beauty in a case of mistaken identity that turned out to be fate.

Would you like to read more about Garrett's friend, billionaire Wyatt Winters? How about struggling restaurant owner Sydney Robinson? They'll meet in *Fetching*! Get ready for Unleashed Romance, a new steamy romantic comedy series, where dogs are part of the family!

Fetching

Wyatt

I'm a self-made billionaire with a soft spot for damsels in distress, so when I move to the quirky lakeside community of Summerdale, I immediately zero in on the woman I most want to…ahem, rescue. Only the stubborn woman refuses to cooperate.

Sydney

When Satan moves to town, aka Wyatt Winters, I do my best to be welcoming as the owner of the historic restaurant and bar that he won't stop showing up at, despite criticizing nearly everything about it. *Deep breath.* I might've lost my cool and made a rude gesture in his direction. And told him off. How was I to know he was considering investing in my place?

Did I mention I'm in debt up to my eyeballs and every bank has turned me down?

Still, there's not a snowball's chance in hell I'd ever work with him. Or admit he fires me up in every way.

And then a snowstorm traps us together and—

I'm melting.

Sign up for my newsletter to be emailed when *Fetching* releases at kyliegilmore.com/newsletter

ALSO BY KYLIE GILMORE

Unleashed Romance <<steamy romcoms with dogs!

Fetching (Book 1)

Happy Endings Book Club Series <<the Campbell family and a romance book club collide!

Hidden Hollywood (Book 1)

Inviting Trouble (Book 2)

So Revealing (Book 3)

Formal Arrangement (Book 4)

Bad Boy Done Wrong (Book 5)

Mess With Me (Book 6)

Resisting Fate (Book 7)

Chance of Romance (Book 8)

Wicked Flirt (Book 9)

An Inconvenient Plan (Book 10)

A Happy Endings Wedding (Book 11)

The Clover Park Series <<brothers who put family first!

The Opposite of Wild (Book 1)

Daisy Does It All (Book 2)

Bad Taste in Men (Book 3)

Kissing Santa (Book 4)

Restless Harmony (Book 5)

Not My Romeo (Book 6)

Rev Me Up (Book 7)

An Ambitious Engagement (Book 8)

Clutch Player (Book 9)

A Tempting Friendship (Book 10)

Clover Park Bride: Nico and Lily's Wedding

A Valentine's Day Gift (Book 11)

Maggie Meets Her Match (Book 12)

The Clover Park STUDS series <<hawt geeks who unleash into studs!

Almost Over It (Book 1)

Almost Married (Book 2)

Almost Fate (Book 3)

Almost in Love (Book 4)

Almost Romance (Book 5)

Almost Hitched (Book 6)

The Rourkes Series <<swoonworthy princes and kickass princesses!

Royal Catch (Book 1)

Royal Hottie (Book 2)

Royal Darling (Book 3)

Royal Charmer (Book 4)

Royal Player (Book 5)

Royal Shark (Book 6)

Rogue Prince (Book 7)

Rogue Gentleman (Book 8)

Rogue Rascal (Book 9)

Rogue Angel (Book 10)

Rogue Devil (Book 11)

Rogue Beast (Book 12)

ABOUT THE AUTHOR

Kylie Gilmore is the *USA Today* bestselling author of the Unleashed Romance series, the Rourkes series, the Happy Endings Book Club series, the Clover Park series, and the Clover Park STUDS series. She writes humorous romance that makes you laugh, cry, and reach for a cold glass of water.

Kylie lives in New York with her family, two cats, and a nutso dog. When she's not writing, reading hot romance, or dutifully taking notes at writing conferences, you can find her flexing her muscles all the way to the high cabinet for her secret chocolate stash.

Sign up for Kylie's Newsletter and get a FREE book! kyliegilmore.com/newsletter

For more fun stuff check out Kylie's website https://www.kyliegilmore.com.

Thanks for reading *Rogue Beast*. I hope you enjoyed it. Would you like to know about new releases? You can sign up for my new release email list at kyliegilmore.com/newsletter. I promise not to clog your inbox! Only new release info, sales, and some fun giveaways.

I love to hear from readers! You can find me at:
  kyliegilmore.com
  Instagram.com/kyliegilmore
  Facebook.com/KylieGilmoreToo
  Twitter @KylieGilmoreToo

If you liked Garrett and Harper's story, please leave a review on your favorite retailer's website or Goodreads. Thank you.

9 781947 379305